Buzzer felt the electricity in the air...

Buzzer took a small step back as all ten men swung up their half-chargers and aimed at him.

Willis stood relaxed and smiled. "Would you please come with me, sir?"

"I'm sorry, no."

Willis blinked in reaction to the blunt refusal. "I think that you are far too outnumbered to play these kinds of games, policeman..." Willis drawled the last word as the ten men surrounding Buzzer snickered.

Buzzer unholstered his blaster and brought it up to bear on Willis' head. The move had been so quick that most of the security guards were still snickering among themselves before they realized the sudden change in events. Willis stared wide-eyed at the small black hole of the blaster's muzzle in front of his face.

Buzzer felt the electricity in the air. Willis was frozen with fear, his eyes totally fixed on the weapon in his face. The room was silent, the only sound was the heavy breathing coming from Willis. "Put down your Goddamn guns already!" Willis snarled, eyes unmoving.

Eight of the guards responded to this order immediately by lowering their weapons, the other two looked skeptical. Willis glared at them and snarled. "Do it now!"

"Negative, Mr. Willis," one of the guards rasped as his finger began to tighten on the trigger of his powerful weapon. "This man is outnumbered and outgunned and he is mine."

The huge blast from the half-charger rocked the wall on the other side of the room. Buzzer came out of his dive and crouched behind one corner of the reception desk. He had fired twice while maneuvering and saw two men go down hard in a spray of blood and gore, one of them being the man who had fired first.

Buzzer was up and running now. Although he was well aware that the entire complex would soon be swarming with well armed security guards, the men on his tail were his most pressing problem. He had to move quickly or he would surely be pinned down somewhere in this room. Buzzer did not intend to allow that to happen. Poorly aimed fire followed him in his sprint down a side corridor. He swung around on the run, fired several rounds from his blaster and watched another man fall dead as several others who were beginning to pursue dove, once again, to the carpeted floor.

Buzzer turned a corner and fired again, hitting another target squarely in the chest from a distance of about ten meters. The body immediately hit the carpet and tripped up another who was close behind. Buzzer took advantage of this man's sprawl in the hallway and put one in the top of his head, the body spasmed jerkily as blood washed into the carpet. He raced down a connecting corridor and found himself surrounded on two sides by lift terminals, with a closed door straight ahead. It was a dead end...

What reviewers are saying about **GUARDER LORE**

"This is an action-packed book, kids, so the squeamish and the laid back need not apply. But even if you aren't a devotee of space-opera-shoot-em-ups...the guy can write. His characters are real, their dialogue tough yet fresh, and they take on a semblance of reality that goes a long way towards suspending that darn old disbelief. If I were writing or directing an action movie, I'd ask Shawn's opinion, and that's more praise than I should be allowed to give anyone."

~Bob Yosco, **Shadowkeep**

"This is a universe in which I would love to read more tales, finding out what happens on some of these outpost worlds that have all-too-brief mentions upon in this work. There is a history here, with wars, treaties and exoduses to the stars that I'd like to explore with the characters. In short I want more! Thankfully there are sequels and other works planned - get writing Shawn!"

~Steve and Lesley Mazey, **The Eternal Night**

GUARDER LORE

by

Shawn P. Madison

Writer's Sanctum Publishing LTD

Writer's Sanctum Publishing LTD publishes books online and in trade paperback. For more information, check our website: www.writerssanctumpublishing.co.uk or email writerssanctumpublishing@gmail.com.

Edited by: Gail McAbee

ISBN: 978-1-9998786-8-9

Dedicated to

Dedicated to Craig Garritano, my biggest fan, my strongest supporter and the best cousin a guy could ever have

And to Dave Bowlin who gave me my very first break and as much encouragement as it took to make this book possible.

MULLENS'S ASSIGNMENT: THE HISTORY BEGINS

Joseph Mullens took a deep breath and entered the large conference room within the Guarder HQ. The great mural of the Falcon Symbol immediately drew the historian's eye; the huge and impressive bird looked truly lethal and larger than life. It amazed him how the place that housed the legendary Guarder Squadron could remain so damnably quiet when, at the same time, it seemed to be teeming with staff. Most government offices were so loud with turmoil he usually couldn't hear himself think, but this entire section of the Governmental Complex on Aegis had been perfectly still since his arrival.

The silence was shattered by the sound of a throat being cleared from the other end of the ornate conference table—and Mullens nearly jumped out of his skin. He turned his head and noticed for the first time the large, dark man who seemed to occupy that entire side of the room.

"Forgive me," Mullens said and took a tentative step or two closer to the man. The historian was transfixed by the cold eyes of this imposing stranger and he had to tear his gaze away as he took a seat about half way down the length of the table. "I didn't know you were already here," Mullens muttered, his voice barely a whisper. "You *are* Mr. Buzzer?" He asked and received a slight nod in return.

The room became completely quiet; Mullens couldn't even hear the big man breathing. He could feel his own heart racing as the impact of what he was doing this day fully dawned on him. He placed his small recorder on the table in front of him and brought his mini-pad up to full charge. Looking up at the room's only other occupant, Mullens attempted a smile and then leaned back in his chair.

"Mr. Buzzer, I have to tell you, what you did today..."

"I was only doing my job," the Guarder said.

"Yes, but...it was amazing, I mean, you managed to..."

"Like I said, I was just doing my job."

Mullens suddenly realized that this would be no ordinary interview and began to search for a way to get this man to open up. "Do you know why I'm here, sir?"

"Yes, Mr. Mullens."

"Good, then you know that this is the first time an official history of the highly secretive Guarder Squadron has ever been sanctioned by the United Earthian Nations," Mullens said, relaxing somewhat as he got into his groove. "To tell you the truth, I don't even know that much about your unit and I'm a historian. Other than the fact that the roots of the Guarder Squadron go as far back as the

New Conflict, there's really not much information out there. Most people in the Known-Grids don't even think your kind exists. They seem to think that you are all nothing but myths and..."

"I know of the legends surrounding this squadron, Mr. Mullens," Buzzer said. "What I don't know is why I am sitting here across this table from you. What do I have to do with a U.E.N. sanctioned history of the Guarder Squadron?"

"Well, surely, you realize that after the events of earlier today you are something of a celebrity?" Mullens asked.

"In my line of work, that type of attention tends to end careers, Mr. Mullens."

"Well, I hadn't exactly thought of it that way," Mullens said and felt himself losing control of the session.

Buzzer bowed his head momentarily and then looked up again, this time with somewhat less of the steely glare he'd possessed just moments before. "I know you are just doing your job, Mullens, and I don't mean to be uncooperative. It's just that I don't understand how a history of this squadron really matters in the overall scheme of things; and I just don't know what you want from me."

"I can fix that for you right now," Mullens said and leaned a bit closer. "I just want you to tell me about yourself and your career. You've been at this for what, twelve e-years now? Just relay some of your experiences to me in your own words. None of this is going to be included word for word in the historical archives; this session is just to give me some background information. Something to help me understand what I'm researching and the events that I will find as I dig through the last four centuries of the Guarder Squadron's history."

"Fair enough," Buzzer said. "Where should I start?"

"Why not back at the beginning of your career; say when you were only at this for an e-year or two, when your feet were just getting wet," Mullens suggested. "Can you remember any mission or event from back then where you just sort of stumbled into something that you weren't prepared for? Some type of thing that happened unexpectedly, that threw you into high gear through sheer reaction alone?"

Buzzer's eyes softened then and he nodded once. "Sure..."

For most of the early 21stCentury, the largest threats to global peace were thewar-like acts of expansion committed by the Red Union (which later became the United Soviet States), the hardcore communist Superpower that arose from the ashes of the former Soviet Union. The U.E.N. owes its very creation in 2045 to the worldwide effort to fight the Soviet war machine as it toppled nation after nation across the globe, resulting in a death toll which numbered in the tens of millions. Most of those who died were the innocent civilians of those countries who wanted no part of the Communist hardliners and their blood-lusting quest for global domination...

(Excerpt*: The U.E.N. Unveiled— The Dark History of Humanity's Greatest Government*by Joseph Mullens)

MISSION ONE: KILLDEVIL STATION

Traffic was heavy all around the orbiting starport, as it loomed large on the view display inside the pilot's helmet. He and his crew wished nothing more than to make a successful dock with one of the outer ports, discharge their two brooding passengers and get on with their long trip to Azuridia. The Berking System's CargoLiner #XXL48723-J was a half-kilometer in overall length and almost an eighth wide, small by Liner standards but a handful nevertheless.

He couldn't believe he'd been ordered to ferry the two silent figures to this speck of a system, so far out of his original course that he cursed the lost time that would go onto his record. But the orders had been clear when he reported for flight pre-check almost three days ago: *unexpected passengers; provide safe transit to Toolis— Killdevil Station; proceed to final destination.*

The two men had said little upon their arrival. The tall one had nodded in greeting and asked where they would be quartered. No one had heard a sound from either of them since then. They had not even reported to the galley for scheduled meals. Although neither man wore any insignia on their black clad bodies, the pilot was pretty sure that they were armed, and he was *damn* sure that they were military.

The U.E.N. must be up to something; but whatever it was, he wanted no part.

"BerkSys CargoLiner on approach vector," a low voice sounded inside his helmet. "Access codes confirmed. Proceed to Outer Port Three-Five and engage docking procedures."

The pilot zeroed in on Port Three-Five and grinned. It was the largest docking port on the entire station, built to handle a rig six times the size of his little vessel. *The star treatment for a change.*

"All the easier to get rid of those two..." he mumbled to himself and cursed his superstitious Berking nature.

His ship's communications system linked with that of the station and the Liner drifted slowly to a stop, coupling perfectly with the docking port.

Less than a minute later, his Cargo Master's voice sounded inside his helmet. "Passengers are clear, ready for de-docking."

The pilot's eyes widened in surprise at the speedy departure of his unwelcome guests. He had thought his ship and crew would be laid up for at least half an hour before the two young men would be ready to leave. He initialized the de-docking procedure, thanked the Killdevil Station Control Center for their hospitality, and the great ringing sound of the docking port separating itself from his ship vibrated throughout the cockpit.

"Good riddance," he said as his ship gained speed.

~*~

The trip to the main hub of the starport from the outer docking port took several minutes.

Everyone else on the hopper had moved forward, as far away from the two men in black as they could.

It was something about the clothes…or the silence, Buzzer thought to himself and smiled. Whatever the reason, people always avoided Guarders, whether they recognized them for what they were or not.

The hopper slowly lowered itself onto a magnetic catch-pad and the other passengers stepped off as quickly as they could.

Buzzer looked at Mestizo and they both shared a silent laugh. They hadn't been Guarders for long…but they were Guarder trained. That meant that they were two very serious and very deadly human beings. It also meant that people usually realized this very quickly upon getting one good look at them—and took great pains to avoid them thereafter at all costs.

The Transport Scheduling Terminal was in sight across the great open area they had just entered. Huge transparent panels gave the visitors to Killdevil Station a perfect view of fiery Toolis below and the myriad ships that were coming and going.

Toolis had been nothing more than a fair-sized fireball when it was discovered several hundred e-years ago. Since then, its potential as a point on the path of one of the most heavily traveled space lanes had been realized and the planet itself targeted for development. It was a long process, of course; but the Hell Planet, as it had come to be known, was slowly being tamed. Soon it would be an industrial center for all types of major corporations, from warehousing to manufacturing, since it was a perfect spot for cargo ships to import and export cargo on their way to any one of a hundred or so hot spots in the NorthWestern Corporate Grid- Sector. In the meantime, the Hell Planet was being artificially cooled, and several large landmasses were either under heavy construction or in various stages of development. The Interim Planetary Government of Toolis was very happy indeed with the speed in which the global project was progressing. The potential profit-making ability of the business powerhouse that Toolis would soon become was off the charts.

The Corporate Conglomerate—which had snatched up Toolis within days of receiving the initial profit-analysis reports—had just secured full-retirement funding for each of their several million current employees, as well as all future hires over the next decade, with this acquisition. The so-called 'Devil of Toolis' would soon be defeated.

Buzzer scanned the arrivals and departures board, looking particularly for listings of the Liner that would be 'sponsoring' the next leg of their journey to Aegis. The two Guarders had contacted Guarder HQ on Aegis just prior to leaving the Berking ship, and all was still clear for their return. Guarder Squadron Commander, Sergeant Harrison Jekel, expected to fully debrief the two young Guarders on their latest successful mission and their ability to work together as a team—an anomaly, and something most Guarders preferred not to do.

"I don't see it listed," Mestizo remarked, not taking his eyes off the huge board. "Maybe there's been a mistake or they've been delayed somewhere else?"

"Let's hope not," Buzzer replied. "The last place I want to spend any time is this crowded station. I'll go find their check-in area and see what the hold up is."

Mestizo nodded and continued watching the board as Buzzer headed across the cavernous room. He wasn't very familiar with this system or the red planet that took up most of the view outside the station but he had heard somewhere that this was soon to be a metropolis of sorts for the NorthWestern Corporate Grid-

Sector. *More power to them*, he thought to himself as he spotted the booth he was looking for and headed toward it.

Buzzer felt a slight vibration under his feet and hesitated, his senses suddenly on alert. His mind immediately registered the location of his primary weapon, a blaster nestled in a speed rig on the left side of his waist, and the quickest path to it; as well as the location of the second smaller weapon strapped to his ankle. *Something's not right*, he told himself; but everyone around him carried on normally, oblivious to any danger.

The vibration started again, and it wasn't a normal starport functioning vibration either. For some reason, this felt like...

Buzzer turned back the way he had come and found Mestizo already walking toward him with the same look in his eyes.

Something was about to go down, and both of them knew it wasn't going to be good. "Did you feel that?" He called toward Mestizo.

"Yeah; it felt like low-level explosives to me."

"That's what I thought," Buzzer answered as they both glanced out the massive viewports, trying to identify where the explosions were coming from.

Less than a second later a third vibration swept through the starport, Buzzer pointed out one window toward one of the outer docking ports. "There."

"Someone's blowing the outer ports," Mestizo said as he watched the remnants of the small fireball dissipate.

With the threat confirmed, both Guarders automatically pulled their blasters. Several travelers saw this and scattered away from them, some screaming as they did so. The two men began to move quickly through the large open area of the main hub, eyes scanning the crowd for potential targets.

"Security!" A man in front of them shouted. "Stop now or I will be forced to open fire!"

Buzzer slowed to a walk and held up a hand for Mestizo to hold fire as they approached the security officer.

"Buzzer, U.E.N. Guarder," he identified himself and pulled out his Guarder Badge and ID for the man's inspection. He could see the sweat on the older man's face as his eyes flicked back and forth between the two large men.

"What the hell is that?" He questioned, not recognizing the Falcon Symbol of the Guarder Squadron.

"We are U.E.N. Guarders," Mestizo offered. "We're here on Killdevil Station between flights while in transit back to the United Earthian Nations Governmental Complex on Aegis."

"I couldn't care less for your travel plans," the man stammered and motioned toward their weapons. "Lay your weapons on the floor and back slowly away."

"Mister, you have a situation here," Buzzer spoke calmly, trying to put the uptight security man at ease. "Someone's blowing up your station bit by bit. All we're trying to do is put a stop to it. We are well trained for such situations. Just let us do our jobs."

"I said lay your weapons..."

The security man was cut off by a larger, closer vibration that actually made him stumble. The fire from this explosion glowed red along the far wall of the Transport Scheduling Terminal.

Amidst the growing cacophony of screams, Buzzer took advantage of the opportunity. He moved in quickly, sidestepping the man's gun arm, twisting the wrist with enough pressure to make the weapon drop, and landing a hard thumping blow behind the older man's left ear. He hated to hurt a man who was just doing his job but, at the moment, all of their lives depended on stopping whoever was responsible for the fireworks. He gently placed the limp body on the carpeting and motioned for Mestizo to follow him toward one of the vacant hopper pads.

~*~

"It's begun," Lieutenant Greely said. "We have received confirmed reports that several of the outer docking ports have been destroyed, along with several docked ships."

"Very good," Commander Antonin replied. "Right on schedule. This should soon be over on the station. How about on Toolis?"

"Thompson reports that he has the High Council of the Interim Planetary Government in custody," Greely snickered. "He found it quite unfortunate that none of them put up any resistance. He says they are all in good health."

"Ah, Thompson," Antonin laughed. "He is a fine soldier."

Antonin stood and walked to the large viewport in his suite on the small transport. Toolis was slowly growing smaller as they made their way up to Killdevil Station, four other transports full of his people close behind. The coup was going very smoothly, just as planned. He could almost smell the enormous wealth, which he would soon be controlling once he got his hands on the reins of the Toolis operation. "Any resistance from Cooper and his small squad?"

"They were actually in the conference room while the High Council was in session," Greely answered. "Thompson says they didn't even have the chance to draw their weapons. They were in a state of shock, or disbelief. He couldn't actually tell which."

"That sounds like Cooper," Antonin shrugged.

It was all clicking together so well, almost too well. No resistance on the ground and no resistance so far from station security. It was Killdevil Station that was the real prize in this operation. Once his forces gained total control over the station, they could control all incoming traffic and dictate who was allowed in or out. If this was over as quickly as he had planned, the fallout could be held to a minimum. Toolis was not yet developed enough to rate any level of importance with U.E.N. Military Forces, so a retaliatory strike was not expected. However, just in case a strike was ordered, the fifteen largest docking ports on the station were being destroyed to prevent the docking of a military cruiser. Once his cover story could take hold, it was just a matter of convincing the Boards of the Corporate Conglomerate that owned the Toolis operation that all was in order, and things would proceed at an even better pace than originally anticipated.

The transit logs of Killdevil Station currently showed no presence of military type transports or personnel. Most of the paramilitary force which had been hired by the High Council of the Interim Planetary Government were a part of this coup. Those who had not joined were either in the brig on Toolis or, unfortunately, dead. Cooper's group was an independent force hired specifically to protect the High Council. A choice the Board Members would later regret, no doubt. Simmons's group was another independent force hired specifically to protect the workers, equipment and supplies at the five operational construction sites located throughout the planet.

So far, Antonin's men had eliminated any threat from Simmons's group, including Simmons himself, or so it had been reported.

"Well, I guess play time is over," Antonin said. "Now it's time to put our cover into play."

~*~

Goodings thanked God that the small pack on his back containing the explosives was getting lighter as he set them throughout the outer docking ports. He settled another small pack around the main joint of one of the connecting rings in this particular docking port, the powerful little magnets taking hold with a loud metallic clang, and set the timer for two minutes. He had set three of the deadly explosives already and he could tell, by the other slight vibrations he had been feeling, that Daniels was also hard at work.

"You can deactivate that now," Goodings heard and the small hairs on the nape of his neck stood on end. He turned slowly toward the voice and saw two shadowy figures pointing big black blasters at him. He stood up slowly and moved the pack of explosives in front of him as a sort of shield. *What the hell was this*, he thought as he examined the two men. "You're not security," he mumbled out loud.

"Deactivate that now," he heard one of them say, although he couldn't see their lips in the darkened tunnel.

"Uh, as far as I know, there is no way to deactivate one of these, mister," Goodings said and took one hesitant step backwards. These men were between him and the exit to safety—and there was about a minute and a half left until detonation.

"Deactivate it now or die," one of them said.

Goodings looked around and found no other way out. "It seems to me that you risk blowing us all to hell if a stray shot hits this pack on the way to killing me," he said and patted the pack now hanging off his chest.

"I don't think so," Buzzer said…and fired.

The blaster bolt destroyed Goodings's head, a wet red spray splashed the walls of the docking port tunnel as the lifeless body slumped to the floor.

Mestizo ran up to the explosive, whose timer read fifty-eight seconds, and scanned it for a deactivation switch as what was left of Goodings still twitched. "Damn," he swore and looked up at Buzzer. "He wasn't lying; this thing's got no *off* switch."

The two men wasted no more time on words as both sprinted down the docking port tunnel in an effort to outdistance the impending explosion. Although the station, like most, would automatically seal off any area experiencing a hull breach, they were taking no chances and continued to run, even after reaching the end of the connecting tunnel and entering a long corridor. The vibration caused by the explosion so near to them was violent enough to knock both men off their feet and send them skidding into the walls. Buzzer picked himself up and continued his sprint down the corridor, Mestizo close behind.

"That guy wasn't working alone," Mestizo stated as he ran and Buzzer nodded in agreement. "It looked like he was wearing a military uniform." Buzzer nodded again. "What does that mean?"

"I don't know," Buzzer answered. "But these explosions are not geared toward destroying the station. I think they are disabling some of the larger docking ports. The ones, for instance, a military transport would use to respond to this threat and land troops here."

"That sounds right," Mestizo agreed. "So you're not thinking terrorists?"

"No," Buzzer said as they kept running, looking up each tunnel as they passed more docking ports, trying to locate other bombers. "Not their style, they would have gone for the whole deal, blown the station to bits."

"What, then?"

"Maybe a hostile takeover?" Buzzer thought aloud. "Maybe someone's realized how much money this place is going to be taking in soon and decided that he should be running the show instead of working for the suits."

"That makes sense," Mestizo agreed.

Another explosion rocked the station, causing them to stumble again, but they both easily retained their footing.

Once these vibrations died down, the two Guarders picked up their pace and zeroed in on their next target.

~*~

Antonin's transport docked in one of the inner ports. They had been able to get a visual on the last two explosions at the outer ports several minutes ago, but there had been no others after that—and Goodings and Daniels were not responding.

Could they have blown themselves up, the idiots, he thought. *Maybe so...but not very likely*.

"Could security have gotten them?" Antonin wondered aloud.

"It's possible," Greely said. "But I don't think Daniels would have allowed himself to be taken by that pitiful bunch."

"I agree," Antonin said as he and Greely stepped off the transport and into the station. Fifty of his men soon joined him in the corridor. He nodded at Greely and the men split into five units, all knowing exactly what they were responsible for. It looked as if the training was payingoff.

Ten men remained with him and Greely as they made their way to the Control Center to take official command of Killdevil Station.

~*~

Buzzer and Mestizo had heard the group of men coming several seconds before, and were able to gain positions on either side of a large bulkhead, weapons drawn and waiting to move. Once they had dispatched the second bomber they had contacted Security and explained to them what was going on. Their Guarder ID's had more effect on the Head of Security when he saw it through the com-link, and he quickly mobilized the other twenty-four men on his team into defensive posture.

What good that would actually do, Buzzer had no way of knowing, but it was a relief to know that they finally had some backup.

The running footsteps were gaining ground on their position and it was almost time. Buzzer could feel the adrenaline pumping through his veins. They had watched the five small transports dock in the inner ports and realized that the station was being invaded. By whom, he didn't know, but that didn't much matter at the moment. He looked across the bulkhead to Mestizo and nodded. On a mental count of three, both men sprang out from their hiding places and began to fire repeatedly into the advancing men. Buzzer's first four shots took out four targets before they even had a chance to respond. Mestizo enjoyed the same success from his side of the bulkhead.

By the time it was over, their enemies had managed to fire three charges at them, all of which splashed into the thick walls of the station, causing only minor damage.

To the Guarders' disappointment, none of the men were alive. Once more, they were unable to secure any type of information about this attack. Buzzer's disgust showed clearly on his face and Mestizo's features reflected the same.

"Let's move," Buzzer said and the two men resumed the hunt.

~*~

Eduardo Sanchez gripped his half-charger tightly from his position near the entrance to the Killdevil Station Control Center. His men were evenly placed between the Security HQ and this corridor leading toward the Control Center. Although he had never fired a half-charger except on the range during practice sessions, he hated to think of the damage a single charge could cause if it hit something vital instead of an intended target. The thing was also extremely heavy, compared to the ultra-lite special issue blaster weapons his squad usually carried. If the half- charger weighed this much, he grimaced at the thought of carrying a full-charger into battle under any conditions. Although the larger version of the weapon in his hands could effectively take down large aircraft with a single bolt, the massive firepower wouldn't matter much if his guards weren't physically able to carry the thing.

The com-link message from the two Guarders had started his heart racing. Guarders? On Killdevil Station? He had always thought the stories he had heard about the Guarder Squadron were nothing but legends, but their U.E.N. ID Badges had looked real enough, and Jeff Kemp had been mumbling something about Guarders after he had regained consciousness in the Transport Scheduling Terminal.

So now, Sanchez and his young squad of inexperienced security men were fully armed and loaded for bear, waiting to unleash on an unseen enemy that was supposedly fast approaching. It only occurred to him now that maybe the ID Badges weren't all that real…and this was just a ploy to throw them off of what was really going down. Sanchez shook his head to clear it. No, he couldn't think like that and second-guess himself. Hell, when Guarders showed up they were supposed to be in control; that's what he remembered. Guarders always outranked anyone else on the scene, something about being judge and jury with those guys. Their word was law and the trouble would come down hot and heavy on anyone who interfered with their plans.

But Guarders...here on his station?

"Mr. Sanchez," one of his men whispered beside him. "They're coming, sir."

Sanchez tilted his head to get a better angle for his ears—and heard the sound of many footsteps getting closer. He nodded once and whispered back, "Okay, everyone get ready."

The young man took a deep swallow and turned back toward the approaching sound. Suddenly the sound lessened…and then almost disappeared. All was quiet for several seconds, and Sanchez began to think that whoever it was had turned down another corridor.

Sanchez felt his heart slowing down and he took a deep, satisfying breath. It seemed like the first one he'd drawn since he'd heard from the Guarders.

It was then that the first shot took out the young man in front of him. Sanchez shook his head to clear the stinging blood from his eyes and the corridor filled with blaster fire. With his vision still unclear, he lifted his half-charger and began unleashing an enormous amount of firepower down the corridor. Several screams from far away were his reward but he could just make out at least eight or nine of his men sprawled on the carpet of the corridor.

"Christ," he muttered and took a second to wipe at his eyes with his uniform sleeve. They had nowhere to pull back to, since they were literally up against the massive doors of the Control Center.

"Cease your fire!" A deep voice boomed down the hall. "You will not be harmed!"

"Bullshit, Mr. Sanchez," another of his men shouted from beside him. "These bastards will

kill us for sure if we throw down our weapons!"

"Wilson, these men will kill us whether we fight or not," he replied.

"I for one would rather die fighting than just crawl out there and let them shoot me."

"Well, we're not giving up just yet," Sanchez said and sprang out into the corridor, his weapon bucking in his hands. Sanchez took a bolt in the chest within seconds, and his eyes went wide with the shock of the impact. As he dropped to his knees and consciousness began to fade, his last thought was of seeing one of the enemy soldiers down the hall get blown away by a dark figure firing from behind...

~*~

Buzzer and Mestizo picked off their targets easily, scoring head shots on five of them before anyone knew what was happening. Looking down the corridor toward the doors of the Control Center, Buzzer could see that the security men had been slaughtered. Two of the attackers branched off from the remaining group and disappeared down a side corridor with a sign reading *Lifts and Restrooms* overhead.

Buzzer knew that he couldn't worry about those two for the time being; he still had trouble here to take care of. More than once, he and his partner had to dodge stray shots coming from the security detail down the hall, but before too long there was only one attacker left and both Guarders hit him simultaneously. The resulting red mess mingled with the rest of the detritus in the corridor and silence quickly took over.

"U.E.N. Guarders," Mestizo's voice boomed down the corridor. "Hold your fire!"

"Yes, sir," came a weak reply. "Thank you, sir!"

"Where's your CO?" Buzzer called.

"Dead, sir," came the same voice.

Buzzer shared a look with Mestizo, both acknowledging that they just hadn't been fast enough.

"All's clear in the corridor," Buzzer called and began to proceed toward the Control Center. He whipped around the corner where the two men had disappeared but, as he had known, there was nobody lurking there. Those two were long gone. There were only two of the security detail left and Buzzer counted eleven bodies on that side of the hall.

"We got ten of them," he said to the visibly shaken young man whose knuckles had gone white around the butt of his ultra-lite blaster.

"They got their share of us too, sir," the youngster replied. "With your CO dead, who's in charge?" Mestizo asked.

"Ah...that would be Denning, sir," he said. "He's with the others down by HQ."

"All right, you two stay here," Buzzer ordered. "When we get to your HQ, we'll send some of them up here for support. Until then, the Control Center must be protected."

"Yes, sir," the two security men said together and then looked at each other with something close to terror as they watched the two Guarders disappear down a nearby corridor.

~*~

"Who the hell was that back there?" Antonin wondered out loud as he and Greely raced toward the Security HQ.

"They weren't security," Greely replied. "Their uniforms didn't look like standard military issue but their skill level fits the bill."

"Dammit!" Antonin screamed with rage. First his bomb squad had stopped responding, then two of his ten-man squads stopped reporting in and now this fiasco at the Control Center.

Another ten men dead; that left maybe twenty of his men still alive on Killdevil Station.

At least it looked as though they had eliminated about half of the security force back there. But those two men in black that had surprised them from behind were unknown quantities, a wrench in the works that could spell disaster if he didn't regroup his men and get back on track.

"Commander," Greely broke the silence. "Once we gain control of the Security HQ, we can shut down major systems and demand the surrender of the Control Center. When we gain that position, there's nothing those two men can do to stop us."

"That sounds good, lieutenant," Antonin agreed. "Let's concentrate on the Security HQ and go from there."

Timothy Denning turned off the com-link on the corridor wall and his jaw hung open with shock. Sanchez and almost everyone with him were dead. These invaders weren't playing around; they meant business. *Damn, but he didn't want to die today*, he thought to himself and gripped his half-charger tighter. Guarders, there were Guarders on the way here for support, that was amazing...Guarders on Killdevil Station. Denning shook his head and took another deep breath.

"Tim, what's going on?" One of his men asked from behind.

"Sanchez and most of the others got fried," he said, and several of his men reacted with sharp intakes of breath. Then the shouting started and he quickly yelled for them to calm down. "Another invading force is most likely heading this way, we have to be ready."

"What the hell, Tim," another man spoke up. "Chasing thieves and catching fugitives is one thing, but I didn't sign on to die up here!"

"Dammit, Carl," Denning shot back. "Shut up and take your position; and you will damn well fight to defend this station if a threat presents itself! Do you understand?"

"Hell, no!" The man snarled. "Not today, not for me..." was all he got out before his head was ripped from his shoulders by the first of many blaster bolts which filled the corridor.

Denning dove to the carpet and rolled against the wall. He brought his weapon up and fired blindly down the corridor. In just the first few seconds of the firefight, he saw eight of his men go down, leaving only him and three others.

He didn't know who was firing at them or how many of them there were—but he knew that the remainder of his team couldn't hold them off forever.

~*~

Buzzer and Mestizo had followed the *Security* directional signs most of the way, knowing that they were hot on the heels of the men who had fled the corridor outside the Control Center. As they got closer, they purposefully sidetracked the long way around, pushing it double-time, so they could approach the Security HQ from the opposite direction. Any designer worth his salt would have built two entrances to the Security HQ, providing an ample escape route in case of an ambush. Both Guarders knew this and hoped to take advantage of it.

As they rounded the last corner and saw the closed entrance to the Security HQ, the sound of muffled heavy-weapons fire could be heard throughout the corridor. As they both picked up speed, Mestizo fired three bolts in rapid succession into the large control panel outside the doors and was rewarded by a spray of fire and sparks.

The door panels slid aside and Buzzer was through first, dashing across the circular room. As Mestizo cleared the blown doorway, Buzzer quickly punched in the *Open Door* command at one of the workstations and the opposing door panels slid apart.

The raging firefight in the outside corridor quickly found its way inside the Security HQ, and the two Guarders let loose with a full barrage from their blasters. The two remaining Security officers literally fell into the room and scrambled to get out of the line of fire.

"Get clear!" Buzzer shouted as he grabbed and flipped the arming mechanism on three marbles—tiny grenades with surprising explosive power.

Mestizo knew the drill and laid down a covering fire as his partner wound up and threw all three of the small explosives into the outside hallway. Buzzer worked the control panel again and the doors slid shut just as the marbles made it through the opening.

The resulting explosion buckled the entrance door panels and smoke began to trickle in through the busted seal. After that, all was quiet...

~*~

Tim Denning picked himself up off the floor and looked at the only other remaining survivor of his twelve-man detail of security officers. Jackson was bleeding from several places, including a nasty gash on his left cheek, but was otherwise in one piece. He wished he could say the same for himself. His left arm dangled limply from his shoulder socket and he had no vision in his left eye. He could feel the badly burned and cracked flesh on the left side of his chest and shoulder but, strangely enough, he could not feel his left arm. He looked over at the two men in black who were standing in the middle of the HQ and knew immediately that these were the Guarders.

Two men, only two—and the horrible firefight which had taken the lives of ten of his detail, and had seemingly lasted forever, had been ended in seconds.

The taller of the two, the one with close cut black hair and stone cold eyes, looked him over to measure his wounds. Denning almost stumbled and caught himself against the wall behind him.

"Would either of you two be Denning?" the man asked.

Denning almost didn't register the question, wondering at how this dangerous man had known his name, then he managed to drawl through cracked and bleeding lips, "Me."

"You did good work out in that corridor."

"Yeah," Denning answered and slumped down the wall to the floor. "Yeah."

"Stay here," the other Guarder said, the one with the long hair and thin face. "We're going to try to finish this little skirmish; but you two need to pull yourselves together and defend this HQ. Others of your team are stationed outside the Control Center. Most of the invading forces have been eliminated but there are still some of them left on this station. It is imperative that you do not give this place up. Do you understand?"

Denning nodded and could see out of the corner of his eye that Jackson did too.

"I don't think you'll have any more trouble," the long haired warrior in black continued. "But, just in case, the doors you just came through are no longer operational. Make sure you have good cover between yourselves and the other doors. If you lose that cover, you'll have to blast your way out the damaged doors or a wall. Either way, if you are forced to leave, try to do as much damage to this HQ as you can. You don't want them to gain control of this room if its major systems are still operational."

"Yes, sir," Denning managed.

"Good," the Guarder who had thrown the explosives said from his position at one of the work stations. "How do I contact the Control Center from this console?"

"Upper-left corner, the blue portion is communications in-station," Jackson offered and the Guarder immediately found the desired controls.

"Control Center, this is Buzzer, U.E.N. Guarder; please respond."

Although the video must have taken a hit during the brief battle, a slight warble came through the open com-link's audio before the response, "Guarder, this is Control Center. The security officers left to defend us have filled us in on the situation."

"Good," Buzzer replied. "How strong are your docking clamps, Control?" Several seconds of silence were followed by, "General duty...sir."

"Strong enough to hold tight the five transports which docked earlier without clearance?" "Yes, sir," the voice answered. "I think so, sir."

"Good, please secure those five transports to their docking ports and do not allow them to leave this station," Buzzer ordered with authority in his voice. "Once you register occupants on any of those vessels, I want you to seal the airlock of that vessel. Am I understood?"

"Yes, sir," the voice wavered. "What do you propose to do, sir?"

"Suffice it to say, Control, that you may want to evacuate those docking ports as soon as possible," Buzzer replied and nodded at Mestizo who was gathering up two half-chargers and some extra charge packs. "And send a medic up here, your wounded need attention."

~*~

Antonin and Greely had ordered their remaining ten men to regroup at the transports and prepare to depart Killdevil Station immediately until they could return with more troops. More than forty men gone...he could hardly believe it. They had beaten a hasty path out of the corridor outside of Security HQ once the doors opened up and he could see the two mysterious soldiers inside. The ensuing explosions had proven correct their decision to flee. All twelve men were packed into the small transport and the pre-flight checklist showed green lights all the way.

Antonin motioned for the pilot to guide them away from the inner docking port and the engines began to rumble with strain. He could feel a heavy sinking feeling in his gut as he realized that the small vessel was not moving. The crowded men began to murmur and the tension level rose substantially in the instant that they realized the docking port would not let them go.

"All right, I've had enough of this game," Antonin rasped and hit the control to open the transport's hatch. A fault tone sounded throughout the transport's cockpit.

The terror that had been threatening to overwhelm him just seconds ago now took full hold as he realized that the airlock had been sealed tight also.

The ship could not leave… and would not let them out.

"What's going on, Commander?" Greely asked, and his idiotic tone of incomprehension grated all over Antonin.

"What's going on is we are going to be supremely screwed!" He shouted in Greely's face. "Those bastards have locked us to this docking port and they won't let us open the hatch!" He screamed and drew his blaster, pointing it toward the small hatchway.

Greely struck his arm and the blaster fell to the floor. Antonin stared at him in shock but Greely responded quickly, "If you blow that hatch, sir, you will destroy the airlock and we will be exposed to the vacuum of space. We can not survive without oxygen. We must think of another way out of this."

"You frigging idiot!" Antonin shrieked. "Those two damn shadows are probably out there right now! Right frigging now!"

That was when they heard the metallic clang of metal attaching itself to metal...

Buzzer had set the detonators of the two explosive charge packs to one minute before attaching both of them to the airlock outside of Inner Port Seventeen. He and Mestizo had gone back to where the corpse of the second bomber still lay, to retrieve the remaining unused explosives before making their way to the inner docking ports, where the five transports used by the invaders had docked. A quick check-in over the com-link with the Control Center had confirmed that occupants had entered a single transport vessel on Inner Port Seventeen and began to power up.

Now, he and Mestizo were running full-speed down the port and into the outer corridor. They were running in the direction of the farthest remaining transport, the one they would use to go down to Toolis and finish what had been started.

Seconds before the transport containing what was left of the invading forces exploded, taking much of the inner port and connecting tunnel with it, the two Guarders dove to the cold metal floor of the corridor to ride out the shockwave. Luckily, the hull-breach caused by the transport's destruction was sealed off immediately where the connecting tunnel met the corridor, just as the emergency mechanisms were designed to do. Buzzer and Mestizo quickly got to their feet and hurried toward their intended transport. Mestizo worked the airlock-access controls and both men scrambled aboard the small ship. Buzzer began the pre-flight checklist as Mestizo secured their weapons. "Buzzer, U.E.N. Guarder, to Control Center," the Guarder called over the now open com-link.

"This is Control Center," an older man's face snapped into view over the com-link in the transport's cockpit. "What in the hell's going on out there?"

"The invasion force formerly on this station has been eliminated," Buzzer answered calmly as his pilot training took over and he readied the vessel for immediate departure. "Please release the airlock seal on this docking port. We are heading down to Toolis. Hopefully, we can put an end to whatever this was and you can get this station back to normal."

"Just the two of you?" The man asked, incredulous.

"Yes, sir," Mestizo added. "We have more than enough firepower, I assure you."

"How can we help you?" A new voice asked and Buzzer could see the face of one of the surviving security guards on the com-link.

"Just sit tight," Mestizo replied with a grin as the small ship cut loose from Killdevil Station. "Don't try to contact your authorities on the planet. You must consider them compromised. We will take care of the situation and return shortly."

"In the meantime," Buzzer said as he scanned the arrival/departure readings for the next day on the small view screen of the pilot's console. "Do you happen to have a luxury cruiser heading to Aegis any time soon?"

MULLENS MOVES ON

Mullens looked up as Buzzer paused and realized that the Guarder wasn't about to continue. "What then?"

Buzzer sat back and looked off to the side for several moments. "I'd rather not divulge what happened after we arrived on Toolis, Mullens," Buzzer said.

"But the historical archives need to reflect the true and complete..."

"The historical archives do not need to divulge the political complexities of the remainder of that mission," Buzzer warned. "Or there could be serious repercussions, even to this day."

"Yes, but Mr. Buzzer, I'm sure for the sake of accuracy and..."

"Move on, Mullens," Buzzer rasped. "I won't tell you again."

Mullens caught the lethal look in the large man's eyes and knew that he had nearly stepped over his bounds. He could feel little beads of sweat running down his forehead and couldn't ever remember being this scared during a research interview.

"Right, moving on then," Mullens stammered and scrolled through his notes to try and regain some semblance of composure. "How about telling me of any encounters you may have had with one of the more powerful businesspersons in the Known-Grids? Any time that you may have had the chance to meet or perhaps work with a well-known member of our society? Are there any of those in your memory?"

"Quite a few."

"Might you elaborate on one?"

Buzzer's eyes left the historian's for a brief instant and Mullens let out the breath he was unconsciously holding in. The man obviously held a wealth of memories of past assignments and combat missions within his brain. If only Mullens could coax out just a few more of those memories before the two-hour time limit for this interview elapsed. He was quickly realizing that he had a gold mine of information seated in front of him, a source of facts and specific events that he wouldn't have been able to find anywhere else.

"Which one would you like to hear about?"

"Well…" Mullens pondered, snapped back to the moment by the unexpected question. "How about one of those incidents that took place not too many years after the events you just described?"

"All right, then," Buzzer said and paused to gather his thoughts before continuing. "You might recognize the event I am about to describe…but I doubt that you've ever heard this version before."

When the United Soviet States destroyed a U.E.N. Military Transport over the Indian Ocean, killing all 838 soldiers aboard in 2096, the two Super Powers had never been closer to the global nuclear holocaust that had been feared for more than a century. To this date, it remains unknown how cooler heads prevailed at a time when a nuclear war seemed imminent and it is yet to be explained just how humanity managed to survive almost certain doom. The attack, weakly justified by the U.S.S. as the logical and tactical defense of its airspace against an enemy aircraft, sparked riots among millions of U.E.N. citizens the world over. With the peoples of both sides clamoring for war, something more than totally unexpected took place in 2097— the signing of the Grid Division Treaty of 2100. With that single act, the human race secured a future among the stars. Within less than three years, more *than 80% of the Earth's population had left the Mother World and ventured out into space— the U.E.N. colonizing the Upper-Grid Levels and the U.S.S. colonizing the Lower-Grid Levels, hopefully never to meet again...*

(Excerpt:*The U.E.N. Unveiled— The Dark History of Humanity's Greatest Government*by Joseph Mullens)

MISSION TWO: BASTILLE

The party was in full swing; the sounds of over ten thousand people eating, dancing and laughing were slightly muffled by the thick walls and rows of books lining the enormous study. It was more than likely that the partygoers had consumed more food in the Great Hall just outside the door to this room in the past three hours than had been eaten by all the people in the sprawling city laid out below him the entire day.

The view from the oversized window, which looked out upon the city of Pari, the capital city of Bastille, was always spectacular, but he found it especially so at night. It seemed a billion multi-colored lights twinkled in the darkness within the city far below. The lights outlining both the Arch de Pari and the Pari Tower brought the city alive at night. Even at this late hour, millions of lives bustled to and fro down there, always rushing to get to wherever it was they were going, always on the move.

Absently he thought to himself, *what could they all be doing?* But he did not have the answer.

Not even the finest talents in his vast organization could possibly keep tabs on the more than eight million rushing citizens of Pari.

A loud crash and the subsequent laughter made him turn his head slightly toward the door. No doubt one of the many servants had already cleaned up whatever mess there was and had just as swiftly disappeared into the crowd.

He raised the wineglass in his left hand, which held nothing but sparkling water, and sipped a silent toast to himself and his corporation. The reason that all of those people were here tonight. A celebration of two hundred e-years of success.

"To Bastille Security Systems," he said and lightly tapped the glass against a meter-wide pane of blast-proof barrier, the only thing that separated him from a certain crushing death upon the rocky foot of Fortress Mount more than six hundred meters below.

"You really should be in there mingling with the guests, John," a soft voice called from over his left shoulder.

"I know, Henri," Bastille answered without looking back at his younger brother. "They came here to be with you, John," his brother continued.

John Domenicus Bastille laughed at that and turned to face his brother. "Those people came here for one reason and one reason only: to be able to say that they set foot inside the legendary Bastille Fortress."

"This is a party, John," Henri said. "Two centuries in business, no small task there."

"Correct," Bastille said and turned once more toward the window. He took a single step closer to the wall-sized window and tried to see the rocks at the bottom of the mountain. "But they don't need me in there to have a party, Henri. Just listen to them. Most of them are drunk, or getting close to it. Dancing, laughing and eating; they don't need me."

After the briefest of pauses, Henri asked, "Why are you brooding on such a great night?"

The elder Bastille brother raised one eyebrow at that and shuddered inside. The cold dead weight of the blaster holstered under his left armpit felt good just now. It felt right.

No need to alarm Henri with news of the plot, he thought to himself. The Fortress Security Unit had been alerted and was fully staffed tonight, mingling with the crowd, trying their best to identify the unwanted guest.

The lower seventy-nine levels of Bastille Fortress, which housed the Bastille Corporate Headquarters as well as the private residences of the entire family, had been closed off prior to this evening's celebration. He had been assured by the commander of his personal security detail that the Fortress had been totally sealed to outside intrusion once the last guest had entered the lift shafts to be whisked away to the party in the penthouse. The other family members had been told that the tighter-than-normal security in place tonight was just a precaution due to the expected size of the crowd.

In fact, he was quite confident that Vlad Gustafa was monitoring the study and his conversation with Henri at this very moment. Why unnerve Henri? Better to let him enjoy the party while everything was under control.

"Of course, Henri," he said and turned away from his brother's reflection in the glass to face him yet again. "I am in a mood tonight and can not explain it. Give me just a few minutes more to get it out of my system and I will rejoin our celebration in good spirits."

"Very good, John," Henri smiled and made his way across the elaborately decorated study and to the door. "Just a few more minutes…or I will be back to fetch you."

"Of that I am sure," Bastille said and watched his brother disappear quickly through the door.

In that brief moment, he saw perhaps a thousand faces through the open doorway, caught the sparkling light of the grand chandelier hanging from the ceiling ten meters over their heads, heard the soothing music of the orchestral assembly playing on the other side of the Great Hall near the entrance, and smelled the great variety of foods that had been prepared for this occasion.

"Report," he whispered and looked up to the eyes of the portrait of his grandfather hanging high atop the far wall, knowing that the unseen camera lens was there.

"Nothing to report, sir," Gustafa's voice sounded low in his left ear, the subcutaneous microphone and speaker implanted there working perfectly.

"Dammit, Vlad," he grumbled. "I can't stay holed up in here all night."

"We haven't located the intruder yet, John," Gustafa said. "It's best if you stay in there where we can monitor you more effectively until we do."

"What if it's not tonight?" Bastille whispered.

"It has to be," his Security Commander answered. "The U.E.N. is certain of it. All of our intel points to it going down tonight. Our contacts confirmed it for tonight. It's going to happen. The assassin is here."

"Well, find this person and do it quickly."

"We're trying," Gustafa said. "Believe me, we're doing everything possible to locate and eliminate this threat as quickly and silently as we can."

Bastille nodded once up toward the picture of his grandfather and resumed his position in front of the blast-proof barrier. It was the furthest point from the door and allowed him the most time to react if an intruder entered the study.

How would it look if this assassination plot succeeded, he thought in dismay. It would ruin Bastille Security Systems forever if the head of the corporation were to be taken out within the walls of the very facility that housed the organizational HQ.

Bastille Security Systems was the premiere security firm throughout all four Corporate Grid- Sectors and had been for the better part of the last century. The intricate security devices designed and installed by Bastille were by far the most advanced and most crime-deterring systems on the market today, for both corporate and residential use. By diversifying into private security force training and staffing and with the launching of a subsidiary specializing in planetary satellite net—defensive/offensive security systems—the corporation was thriving under John's reign. His corporation was directly responsible for substantially lower crime rates in all four Corporate Grid-Sectors over the past decade, and partially responsible for the new trend of declining crime rates among corporate employees, which had been announced by the Universal Corporate Council during last month's State of The Union address broadcast from Cazara.

As a result, many of the major crime syndicates operating throughout the Known-Grids wanted the head of John D. Bastille on a platter. But he had always been considered untouchable by the crimelords...until now, that is.

Word had come several months ago, directly from the United Earthian Nations Judiciary Board, that a price had been put on his head by each of the three major criminal organizations known to exist in the Known Grid-Levels of Space. A bounty worth more than ten billion to the man or woman who could take out John Domenicus Bastille before the end of his corporation's Two-Hundred-E-Year Anniversary Party, with an extra billion thrown in if it happened within the confines of the Bastille Fortress itself.

Not exactly small change, by any standards.

The Fortress was known to be one of the most formidable structures in existence, second only to the enormous U.E.N. Governmental Complex on Aegis. Built as a near-exact, though greatly enlarged, replica of the Bastille Prison in France on old Earth, the towering structure stood eighty stories tall atop the majestic mound of stone often referred to as Fortress Mount; and obviously it did not include the legendary dreaded dungeons and implements of torture as its predecessor had. With eight magnificent rounded towers linked by walls meters thick and tipped with classic castle-style turrets, the Bastille Fortress was a marvel of modern architecture—and one of the most securely fortified structures ever built.

And right now it truly seemed like a prison to John Domenicus Bastille. One which he was just dying to get out of.

"For Chrissakes, Vlad," he grumbled. "How long can it possibly take to locate one person?" Silence was the only response.

A faint electric current, barely there, seemed to race across Bastille's entire body as the silence continued.

So, it happens, he thought to himself and smiled. Somehow, they did it. The Fortress had been penetrated. Incredible!

Bastille's mind soared with the implications that this structure, once thought impregnable, would allow an assassin to enter the gates undetected. As soon as this ordeal was over, he would begin to pick apart every aspect of how this intrusion was accomplished and study it raw, study it until he could be sure that it would never happen again.

The sounds of the crowd could still be heard but his security detail would not respond.

Interesting, he thought, and realized that he stood unmoving, facing the glass, a perfect target.

His eye caught a slight reflection of movement in the glass of the blast-proof barrier before him. The slightest hint of movement and he knew that it was now...

Time stood still for several heartbeats as the analytical mind of John Domenicus Bastille swiftly sorted through the data available to him and devised a strategy, quickly throwing his body into action.

Instantly, the blaster filled his right hand and he dove to his left, away from the window. The blaster bolt that had been heading towards him splashed harmlessly against the glass, another exploding into the wall just above his head.

Funny, he thought, as he stood to take aim across the other side of the study, that he could still hear the raucous sounds of the party on the other side of the closed door.

While someone tries to take my life in this room, the party rages on in the next with no one the wiser.

Bastille smiled at the simplicity of the assassination plot and took aim away from the man who was firing at him, at some yet unseen target on the other side of the room.

From the deeply shaded arches near the door of the study, a black form emerged, exploding into action and triggering three quick blaster bolts towards Bastille's assailant.

Bastille pulled his trigger three times also as an ill-aimed blaster bolt tore into the wall just behind him.

Out of the corner of his eye he could see the man who had been shooting at him fly apart in a bloody spray of bone and tissue.

Bastille's first shot slammed into the column on the opposite side of the door to the study, fracturing the mostly decorative fixture and exposing the man hidden behind it.

The dark form across the vast room seemed to be moving at blinding speed but Bastille's heightened senses interpreted everything in slow motion.

Bastille's second shot slammed into the newly exposed man's chest, shoving him back three meters to thud against the wall. A thick cloud of red mist seemed to surround what was left of the intruder as he began a slow slide to the plush carpeting of the study.

The dark form swung around to take aim at this second intruder but held his fire as Bastille's third shot exploded into the head of his target, staining the walls in that area with thick red blood and gray brain matter. The headless corpse slumped to the carpet with a muffled thud.

And just as suddenly as it had arrived, the threat was over. Two targets were down and out for good. The rest of the room was once again secure.

The smell of spent blaster bolts and charred human flesh filled the study. A slight haze of pulverized building material hung suspended in the air, but all was quiet except for the muffled sounds of the party in the Great Hall.

Bastille turned his head to look at the large dark figure as it emerged from the shadows and became fully visible. The head of Bastille Security Systems held his blaster up, pointed toward the ceiling in a non-threatening posture, realizing immediately that he was in the presence of a dangerously lethal individual.

"I thank you, Guarder," Bastille said, recognizing the man for what he was, and slowly holstered his weapon. The large man dressed entirely in black merely nodded in response but kept his weapon in his big right hand.

"My family and I owe you a debt of gratitude this day," Bastille said and approached the Guarder, hand outstretched.

The warrior deftly switched his blaster to his left hand and met Bastille with a firm unwavering grip.

"Buzzer, U.E.N. Appointed Guarder, Squadron Number Zero-Four-Four," the man stated. "And I was only doing my duty, sir."

"You saved my life, Guarder," Bastille said.

"You seemed to have the situation under control," Buzzer said. "I simply provided some assistance."

Bastille considered this for a moment. "How did you get in here?"

"The same way the two of them did," Buzzer replied.

"Are my security forces that lacking?"

"Actually, no," the Guarder said and holstered his weapon, apparently satisfied that the threat had been eliminated. "Your security is tight. Your personal detail should arrive momentarily.

These two just happened to be the best that the syndicates had to offer. They managed to install a scrambling device specifically tuned to the security hardware contained in this room, just moments before you entered almost an hour ago. They activated it immediately before the attack. They were pretty good, but no match."

"For you, I should say not," Bastille said.

"No, for you," Buzzer answered. "You knew I was there. You saw the first assassin yet you ignored him after his first two blasts. You were confident that the U.E.N., despite your insistence that your security could handle any intruders, would not allow your assassination to occur, and you targeted the second assassin. That was an incredibly calculated risk."

"Not really," Bastille said and smiled. "I know how things work in this universe. As soon as I became aware of the attack and how it was being implemented, I simply became a bystander. You were more than capable of taking them both out. I just felt compelled to take one of them myself."

"And yet I allowed the first assassin to get three shots off."

"I was already moving and in no real danger at that time," Bastille countered. "Surely you were aware of that?"

Buzzer smiled himself then and nodded once toward Bastille as he began backing toward the shaded archway from which he had emerged. "I like to keep things interesting," he said and promptly disappeared.

Standing alone in his study with two corpses and a fair amount of destruction surrounding him, Bastille laughed once.

"I just bet you do, Guarder," he said as Vlad Gustafa and three other of Bastille's personal security detail burst through the door.

MULLENS DIGS DEEPER

"That was *you*?" Mullens whispered. "You were there on the night of the two-hundredth anniversary celebration of Bastille Security Systems? This is unbelievable."

"Believe it."

"I have interviewed Mr. Bastille for the historical archives several times in the past and I have to tell you," Mullens laughed. "He never mentioned a word of it to me. He always said that he didn't recall much of that night, and that he was lucky to have survived the attack."

"John Domenicus Bastille is a very honorable man," Buzzer said. "He would never do anything to put my identity at risk or say anything to a historian that might get back to the wrong people. Assassins work cheap and can be found rather readily throughout the Known Grid- Levels of Space, Mullens. The trick to staying alive in this business is to keep them all guessing. If they don't know who did what, they don't know who to try and kill."

"You make it sound like crime is running rampant all over the four Corporate Grid-Sectors," Mullens joked but quickly swallowed down his laugh when Buzzer fixed him with a glare. "You *are* exaggerating, aren't you?"

"If there wasn't a problem to be dealt with out there each and every day, Mullens, why would there be a need for people like me? Why would the Guarder Squadron even have to exist if there weren't any missions to send its members on?"

"Are you saying that there are killers and assassins walking the streets of every major city in the Known-Grids?" Mullens asked.

"Not only each and every major city that you can think of but most of the smaller and insignificant ones as well," Buzzer rasped.

"That is remarkable," the historian said and sat back in his chair to digest this bit of news. Coming from anyone else, he would have laughed such a statement off as sheer lunacy; but coming from this dark and brooding fellow before him, he somehow knew it was true.

"How about within your own squadron?" Mullens asked and Buzzer's head snapped around fast. Mullens's heart skipped a beat but he pressed on. "Has there ever been any type of dissension in the ranks of the Guarder Squadron? Any Guarders gone bad?"

"Where are you going with this, Mullens?" Buzzer asked and stood from his chair. "Nowhere, sir," Mullens said quickly and pulled his mini-pad close to his chest. "It was just a question. You said that crime is running rampant nearly everywhere…so I was just wondering if you Guarders had ever experienced some of it from within."

Buzzer slowly regained his seat and some of the tension in his jaw line visibly dissipated. But the veins in his neck still bulged with seething anger and Mullens could see the man's fingers spasming with barely controlled rage.

"It seems I've touched a chord with that question, Mr. Buzzer," Mullens said, trying to squeeze a breath in through the tightness of his chest. "Would you care to relate the memories of whatever incident transpired for the historical record?"

"Not particularly, Mullens," Buzzer said. "But the answer to your question is, yes, the Guarder Squadron has experienced evil from within. I'm surprised you haven't heard about it, actually. It wasn't all that long ago either…"

Prior to the New Conflict, the bloodiest war in human history took place in the Concordian Frontier, a vast region of non-populated space, rich with celestial bodies in various shapes and sizes. Shortly after the renowned explorer Tate Concord discovered the region, InterGridactic Mining, Inc. claimed sole ownership of the ore-infested system and quickly stripped each and every rock of all that was valuable. Left abandoned once the mining was completed in 2136, the entire region lay dormant until 2140, when InterGridactic Business Machines laid claim to the Rights of Ownership. Although the allotted four-year period had expired and IGBM had taken care to ensure that their claim had been made within all known legal boundaries, InterGridactic Mining responded with force in an attempt to thwart the IGBM takeover. What started as a simple skirmish, a mere disagreement between enormous corporate entities, exploded into what became known as the Concordian Post War. Ten years and 800 million lives later, IGBM accepted InterGridactic Mining's surrender and The Concordian Post War came to a close. Even now, centuries later, the mere mention of the ghosts of The Concordian Post War sends shivers down the spines of children and adults alike...

(Excerpt: *The U.E.N. Unveiled— The Dark History of Humanity's Greatest Government* by Joseph Mullens)

MISSION THREE: GUARDER RAGE

The lights of the landing platform temporarily blinded Buzzer as he stared down at the Aegis New Arrival Customs Center through the portholes of the small ship. It had taken just a few minutes for the shuttle to descend to the planet's surface after departing the Aegis Spaceport in orbit above the giant planet.

The immense bulk of the U.E.N. Governmental Complex loomed before him in the far distance. Buzzer hardly noticed the slight vibration under his feet as the shuttle's docking clamps secured themselves to the landing platform.

"All passengers, it is now safe to debark," a soothing computerized voice sounded throughout the passenger compartment. "This shuttle is scheduled to return to Aegis Spaceport within the hour. All passengers, it is now safe to debark..."

Buzzer left the shuttle, noticing that the other passengers took great pains to get out of his way; most could not bring themselves to look him in the eye. Although he wore no actual uniform or displayed any type of military ID, most people on Aegis could usually recognize the menacing presence of a Guarder when they saw one.

The Aegis New Arrival Customs Center was bustling with activity, as usual for a facility located so close to the Governmental Complex. Thousands of people and a multitude of vehicles were rushing everywhere, performing millions of different tasks simultaneously. It was the mark of civilization, the mark of technology and the mark of humanity.

Buzzer didn't like it, not at all. He'd much rather stay out on assignment, on different worlds, traveling all across the Known Grid-Levels of Space. He despised returning to this dismal planet of massive crowds, dirty streets and boisterous politicians; but he knew that something important must be brewing if it resulted in his recall to Guarder HQ before the completion of his last assignment.

Glancing up at the massive viewscreens lining the Customs Center's lobby, Buzzer made his way across to the exits. Each screen blared a different newscast, some local and some off world, but none of them caught Buzzer's interest. Just then a feeling came over him, as if he were being watched. Although it was just a tingle, Buzzer hadn't survived this long in the ranks of the Guarder Squadron by arbitrarily dismissing his hunches, no matter how small.

He quickly took mental stock of his weaponry and considered his options within the crowded confines of the Customs Center. If something was going to happen, he would rather it be outside, away from the bustle of innocent civilians. He had two blasters secured on his person underneath the thin black jacket; one in a speed-rig under his left shoulder and one strapped to the small of his back. Several small knives and marble grenades were also within easy reach.

The feeling was creeping up his back now, telling him that the threat, if any, would come from behind. Buzzer couldn't explain it and had stopped trying long ago, but he had learned to trust his instincts. He moved swiftly toward the exit doors, where a row of aircars waited, anxious to ferry newcomers to their destinations on Aegis. His right hand started to flex, fingers twitching with anticipation as he almost reached the doors.

"Buzzer," the low voice called from behind and, with an incredible display of speed, Buzzer turned sideways towards the voice, both of his hands filled with blasters. The one in his right hand was pointed dead center at the chest of the man standing just meters away; the one in his left was pointed safely upward toward the ceiling at his left shoulder. Gasps and a few shouts came from some of the people around the two men but Buzzer didn't allow those to distract him.

"Mestizo," Buzzer said and nodded at his fellow Guarder as the urgency of the situation suddenly dissipated. "It's been a long time." The other man stood stiffly less than three meters away from him, smiling.

"I'm surprised you let me get this close," Tony Mestizo said.

"I wasn't expecting you," Buzzer replied and holstered his weapons. The two friends shook hands briefly and exited the Customs Center together. "Why the pick-up?"

"Sarge said to get you to HQ as soon as possible," Mestizo said and motioned toward a particular aircar. "Many of the others are already here."

Buzzer paused at that and let the implications of Mestizo's statement sink in. "How many of us were recalled?"

"Dozens, from what I've heard," Mestizo said.

"What's this all about, Tony?" Buzzer asked as he entered the tiny vehicle.

"Sergeant Jekel will have to fill us both in on the details," Mestizo offered as he piloted the aircar toward the sprawling Governmental Complex of the United Earthian Nations. "But I've got a very bad feeling about this…"

~*~

Upon entering the Guarder Squadron HQ, Buzzer and Mestizo were instructed to proceed directly to their CO's office deep inside the complex. Without taking the time to check into temporary quarters or filing the standard status reports, both men arrived at their destination within minutes. Jekel saw them enter his outer office and beckoned the two Guarders inside.

"Good to see you, Buzzer," Jekel said and motioned for the two men to sit in chairs opposite his desk. "I'm glad you were able to make it here in one piece."

The doors to Jekel's office, normally left open during the day, silently closed behind them.

Buzzer saw the intensity in the eyes of the large figure of Harrison Jekel and knew immediately that he wouldn't like whatever it was his commanding officer was about to say. "Although Mestizo arrived here yesterday, I wanted to address you both at the same time about what's been happening."

The two Guarders shared an ominous glance with each other before settling their attention back on Harrison Jekel.

"I'm going to provide the two of you with a lot more information than I've given to the others who have arrived so far. Since I'm looking for you two to head up this little mission, I'm going to give it to you straight."

"We're being sent out together?" Buzzer questioned.

"Yes, Frank," Jekel nodded. "I'm adding a few more to your group also. In fact, you'll probably need to make use of as many resources as you can get your hands on before this mission is through. I need you both to listen to what I have to say without interruption; I need your undivided attention and I need you both to deliver quickly on what I'm going to ask of you. Understood?"

Both men nodded and Jekel continued. "When I first put out the recall, there had only been twenty hits. While you both were in transit, there've been eighteen more. This problem is extremely serious, in fact it's unheard of; but the killing has to be stopped."

"The killing of who, Sarge?" Mestizo asked and Jekel frowned at the interruption. "Guarders," Jekel said and stood up to hover over them. "There have been thirty-eight confirmed kills on Guarders in the past week, Aegis standard. Thirty-eight!" Jekel boomed. "I don't know by who or why, but that's where you two and your team come in."

Buzzer was shocked; he couldn't believe what he had just heard but he was pretty sure it was no joke. By the look on Mestizo's face, the other Guarder couldn't believe it either.

"I know it's hard to swallow, I know it's unbelievable, but those are the facts," Jekel said. "For over four centuries, this Squadron has been invincible, the very best fighting force to ever exist in the history of mankind. Guarders have proven themselves again and again throughout the history of the U.E.N. and even through the New Conflict; but never before has such a threat as is facing us now surfaced to plague our ranks. Back then, when our indelible reputation was first being earned through precision strikes and overwhelming force against our opponents, the people of the Known-Grids learned to respect us and fear us. The legendary wrath and vengeance of the U.E.N. Guarder Squadron has been in place for centuries; we have taught our enemies to cower before us and they dare not stand against us." Jekel paused and looked each of the two men before him in the eye. "Now that's changed. Someone has taken our group of two hundred and reduced it by thirty-eight. *Thirty-eight!*" Jekel shouted, pounding his fist down on his desk. "Yes, I'm angry. I can see it in both of you, too. This has to stop! We have to find out who has been targeting the members of this Squadron and eradicate them. Permanently. Am I understood?"

"Yes, sir," Buzzer said, nearly growling with rage.

"Buzzer will be Mission Commander," Jekel said to Mestizo. "You'll be number two. Any problems there?"

"No, sir," Mestizo answered, his right hand tapping the blaster holstered at his side. "Who were some of the victims, Sarge?" he asked.

"You both knew many of them," Jekel sighed. "Loner, Rival, Navajo, Slammer, Mercury and Cyclone were just a few of the first to get hit. Some, not on the list of dead, have been missing now for quite some time. Since we haven't found any bodies, we can't be sure if they are dead or being held up somewhere; but we haven't received word from at least twenty others and they are long overdue to check in."

"What are some of the names on the missing list?" Buzzer asked.

"Kozar, Serpent, Stryker, Rizzo, Snaker and a bunch of others," Jekel said. "Stoner was the first to disappear."

"There're a lot of good men on both those lists," Buzzer said. "Have there been any casualties at all on the other side? Have any of our men managed to take even one of their assailants out?"

"None that we know of..." Jekel almost whispered, knowing what his answer implied. "Each hit was performed execution style, up close and personal. So far, no witnesses, at least none that the local authorities at the crime scenes could turn up. Only those bodies that were still intact enough to be shipped were brought back here. For the others, I've instructed the local authorities to provide burials with honors."

"Any suspects?" Mestizo asked. "Guarders..." Buzzer muttered. "Guarders?" Mestizo asked in amazement.

"I have to agree with you, Buzzer," Jekel said softly. "However much I hate it, that's the only thing that makes sense."

"Who in their right mind...?" Mestizo started.

"Guarders are the only human beings capable of moving in close enough to other Guarders to take them all out," Buzzer said. "No one else would have this much success against us. We're too well trained and too damned suspicious to allow anyone who we are not fully comfortable with to approach that closely. Especially when out on assignment."

"My thoughts exactly, Buzzer," Jekel said. "Incredible as it sounds, I believe that we have a renegade group of Guarders on our hands that are intent on doing away with everyone else who is not a part of their little rebellion. And so far, they've been damn busy at it."

43

"For what possible reason?" Mestizo wondered aloud.

"For greed," Buzzer said and saw Jekel nod in agreement. "Think about it, Tony. A group of Guarders get greedy seeing all the money that the slimeballs they are sent out to terminate are raking in. They figure to hire themselves out as mercenaries, or maybe move in on a particularly lucrative criminal operation, and get rich in the process. The only problem with that is the other Guarders who aren't a part of their group. Knowing the Guarder wrath as well as anyone, they know that the only way around this problem is to eliminate the threat—meaning *us*. Once all the Guarders who aren't willing to join them are dead, who else in all of the Known Grid-Levels of Space could stand against them?"

"It's a devious scheme but, if implemented properly and ultimately successful, this group of renegades could wreak total havoc throughout each of the four Corporate Grid-Sectors. We have to assume that they've just gotten started and look at how much damage they've done already," Jekel said. "The one thing they didn't count on was our periodic checks on your vitals, little scans we run on your sequencers, which let us know if you are all still alive and well out there among the stars. When some of these vitals came back negative, we thought it was an equipment malfunction. Once we started getting calls from off-world law enforcement agencies, all wanting to know just what in the hell to do with Guarder bodies, we knew we had a significant problem."

"So, the renegades are not yet aware that Aegis knows what's going on?" Buzzer asked. "That's correct; one of the reasons why I rushed you both back here," Jekel said. "If your team can locate them and take them out before they are aware that they are being hunted, we could save a lot of bloodshed and restore a little dignity to our squadron before news of this explodes across the Grids. I leave it in your hands. I will monitor things from here and pass along any new intelligence as it comes in. Anything you want on this mission is yours, just ask for it. I have recalled as many Guarders as I could without arousing immediate suspicion. I have more recalls going out discreetly as we speak. But since I don't know who is part of this rebellion and who isn't…I can't come right out and tell them why they are being recalled. This is a damn mess. I feel like I can't trust half of my own men and some of the other half might just get killed because of it."

"Who did you recruit among those of us you trust, Sarge?" Buzzer asked.

"You two will be joined by Thunder, Psyches and Skinner," Jekel said. "I'm hoping that a grouping of the five best Guarders in the ranks will put this whole fiasco to rest."

"Good men," Mestizo said. "We'll make a solid team."

"That's what I'm hoping for," Jekel said and stood. "There will be a short group-briefing in the conference room in one hour. You'll leave immediately after that. Dismissed."

Jekel looked into the eyes of Frank Buzzer, his best soldier, as he stood to leave the office…and saw something very dark in the recesses of the man's mind. A dark and cold thing that threatened to boil over at any moment, threatened to explode into action and bring vengeance to the men who had betrayed him. Jekel suddenly realized that the specter of death stood before him, a specter who would stop at nothing to deliver justice for those who were murdered, and absolute terror to all those responsible.

Funny, Jekel thought to himself as he watched the two Guarders leave his office; he remembered a time when he had possessed that look himself...

~*~

Buzzer sat alone in one corner of a VIP cubicle deep inside the immense bulk of an Aegis/Corpura Express TransitLiner. The ship, although incredibly huge, moved swiftly through space and was already more than halfway to Corpura.

The cubicle he and his team of Guarders occupied was usually reserved for high-ranking

U.E.N. officials who liked to travel in secrecy; but it had been secured for them immediately upon the news that Snaker and Serpent, two of the Guarders on the 'missing' list, had both been spotted in the vicinity of Corpura. With all of the resources of every branch of the U.E.N. Military at the Squadron's disposal, most Guarders operating in the field had instant access to an enormous wealth of intelligence normally unavailable to field agents of other governmental agencies.

Buzzer knew that the identities of most of the renegades could probably be found on the 'missing' list—those who had mysteriously missed their last scheduled check-ins with Aegis and whose command sequencers had stopped submitting vitals. If Snaker and Serpent had both been seen together in one area after they were put on the 'missing' list, it could only mean one thing— they were part of the rebellion and could lead Buzzer and his teammates to the others.

He had also just received word over his command sequencer that Tracer and Eskimo had been added to the list of the dead; their bodies had been found on the resort world of New Africa just hours ago. Eskimo had managed to key in one word on his sequencer before succumbing to his wound, and that one word— *Stoner— was the answer to many of Buzzer's questions.*

Stoner had been a member of the Guarder Squadron just a little longer than Buzzer. He had joined the squadron by filling the spot left open by Gryphon, a Guarder who had died under mysterious circumstances. Stoner came from a deep-rooted military background, having served in the U.E.N. Army Special Forces Unit through two tours before moving into OWOP, the Off-World Operative Program. He had built his reputation there as an ambitious and power-hungry officer, eager for promotions and more responsibility. After just one contract-renewal with OWOP, he asked for, and was granted by the U.E.N. Judiciary Board, a commission in the lower ranks of the Guarder Squadron. Since then, his career had stalled.

Now, it seemed, he was trying to take it up a notch.

Buzzer knew that speed was of the essence if they had any chance of saving the two Guarders, Calico and Blitzer, who were both currently on assignment on Corpura. As far as Buzzer knew, neither Guarder was aware of the escalating rebellion taking place among the Guarder ranks. On the other hand, there was no telling if Serpent and Snaker were on Corpura for a little rebellious rendezvous with the two Guarders already there.

Stoner, Serpent, Snaker...Buzzer couldn't wait to get his hands on any one of them. They may have been Guarders at one time in their lives, but after deciding to turn on their own, they had become nothing but targets. He looked over the other members of his team, sitting at various positions throughout the cubicle. Good men, talented Guarders. All of them seething in their own hatred of those who had decided to become traitors.

He could see each of them concentrating inwardly on their ultimate goal— bringing the rebellion and the rebels themselves to an immediate...and *permanent...end.*

~*~

Calico stiffened. His sixth sense was tingling, telling him that something was about to happen.

It was strange, though, since everything seemed quiet enough out here on the street. Nothing seemed in any way out of the ordinary. He activated his command sequencer, setting the device to *Internal-Com*, and looked toward the bar that Blitzer had entered almost an hour ago for a little investigating on their current assignment.

It wasn't like Blitzer to take this long before checking in by sequencer and now Calico was more than a little on edge.

"Blitzer," he whispered even though no one could hear his voice emanating from the subcutaneous receiver implanted behind Blitzer's right ear. "How's it going in there?"

"I have some company, Calico," Blitzer's voice responded from his sequencer in a very neutral tone. "Why don't you come on in and we'll have a group discussion."

"What kind of company?" Calico asked as he primed both of his blasters and opened the door to his aircar. "Good or bad?"

"Guarder company, believe it or not," Blitzer answered, a slight tremor in his voice. "Serpent and Snaker were already in here when I came in."

"What in the hell...?" Calico said and paused for a moment. It was extremely odd to meet up with two other Guarders who were not participating in your assignment, especially when the meeting was unannounced. "I'll be right there, Blitz," he said and closed the door to his vehicle.

The hand came out of nowhere and grabbed him tightly around his neck, effectively immobilizing him for one brief instant. Calico stiffened, prepared his counter-attack but heard the familiar voice behind him and was even more confused. "Stay cool, Calico, it's Psyches."

Psyches released some of the tension around the Guarder's neck and allowed Calico to turn around and face him.

"How many of us are on this damn planet anyway?" Calico asked.

"Listen to me," Psyches said with authority and Calico noticed that his hand rested on the blaster strapped to his left hip. "There's some trouble in the ranks. Snaker and Serpent have turned renegade...can't you feel the tension?"

"Yeah, I felt something," Calico agreed. "But that doesn't explain what you're doing here, Psyches."

"There's no time for details, Calico," Psyches said and pulled his blaster free from its holster. "Your partner on this assignment is in there with those two, and so are Buzzer and Mestizo."

"What?" Calico asked in exasperation.

"We'll fill you in later," Psyches said and began to slowly make his way toward the entrance of the Blue Olive Bar. "You're going to have to trust me on this. Stay alert. If we're right about those two, someone's going to get fried."

~*~

"Snaker," Buzzer growled from behind the Guarder's seated back. Serpent and Blitzer were also sitting at the small table in the dark near the back of the bar. Buzzer could see the nervous tension and confusion on Blitzer's face. "Imagine seeing you here. And Serpent, too?"

Snaker had visibly stiffened in his chair several moments earlier, obviously warned by Serpent of Buzzer's approach.

"Buzzer," Snaker said without bothering to turn around, relying on Serpent to tip him off if any real trouble began. Buzzer wondered at that lapse in Snaker's Guarder training.

"Well, I haven't seen this many Guarders grouped together off of Aegis in a long time," Buzzer continued and pulled up a seat next to Blitzer.

"What brings you to Corpura, Buzzer?" Serpent asked.

"Vacation," Buzzer rasped, not taking his eyes off of Snaker. With Snaker's proven ability on the firing range and his reputation for completing missions in a coldly methodical manner, Snaker was easily the more dangerous of the two. "How about you, Serpent? According to Sergeant Jekel's placement schedule back at the HQ, your current assignment isn't on Corpura."

"You're right," Snaker said and flashed Serpent an angry glare. "We're just passing through and happened to meet up with Blitzer here."

Buzzer nodded. "Sounds like a good enough reason, I guess," he said and looked at Blitzer. "Can I talk to you for a moment alone, Blitzer?"

"Sure thing," Blitzer replied immediately and the two Guarders stood up from their chairs. As they began to back slowly away from the table, Buzzer saw Serpent make his move.

"Down!" Buzzer shouted and he and Blitzer dove in different directions. Ignoring Serpent, Buzzer concentrated on Snaker.

Serpent swung his blasters toward Buzzer and was just about to fire—when a blast from Mestizo's half-charger cut him down from behind.

Snaker had weapons in both hands and was trying to aim for Buzzer as a blast from Blitzer exploded into the table in front of him, sending Snaker sprawling for cover.

Serpent's blood and guts flew across the room as his body thudded to the floor of the bar.

48

Buzzer covered the short distance between him and Snaker in less than a second and delivered a vicious kick to the man's left temple. People scattered throughout the bar, running for the exits or diving under tables. Snaker hit the floor hard and was already turning when Buzzer struck him with the butt of his blaster in the same temple.

Snaker tumbled over, grabbed a downed table and flung it at Buzzer. In the moment that it took Buzzer to kick aside the table, Snaker snapped off a shot with his blaster. The shattered table bore the brunt of the blaster bolt but Buzzer was no longer behind it. He came out of his shoulder roll about five feet away, ignoring the flare of pain in his left shoulder from a collision with several chairs, and fired once toward Snaker.

Snaker's gun hand was obliterated by the blast, and the wounded man fell to his knees in agony. Despite his tremendous pain, Snaker was reaching inside his jacket for another concealed weapon when Buzzer pressed the muzzle of his blaster against the man's forehead. Distantly, Buzzer heard the muffled sounds of weapons fire coming from outside the bar and hoped that the others were all right.

"Game's up," he muttered at Snaker and pressed the man's head down with his blaster until Snaker was lying flat on the floor. Mestizo appeared at his side and nodded toward Serpent.

"That one's dead," Mestizo said and Buzzer could see that he had already gathered Serpent's weapons and ID.

"So's this one," Buzzer said—and stomped his foot down hard on Snaker's handless arm. The scream was short but it escaped Snaker's mouth before he was able to stop it.

"Hear that, Snaker? You're dead, too."

"Jesus Christ, Buzzer," Snaker rasped through gritted teeth. "What in the hell's the matter with you?"

"Enough with the small talk," Buzzer said and pressed down a little harder on the bloody stump of Snaker's arm. "Where's Stoner?"

"How would I know?" Snaker answered.

"Wrong answer, Snaker," Buzzer said and motioned to Serpent's dead body. "Look long and hard at your co-conspirator over there, Snaker. Those eyes aren't looking at anything. They're dead. The Sarge knows all about you and Stoner and your upstart rebellion. Forty Guarders have been fried by you traitors already. But now, that's over."

"I'm telling you that I don't..." Buzzer leaned all of his weight forward on the stump of Snaker's wounded arm and watched deep red blood gush out.

"Once again, wrong answer," Buzzer said.

"Kill me, then, you son-of-a-bitch!" Snaker yelled between gasps.

"If I don't your wounds will, and soon," Buzzer said. "Unless, of course, we get you some medical attention pretty quickly. Do you want to die, Snaker?"

Snaker took several controlled gasps between the seemingly unending waves of pain which flowed through his right arm and settled his gaze on the face of his tormentor. "You'll get me medical attention, Buzzer?"

"Not before you tell us what we need to know," Buzzer said. "Now, where's Stoner?"

Snaker let his head slowly settle to the floor of the Blue Olive Bar and took a deep breath.

"He's in a safe-house somewhere on Adonis."

"Who's the next hit?"

"Damn, I don't know," Snaker said. "That's Stoner's thing, Buzzer. All I know is that he's devising his attack strategy now."

"Attack on who?"

"Not who," Snaker sighed. "He's going to attack the Guarder HQ, inside the Governmental Complex."

Buzzer's eyes widened at this new information.

"When?"

"Four or five days from now, Aegis Standard," Snaker said. "I don't have any of the details because I wasn't supposed to be a part of that action."

"How many Guarders has Stoner turned renegade, Snaker?" Buzzer said.

"There were twenty of us," he replied and looked over at Serpent's still form lying in a puddle of blood not three meters away. "Now I guess there's only nineteen."

"Wrong," Buzzer said and pressed the muzzle of his blaster to Snaker's head once more. "There's only eighteen..."

Buzzer fired once and Snaker's head blew apart. The traitor's headless body spasmed for a second or two, then lay still.

Buzzer picked the body clean of weapons and ID's, then motioned for Mestizo to follow him out of the bar.

To the well-dressed man standing in the doorway, obviously the establishment's owner or the owner's representative, Buzzer said, "Contact Aegis for a credit voucher, tell them it's authorized by Buzzer, U.E.N. Appointed Guarder, Squadron Number Zero-Four-Four. They'll take care of this for you."

The man nodded once and stepped aside.

Buzzer left the bar with Mestizo close behind. Although the bright sunshine was a welcome relief from the dimly lit confines of the Blue Olive Bar, the stench of death Buzzer had just left inside remained with him out on the street. About five meters away, Calico and Thunder were standing over the body of Kelly Psyches, a gaping hole in his chest, lying in the dirty street. The body of another Guarder, Caballero, was lying about twenty meters further up the street. Skinner stood over the still form.

"What happened?"

"Caballero came out of nowhere," Calico said. "He only fired once before he took off. I fired back several times. I swear I hit the bastard in the back twice but he kept moving."

"Caballero liked his body armor," Buzzer commented.

"Skinner fried him with his half-charger before he could clear the corner," Thunder said, then motioned toward the bar. "What happened in there?"

"Scratch Serpent and Snaker," Mestizo said.

Thunder just nodded and flashed a thumbs-up signal to Skinner down the street.

"I want everyone but Mestizo to head back to Aegis," Buzzer said. "Stoner is planning to attack the HQ; he probably wants to waste Jekel."

"Where are you and Mestizo going?" Thunder asked.

"To Adonis," Buzzer said. "We have some unfinished business with what's left of this rag-tag rebellion. Any questions?"

"Yeah," Calico said and raised his arms in bewilderment. "Will someone please tell me what's going on?"

~*~

Mohican caught sight of Buzzer and Mestizo in the busy shopping square again. For a few seconds there he had lost the two of them in the crowd.

He had been tailing them since they had debarked a SleekLine Cruiser several hours earlier at the local spaceport. Although he had been stationed there to look for the unexpected arrival of uninvited Guarders, their sudden appearance had still managed to shock him.

Stryker had warned him that it wouldn't be long before the Sarge figured out what was going on and sent the best Guarders he could after their small group of rebels. But Mohican had had no idea that it would happen so soon.

The mere presence of Buzzer on Adonis was enough to convince Mohican that the Sarge had dispatched the most skillful clean-up crew available to search out the rebel band and destroy them. The presence of Mestizo as well only served to solidify that assumption. Buzzer was supposed to be deep in the Axtell System, several hundred Grid-Levels away from Adonis, for at least another week, Aegis Standard. There was a very serious problem arising on Axtion-3 and the U.E.N. Embassy there had requested some assistance.

Mestizo was also supposed to be on assignment, nowhere near where he now stood on Adonis. Big trouble was brewing and Mohican started to question the ultimate wisdom of his decision to join up with Stoner and the other renegades.

Only the fact that he hadn't really had a choice—other than death—when he said 'yes' to Stoner made him feel somewhat better...but only somewhat…

Buzzer and Mestizo were the two best Guarders in the ranks, surely more than a match for most of the Guarders who had joined Stoner's rebellion. A teaming of the two best personnel was a very rare thing in Guarder history.

Mohican didn't like it, not one bit.

He had to get word of the two unwelcome visitors back to Stryker before things began to heat up. In fact, Mohican thought to himself, it might take him up a notch or two with Stoner if he could manage to take out the two unsuspecting Guarders before they knew what was going on.

It was the perfect opportunity, one that wasn't likely to present itself again anytime in the near future. Mohican reached inside his jacket and gripped the cold metal of his half-charger.

~*~

"Something's up," Buzzer said casually as he and Mestizo walked through the business district of Center City. The busy shopping square was bustling with salespeople shouting out their deals, customers griping about prices and hundreds of other people who were rushing through the area. "Keep your eyes open, Tony."

"I'm already there," Mestizo said and casually glanced backward over his shoulder.

All looked normal, exactly as it should be within the midst of a busy shopping center. But something was nagging at the back of Buzzer's mind. One word kept popping up back there— Danger.

Buzzer suddenly stiffened—he could almost feel the bull's eye that had just appeared on his back.

The glint of sunlight on metal about a block away snapped him to attention and he dove to the ground, dragging Mestizo with him. The air above them exploded with charger fire and the storefront behind them erupted in a fireball. Buzzer rolled out of his dive with both of his blasters filling his hands and took cover behind a merchandise display. More charger blasts were pouring into the area, sending people running hysterically through the fire-zone.

Mestizo snapped off two quick shots in the general direction of the source of the weapons fire and the charger blasts abruptly ended. He took the sudden lull in the action to take stock of his surroundings and attempt to locate any additional opponents.

As the dust began to settle, Buzzer could see Mestizo several shops over, with blasters also in both hands. That one had been close, too close for his taste. He cursed himself for not sensing the danger sooner. He hated to think that his skills were getting rusty, that he had lost his edge, his sharpness. Buzzer could feel his rage begin to boil as he realized that he and Mestizo were most likely being fired upon, once again, by a fellow Guarder. His overwhelming desire to kill this attacker was threatening to burst through and take over his senses.

The crowd that had been milling about just moments ago had abruptly disappeared from view, leaving the square empty and silent. Mestizo, staying low, moved out of eyesight around the back of the small shop he had chosen for cover. Buzzer gave him a few seconds to get into position and then jumped up from his hiding spot, sprinting across the empty square to draw their assailant'sfire.

Charger blasts immediately began to chew up the paving stones just behind his heels. Buzzer suddenly swerved to his right and leapt behind the ornamental sculptures and carvings that occupied the center of the square. As Buzzer came down on the cold unforgiving stone and rolled with his momentum, Mestizo opened up with his blasters.

For several seconds after Mestizo's onslaught had ended, Buzzer lay motionless and listened to nothing but the pounding of his heart. The silence was almost deafening in the now deserted shopping square.

Almost as if on cue, the two Guarders both jumped from cover and headed directly for the area in which the shots aimed at them had come. Reaching the corner, they took up position at the edge of a large brick storefront, Buzzer low and Mestizo high.

Buzzer snuck a quick look down the shop-lined street beyond and saw a thick trail of blood leading to a badly limping man about forty meters away. Buzzer took careful aim, lined the man's wounded leg up in his sights—and fired. His target howled as the blast took his left leg off at the knee. The man crumpled to the street, his half-charger skidding away, and rolled over in an effort to cradle what was left of his shattered leg.

"Mohican," Mestizo said and swore under his breath as he recognized the face. Buzzer rose to his feet and motioned for Mestizo to follow as they began to walk slowly down the street toward the fallen former member of their Squadron. Mohican had crawled over to where the lower half of his left leg had fallen. Grabbing up the shattered member, Mohican began to drag himself slowly toward where his half-charger had landed, still some meters away.

Buzzer reached him first; he kicked the large weapon out of the man's reach just as Mohican's trembling fingers were about to grab its stock. Mestizo bent down and grabbed the wounded man from behind, twisting his arms around his back and pinning them there with his knee.

Buzzer leaned down and pressed the muzzle of his blaster to Mohican's left temple. "Where's Stoner?"

By now, most of the shoppers who had run for cover during the brief battle were now grouped around the corner the two Guarders had just left. There seemed to be at least two hundred people gawking at the spectacle less than forty meters away.

Mohican returned Buzzer's question with a broad sarcastic smile. Buzzer lashed out with incredible speed, connecting with the butt of his blaster across Mohican's nose. Blood spurted from Mohican's face and he shouted with rage at the two Guarders who held him captive.

Buzzer kicked the heel of his boot into the bloody stump below Mohican's left knee and the crowd gasped in shock. Mohican let out an agonized scream and tried to wrestle free from Mestizo's iron grasp.

Buzzer restored the contact of his muzzle to Mohican's head. "Let's try this again," he snarled. "Where's Stoner?"

"Go to hell, Buzzer," Mohican panted between breaths. "I'm not saying anything."

"You have fired on U.E.N. Appointed Guarders, members of your own Squadron, with intent to kill. An act punishable by death at this very moment, Mohican!" Buzzer screamed at the man. "I am not messing with you; where's Stoner?"

Mohican spat at him. Buzzer grabbed Mohican's face viciously by the chin and looked deep into his eyes, trying to determine what had pushed the man to fire on his own. "If you don't tell me, you will die...whether by my blaster or by blood loss, it really doesn't matter."

"If I talk, I'll be just as dead," Mohican growled. "Stoner will have me killed."

"Stoner won't be around," Mestizo whispered in his ear and Mohican stiffened.

"Go screw..." he said and Buzzer lashed out again with his boot, sending a river of fresh blood squirting from Mohican's tortured leg. The angry sounds of the crowd behind them grew louder at this blatant display of cruelty and torture.

"Let's finish this up fast, Buzzer," Mestizo said. "That crowd could turn into a mob, and I really don't feel like firing on a bunch of civilians today if I can help it."

Buzzer nodded once and met Mohican's terrified eyes. "What will it be, Mohican? Do you talk or do you want another kick? I can keep this going for a while yet, and I know how to wake you up if you pass out from the pain."

"What about the crowd?" Mohican snarled.

"What about them?" Buzzer answered and pressed down lightly on Mohican's bloody stump with his foot.

"Dammit!" Mohican screamed and glared at Buzzer. "All right, all right, but I want protection after this."

"I already told you," Mestizo said. "Stoner's not going to be around much longer. Just tell us what you know."

Mohican swallowed and took a deep breath. "He's in transit."

"To Aegis?" Buzzer asked and Mohican was surprised at Buzzer's guesswork. "That's right; he's got a surprise planned for the HQ."

"It's no surprise, we know all about his plans to attack the Governmental Complex," Buzzer said. "But he's on his way there already?"

"Yeah, but..." Mohican stumbled. "Who is with him?"

"Nobody," Mohican said. "He's acting alone on this one."

"Stoner is going to attack Guarder HQ by himself, with no back-up?" Mestizo asked. "That's his plan," Mohican confirmed.

"What's he going to use for weapons?" Buzzer asked.

Mohican looked at the two Guarders before him and realized the deadly seriousness in their faces. Gulping once, he answered, "A nuke."

"Goddammit!" Buzzer rasped and looked at Mestizo. "He's going to try and take out the entire complex, not just the HQ."

"Where did he get his hands on a nuclear?" Mestizo asked.

"We raided an old deserted mine on Craxton," Mohican said. "One of the nuclear packs was still intact."

"How's he going to save himself?" Buzzer asked, still leaning on Mohican's leg.

"He's going to do a fly-by with an Eagle-44J over the complex, drop the nuke and pull up through the atmosphere," Mohican said through gritted teeth. "He'll be gone before the bomb goes off."

"Where's Stryker right now?" Buzzer asked.

"He's here, in Beacon's Port," Mohican said. "So are most of the others. We were to wait here for Stoner to finish his mission and come back."

"Good enough," Buzzer said to Mestizo. "Let this piece of garbage go."

Mestizo lifted Mohican a few inches from the ground and threw him down harshly. Buzzer kicked the man's half-charger to just within his reach and said, "You're free."

"What about my protection?" Mohican said, eyeing the weapon, trying to decide just how far away it was from his fingertips.

"No protection," Buzzer said. "You're lucky to still be breathing."

"What about my leg?" Mohican screamed at the two Guarders as they turned back toward the square and began to walk away.

Neither man answered and Mohican screamed in rage. Scrabbling on his hands past what was left of his leg, Mohican grabbed up his weapon and began to swing it around. The crowd at the corner scrambled back as, once again, screams of terror filled the streets.

Before Mohican could let loose a single charge, three blaster bolts slammed into his chest, knocking him six or seven meters across the street to crash into a storefront in a bloody heap.

Buzzer held his blaster clear, pointed toward the sky, and watched as Mestizo walked over to retrieve the dead man's weapons, ID and Guarder Badge.

~*~

Cougar came running into his CO's office and stood at attention in front of the massive desk. "Sergeant Jekel, sir," he said before noticing the presence of Thunder and Skinner in the

office as well.

"What is it, Cougar?" the formidable bulk of the Guarder Squadron Commander asked as he stood to face his Communications Officer.

"We just received this message from Buzzer on Adonis," Cougar said and held the data-sheet out to Jekel.

Jekel grabbed the short message and looked it over. It read:

...HQ...TARGET IN TRANSIT...WILL ARRIVE SHORTLY IF NOT ALREADY THERE...WILL ATTACK HQ ALONE USING EAGLE-44J AND MINI-NUCLEAR WEAPON...PROHIBIT ALL LAUNCHINGS...CLOSE ALL SPACEPORTS... ENFORCE GLOBAL TRAVEL RESTRICTIONS ON AEGIS...CLEANING UP HERE...

BACKSOON...B...

Sergeant Harrison Jekel let out a sigh and sat back down in his chair. "Christ Almighty, that maniac is going to try to nukeus."

"Nukes?" Thunder asked. "Stoner has access to nuclears?"

"Apparently so," Jekel said. "Skinner, make sure that an order for global travel restrictions goes out to each and every spaceport and transit terminal on this planet, even the ones way out in the outback. Tell them that all violators will be prosecuted to the full extent of my powers; they'll know what that means."

He turned to Thunder as Skinner left. "Thunder, get down to Technical and tell Needle that I want the entire planet blanketed to warn us of all incoming vessels, maximum range. I want that blanket tuned to Stoner's vitals just in case he has decided to reactivate his command sequencer. That lunatic has got himself a nuclear and he has the balls to use it. We've got to make sure this insane plot of his does not succeed. Am I understood?"

"Very clearly, sir," Thunder said and quickly left the office.

Jekel sat alone with his thoughts for several seconds before getting up and storming out of his office after Thunder.

~*~

Night was usually very dark on Adonis, with no moon in orbit to provide any light, but not in Beacon's Port. The lights surrounding the crowded popular night-spot flared brilliantly across the vast plaza sitting above the marina but left most of the riverside in darkness. There were several yachts bobbing in the shadows alongside four small docks that jutted out into the Beacon River. Above the docks a series of restaurants and open-air bistros crowded with patrons lined the riverbank.

Mestizo could see the lone sentry standing beside the yacht that was their target. He also recognized that sentry and shook his head in disbelief. The Guarder had been a friend of his in the ranks; someone he would have never thought could turn renegade.

He broke away from the small crowd of people strolling along the walkway that lined the riverbank, and stepped on to the dock about twenty meters from his quarry. The lone sentry looked up and visibly stiffened.

Mestizo kept walking toward the man, both hands empty and at his sides in plain view. He stopped about two meters from the man and stared into his eyes.

"Chaney," he said and shook his head.

The man's face betrayed no emotion, his eyes boring straight back into Mestizo's own. "Sorry, Tony," Chaney said and made his move.

Mestizo stood motionless as Buzzer stepped from the shadows behind Chaney and silently slit the man's throat from ear to ear with a single stroke of a long thin blade. Chaney gurgled in his own blood and dropped to his knees, the blaster in his right hand now useless. Buzzer lowered the dying man lightly to the dock, not wanting to make any noise, and watched the pool of dark liquid spread across the wooden planks. Chaney's blood looked black in the light filtering in from above the docks as Buzzer cleaned the knife on the slain man's shirt.

"Sorry, Mestizo," Buzzer said. "I know you two were friends."

Mestizo barely nodded and turned to face the yacht. "Let's get on this boat and finish what we came here for."

Buzzer sheathed his blade and nodded in return.

58

All was silent on the large vessel. Almost too silent. With Chaney now dead, they knew that there were at least fifteen renegade Guarders still alive. Stoner was in transit to Aegis. They had watched Sahara, Python, Mirage and Taurus leave the yacht during the afternoon, probably to check up on Mohican.

That left ten others who were hopefully still inside the boat.

Ten Guarders against the two of them. Buzzer didn't like those odds one bit, but he and Mestizo had the element of surprise on their side, as well as their superior skills. It might just be enough to tip the scales in their favor.

They climbed aboard ship near the stern and proceeded silently forward. They could hear voices coming from the cabins below decks but couldn't recognize any of them.

Suddenly, a door opened, slamming into Buzzer and nearly sending him careening over the rail. The man gasped at the sight of the unexpected visitors and reached frantically for his blaster. Buzzer could see a stairway descending into the ship behind their opponent as his hands found purchase on the rail. Luckily there wasn't anyone else climbing up to the deck.

The renegade Guarder was just about to scream for his comrades when Mestizo's small dagger struck him through the right eye and penetrated his brain. The body began convulsing and Buzzer grabbed the corpse before it fell to the deck. Together, he and Mestizo were able to carry the body several meters further along the deck and out of the way.

"It's Phoenix," Mestizo muttered as he removed the dead man's weapons and ID.

"Not anymore," Buzzer said and turned back toward the still open doorway. Voices were coming from the stairway behind the door now. Buzzer and Mestizo immediately assumed battle crouches, weapons filling their hands.

Buzzer recognized the first man to stick his head through the doorway; it was River, one of the newer Guarders with less than two e-years of experience in the ranks. Before the renegade Guarder could react, River received the thrust of Buzzer's knife through his left temple where it sliced cleanly into his skull and penetrated deep into his brain. Buzzer kicked the corpse free of his blade, sending the body tumbling over the railing where it splashed into the murky water of the Beacon River.

Commotion below decks told them that the surprise part of their advantage was now over.

Their original plan of boarding the ship silently and taking the band of rebels by surprise within the vessel would have to be scrapped.

"Marbles?" Buzzer suggested. The fireworks would attract some undue attention from the crowd in the plaza above but a firefight with other Guarders in and around the shadowy docks was not something that Buzzer felt comfortable with.

"I've got five," Mestizo answered as he pulled them from a pocket in his black skinsuit. "Three here," Buzzer said and primed the three little explosives in his hand. Looking up at

Mestizo, he said, "Down the stairs in three...two...one..."

Both men let the small metal balls roll off their fingertips through the open doorway, where they clattered down the stairs. The sounds of feet fast approaching echoed throughout the metal walls of the stairwell. Buzzer and Mestizo leapt over the railing of the small yacht simultaneously and splashed into the slowly moving waters of the Beacon River.

Just as the first of the passengers on the ship reached the top of the stairs—all eight marbles exploded.

The eruption was incredible; the entire top half of the ship disintegrated in an enormous fireball that rose high into the sky. Mere seconds later, the fuel stores ignited and the ship's four Quirnower-12 hi-speed engines exploded, lifting what was left of the yacht into the burning sky where it hung suspended for the briefest of moments.

Buzzer reached the surface amidst a rain of debris about twenty meters away from the ship just as the hollow hull splashed back into the water.

Mestizo surfaced about five meters from Buzzer's position and the two men began immediately to swim back to the docks. People along the riverbank walkway were running and screaming, not knowing if more explosions were to follow. Buzzer pulled himself out of the water and on to the dock beside Mestizo. Although many of the bystanders looked ready and eager to help, one look at the two dripping Guarders convinced them all to keep their distance.

Buzzer spared one more look at the burning wreckage of the former renegade Guarder hideout, and turned back to face Mestizo.

"I guess we can scratch that bunch," Mestizo said. "That's if they were all on the boat," Buzzer noted.

"Where else could they be?" Mestizo asked. "We watched that boat a long time." Buzzer paused for several moments. "There's still four more on this planet.

"Yeah, but they have no leader now," Mestizo said. "We just fried Stryker in there."

"They don't know that yet," Buzzer offered and Mestizo didn't answer.

Without another word, they proceeded up the dock to the walkway and disappeared into the growing crowd.

On the other side of the flaming wreckage, a shadowy figure swam to shore, climbed up to the walkway along the riverbank and quickly lost himself in the night.

~*~

Buzzer glanced across the crowded bar and caught sight of the four renegade Guarders again.

They were all here, all four of them. It seemed much too easy and Buzzer's senses were at a state of heightened alert. Mirage and Python were drunk and getting drunker. Taurus seemed almost catatonic as he sat at the table and Sahara was returning from the counter with more bottles of a green, viscous-looking liquid.

The four of them had obviously spent most of the afternoon and early evening in the bar. Their awareness levels would be way down, and their reaction time slowed drastically by the alcohol.

The four should be easy prey.

The spaceport bar seemed too heavily crowded for a Sixth day evening, yet the patrons knew enough to keep a safe distance from the group of four dangerous-looking men seated at the table.

Buzzer and Mestizo had checked back in Center City to find out if any inquiries had been made about the shooting incident in the shopping square earlier in the day. This had turned up nothing so they had decided to check out the major drinking spots, beginning with this one in the city's spaceport.

Amazingly enough, all four of their targets had been sitting at a single table. That had been almost three minutes ago. That last three minutes had been spent trying to figure out the best possible way to eliminate the four men without endangering any innocent civilians.

Now Buzzer began to approach the group of renegade Guarders, his blasters filling both hands. Several patrons spotted the guns and began to scamper out of the bar, although no one had begun screaming at the sight of his weapons. Mestizo had a half-charger out, confiscated from Mohican's corpse earlier in the day, and was approaching the group from the opposite side. Buzzer was amazed that anyone, even scum like these four, could forget their Guarder training so easily and let their guard slip so completely.

The bartender saw what was coming and ducked quickly behind the counter. Something must have been left of Sahara's awareness, because he suddenly stiffened as he sensed the danger approaching his back and caught sight of Mestizo approaching from his front. The other three were still oblivious to the danger they were in.

Although his field of fire wasn't exactly free and clear, Buzzer felt sure that no one else would suffer but his intended targets. He made brief eye contact with Mestizo from across the table and gave the silent signal to commence the elimination of their targets.

Sahara almost made it to his feet before Buzzer's blast cut him down from behind. The dead man's blaster clattered to the hard, cold floor of the bar, followed soon after by his corpse.

Mestizo fired twice with his half-charger, sending blood and bone and bits of flesh flying throughout the immediate area. Python had made a pathetically sloppy move for his weapon, but had not even come close before he took numerous hits, pieces of his body went skidding across the floor. Mirage hadn't even cleared the holster strap securing his blaster to his body before being ripped apart by one of Mestizo's charges.

Throughout the four-second firefight, Taurus had not moved. He sat trembling at the table as Buzzer approached him with his blaster pointed toward his chest.

Something didn't feel right; adrenaline surged through Buzzer's body. Out of the corner of his eye he could see Mestizo checking the other three corpses, retrieving weaponry and Guarder ID's. Taurus looked up into Buzzer's face with terror in his eyes.

"It's over, Taurus," Buzzer said. "Relinquish your weaponry and your Guarder ID and it's all over."

"What in the hell are you talking about?" Taurus managed to say between trembles.

"The only one left is Stoner," Buzzer said. "But we'll catch up to him soon enough. I'm not going to fry you unless you give me a reason to. I'd much prefer to drag your ass back to Aegis to stand trial for this mess."

"I don't know what..."

"Shut up!" Buzzer roared and nudged Taurus in the chest with his blaster. "Weapons and ID, on the table; now!"

"Jesus Christ, Buzzer," Taurus mumbled. "Just give me a minute."

Buzzer saw Taurus steal a glance at his blaster, riding in a speed rig underneath his left arm.

He smiled at the man's audacity—and blew him away.

The blaster's bolt exited the man's chest and burned into the floor…as the bar erupted in more gunfire.

Diving over the still twitching body of Taurus, Buzzer could see the menacing figure of Stryker in the doorway of the bar, blaster in hand. Mestizo was trying to dive to the side and bring his half-charger around at the same time but Stryker was one split-second ahead of him. Two blaster bolts buried themselves into Mestizo's chest, driving him through the air to slam against the counter-top of the bar. The explosion of blood and ravaged internal organs from Mestizo's back made a wet-sounding *whack* as they hit the mirror behind the bar's counter and began a slow slide to the floor.

The next few instants seemed to slow down dramatically for Frank Buzzer. Mestizo's eyes were wide with shock as his brain realized that death had come to claim him. Stryker was trying to adjust his aim to target Buzzer but the Squadron's best Guarder was no longer there.

Buzzer rolled out from behind an upended table halfway across the room with both blasters in his hand and, with a primeval war cry screaming its way from the depths of his chest, poured six rapid shots toward the doorway.

Stryker's face filled with fear in that moment…as he realized that he was going to die.

The first two blasts hit him high in the chest, separating his head and shoulders cleanly from the rest of his upper torso.

The next two hit what was left of his body in the abdomen, splashing his guts into the hallway outside the bar for meters in all directions.

The last two blew the corpse's legs apart, one in the left thigh and one in the right knee.

There wasn't much left of Stryker by the time Buzzer lifted himself from the floor. A group of five Spaceport Security personnel rushed into the bar with weapons drawn but Buzzer already had his blasters holstered and his Guarder ID held high over his head. He heard one of the security men grumble, "Jesus Christ," just before throwing up out in the hall.

Buzzer walked over to stand beside the body of his best friend, the former number-two Guarder in the ranks.

"You," Buzzer said, pointing toward one of the security men as he bent down to remove Mestizo's ID necklace and badge. "Call your supervisor and have him contact the local coroner. I don't care what you do with all the other garbage in this place...but I want this body processed and prepped for transit to Aegis."

~*~

Jekel grabbed the Hi-D data-sheet from Cougar's outstretched hand and read the message contained there:

...HQ...MISSION COMPLETE...SCRATCH 17 ON ADONIS...16 NEGATIVES AND 1 POSITIVE...CARGO IN TRANSIT EQUALS

REMAINS OF POSITIVE...WILL CONTINUE TO SEARCH FOR TARGET IN NEARBY SYSTEMS...TERMINATION OF TARGET WILL RESULT ONCE FOUND...BE SURE TO KEEP SECURITY BLANKET IN PLACE ON AEGIS...NEXT COMMUNICATION SOON..B...

"Damn!" Jekel growled and thrust the data-sheet back at his Communications Officer. "Mestizo's remains have been confirmed in-transit on REX— CargoLiner 22190," Cougar said solemnly. "But we can not locate Buzzer anywhere." Jekel looked up and sighed. "That figures..."

~*~

Rex-CargoLiner 22190 received special clearance to dock at Aegis Spaceport, despite the global travel restrictions still being enforced. The specific orders relating to their clearance called for only a single item of cargo to be offloaded— the coffin containing the remains of Anthony Mestizo, U.E.N. Appointed Guarder, Squadron Number One-Thirty-Two. As per the terms of the restrictions, all other cargo and all personnel would remain on the ship until such time as the restrictions were lifted.

Buck O'Grady and Ken Olmstead, being punished for several in-transit violations during this last trip, were ordered down to Cargo Hold 57 to retrieve the sealed coffin which was to be immediately offloaded.

O'Grady took one look at the large metal coffin resting on its cart in the middle of the hold and froze in his tracks. *Who in the hell could be in there*, he thought to himself as shivers ran up and down his spine. Wild rumors had been circulating throughout the kilometer-long cargo ship ever since they were given clearance to dock at the ancient-looking spaceport that orbited Aegis.

He didn't know who was in there but he knew that he didn't like being in the same room with the spooky object.

"What are you doing, Kenny?" He asked his co-worker as Olmstead knelt down beside the coffin, searching underneath for something.

"I'm looking for the control panel," Olmstead said. "I'm going to break the seal on this damn thing."

"You're *what*?" O'Grady asked.

"Hey, they want to send us down here to deal with this mess," Olmstead said and pulled on a lever. "Then I want to see just who is inside this thing."

A rush of air escaped the sealed coffin and a faint glow could be seen emanating from underneath the lid. "Help me with this thing, Buck."

"You're out of your mind," O'Grady said and took a nervous step backward.

"Come on, O'Grady," Olmstead said. "Don't you want to see some dead VIP? It has to be somebody important for us to get clearance to dock with the restrictions in place."

"Take a look if you want to, you crazy bastard," O'Grady choked. "There's nothing in there that I want to see."

"Suit yourself," Olmstead said and, with a strained heave, lifted the lid from the coffin.

A hand shot up from within the coffin and grabbed Ken Olmstead around the throat. O'Grady screamed and ran out of the cargo hold as Olmstead promptly fainted and slumped in the hand's strong grasp.

Buzzer quickly climbed out of Mestizo's coffin and removed the oxygen mask from his face.

Allowing Olmstead's body to slowly settle to the hard metal floorplates of the cargo hold, he tore the plastic partition, which had separated himself from his friend on the short trip, out of the coffin and took a final look at the face of Anthony Mestizo.

Buzzer knew that he was over the edge with rage at the death of his friend and all the other Guarders who had been killed over the past few weeks. It had taken every method of mental control that he had learned since becoming a Guarder to lay unmoving in that coffin throughout the trip from Adonis back to Aegis, while the heat of rage coursed through his entire body.

Knowing that the dead body of Mestizo lay mere inches underneath his in the oversized metal container had succeeded in playing tricks on his brain. Several times he thought he had heard sounds coming from underneath the partition, felt movement within the confines of the coffin.

Buzzer had fought these mental glitches by planning out his strategy against the leader of the renegades, John Stoner. He was almost certain that he knew how Stoner would penetrate the HQ now that the global travel restrictions had been placed around Aegis. Due to those restrictions, he was positive that the renegade Guarder would have to scrap his plans for flying the Eagle-44J in as Mohican had described. Buzzer had also realized that Stoner must have an accomplice within the Guarder HQ, feeding him mission assignments and communications between Guarders, in order for the renegades to have been able to track down and kill so many among their Squadron.

There was only one member of the Guarder Squadron who possessed the technical skills to pull off such an inside job—Needle. As soon as he could get a message to Thunder down on Aegis, that hole in Guarder security would be permanently closed. For now, he decided to keep his command sequencer inactivated, ensuring that his whereabouts remained unknown. There were very few Guarders alive whom he trusted right now…and he always worked better alone.

"Rest in peace," he whispered to Mestizo's still form as he closed the lid, re-sealed the coffin and left the hold.

~*~

Before the start of the New Conflict, which ended in the Universal Treaty of 2182, the Upper Grid-Levels of Space had been successfully colonized by the United Earthian Nations and the Lower Grid-Levels by the United Soviet States. Decades before, the immense population of Old Earth had left for the stars in accordance with the Grid Division Treaty Of 2100. As a result of this, the U.E.N. Governmental Complex, the official headquarters of the U.E.N. Governing Body, had stood on Aegis for over four centuries. When the giant planet had first been discovered in 2099, it was quickly considered the best choice for the location of the first off- Earth Governmental HQ, due to its central location within the Known Grid-Levels of Space and the highly defensible nature of the entire Adirondack Solar System.

The decision had been made to implement on Aegis the same technology used by the U.E.N. Department of Space Exploration several e-years earlier, when an artificial atmosphere had been pumped around the fifth planet in the Percom System, creating a totally human-habitable environment.

Within a very short time, the original two-hundred-story structure of the Governmental Complex was complete and the U.E.N. Headquarters had found a permanent home.

Since then, the Complex had remained in a state of constant construction, with hundreds of additions and expansions adding to its already enormous proportions. With over ten million employees working within the confines of the Complex, day-in and day-out, the building literally hummed with activity. In order to consistently clean and circulate the air for so many employees around the clock, a massive five-story, state-of-the-art air-intake duct system was constructed among the very top levels, high above the surface of Aegis.

It was these air ducts that Buzzer was aiming for now. His transport was a small life pod that had been attached to the underside of the shuttle that was carrying Mestizo's coffin home. Buzzer had disengaged the lifepod's holding clamps several seconds earlier and felt the thrill of freefall overwhelm him as the small pod plummeted toward the large planet below.

At 3,000 meters altitude and nearly six kilometers distance from the looming bulk of the Complex, Buzzer disengaged the canopy of the life pod and allowed the wind to tear his body from the small cockpit. He had rigged the shuttle's instrument panels to ignore any warnings about the pod's detachment—and subsequent destruction—when it splashed into the vastness of Shepherd Lake just beyond the Complex. The pod was also small enough not to raise any security alarms within the Governmental Complex itself.

Battling against the high winds battering his body, Buzzer activated a compact personal survival device known as a Back-Pack-Glider or BPG. The fully maneuverable glider, standard survival gear aboard any atmospheric vessel, had been liberated from the shuttle's stores just prior to the loading of Mestizo's coffin.

Buzzer watched the shuttle descend toward the Governmental Complex in the eerie light of early dawn and struggled to steer the small machine toward the air-ducts far below. He didn't like breaking into the Complex this way but he was just proving to himself that it could be done, by the right person and under the right circumstances. Actually, he was pretty sure it had already been done by Stoner in the very recent past. It was the only conceivable way for anyone to gain access to the building without leaving any record whatsoever of his or her arrival or travel arrangements on Aegis. There was no way that Stoner was getting a nuclear into the building on the ground and the atmospheric blanket installed along with the Global Travel Restrictions would prevent his flying in a ship, even one as small as a shuttle, to deliver the weapon.

No, this was the only way, Buzzer thought as he saw the bulk of the Complex rushing toward him.

Deftly applying light touches to the air brakes of the BPG, Buzzer was able to maneuver the small machine strapped to his back directly toward the massive air-intake ducts. His destination was a large piece of grillwork covering a duct three levels down from the top. He knew from his studies of the Complex while in the academy that this particular section of grillwork contained a maintenance access hatch.

As the enormous air-intake ducts grew closer, Buzzer could feel the strong pull of the air as they tried to suck him in. He applied full air-brakes to the BPG and slowed his descent to approximately twenty kilometers per hour…just as the glider's engine began to sputter as its fuel supply was exhausted.

Buzzer braced himself for the impact, twisted the controls to swing the glider's left wing around toward the duct—and rammed into the grillwork. The wing collapsed into three accordion-like folds, just as it was designed to, and Buzzer frantically grabbed with his gloved hands for a purchase within the sharp metal grillwork

After a few deep breaths, Buzzer attached several fasteners from his harness to the grillwork and worked his way towards the maintenance hatch. It was a lot of work, readjusting fasteners every meter or so, but soon the hatch was in reach. As he had assumed, the hatch had been forced with a mini-torch from the outside and resealed from within. Peering through the grillwork of the hatch, he could see another folded BPG just inside the duct.

Buzzer pulled out his own mini-torch and duplicated Stoner's actions. Once safely inside the duct, he struggled out of his harness and folded his BPG. Grabbing the other survival device, he walked over to a large airshaft that disappeared deep inside the confines of the Complex and dropped both machines in. The clanging sounds of metal on metal could barely be heard through his earplugs and against the constant thrum of the air handlers as Buzzer moved toward the access-door that led into the maintenance walkway of the duct system.

Just outside the door, Buzzer unfastened his oxygen mask and placed it into the pack he had worn strapped underneath the BPG and removed his two blasters and holsters. Stepping through the access door and into the walkway area, he slowly allowed his eyes to adjust to the sudden bright light and went over his mental checklist to make sure he was fully prepared to infiltrate the Complex.

Once ready, he navigated the twisting labyrinth of the maintenance walkway, leaving the almost painful thrum of the duct system behind, until he stood before a door leading into the Complex itself. Buzzer removed the earplugs which had been necessary while within the massive air-duct system, and pressed his ear to the door, hearing nothing. Reasonably sure that there was nothing on the other side of the door, he grabbed the handle and swung it open.

He had done it; he had infiltrated the U.E.N. Governmental Complex. In fact, during a time of Global Travel Restrictions and High Alert on Aegis, the central point of the entire U.E.N. Government had been infiltrated twice. The Sarge wasn't going to like this one bit, Buzzer thought to himself.

The first phase of his current mission—infiltration—had been completed.

Now the second phase—target location—was about to start…and Stoner could be anywhere.

~*~

Sergeant Harrison Jekel allowed his eyes to roam the massive expanse of Assembly Center, where the coffins of twenty-three of his Guarders lay in state.

Mozart Livingston, the Honorary Chairman of the Judiciary Board, had insisted that the mass funeral be held as scheduled upon the arrival of Mestizo's remains, regardless of the expected attack on the Governmental Complex. He had insisted to U.E.N. President Harry Alderman that all must go on as if nothing was suspected, in order to flush the last remaining renegade Guarder into the open.

Although Jekel had initially protested, he now saw the urgent need for closure on the faces of those members of his Squadron who were in attendance. These twenty-three coffins consisted of only those Guarders who had remained more or less intact upon their deaths. Many others had suffered far too much physical damage to be shipped and had been buried by local authorities throughout the Known Grid-Levels of Space.

Of course, the remains of any renegade Guarders would be cremated locally on their planet of death, without any honors or any mention of their previous posting to the U.E.N. Military's premier fighting force.

Thunder entered Assembly Center and quickly made his way toward his CO. "Needle has been taken into custody," Thunder whispered. "He did not resist."

69

"Too bad," Jekel answered and continued to scan the many coffins. "Still no sign of Buzzer?" "None," Thunder responded and then was silent. The entire chamber was silent except for the muffled voices of a few people here and there.

While the highly trained Guarders faced death daily in the performance of their deadly and dangerous duty, never had so many died so close together—and never from murder by members of their own Squadron. Hopefully, once the disease that was John Stoner was eliminated, nothing like this would ever—*could* ever—happen again.

The chamber, which usually hosted meetings of the U.E.N. Executive Session, was today filled with several thousand government officials, all wanting to pay their respects to the mysterious members of the Guarder Squadron.

Jekel had a tingling in the back of his head; something wasn't right and he didn't like it. Every single Guarder and each member of the U.E.N. Governing Guard in the Complex was on the lookout for John Stoner. He found it hard to believe that the renegade Guarder could ever work his way inside this chamber, but stranger things had been done and he wasn't about to take Stoner's abilities for granted.

He couldn't afford to—they were the abilities of a Guarder.

~*~

John Stoner, the man everyone was searching for, was in Assembly Center at that moment, mingling with the upper echelons of the U.E.N. government and the off-world delegates who crowded the large chamber.

Ambassador Fariq Al'Samil of Pakistaria lay dead in one of the thousands of offices made available to visiting off-world officials within the lower levels of the Complex. Although the brightly embroidered ambassadorial robes and the customary hood of the Pakistarians served to hide Stoner's face from the crowd, the intense coloration of his borrowed costume also served to draw the attention of other dignitaries his way. Stoner tried to keep these chance encounters to a minimum. He remained on the move, scrambling for believable excuses whenever he found himself cornered by questions about the missing ambassador.

He could see the looming figure of Sergeant Harrison Jekel as well as a slew of other Guarders scattered throughout the crowd. He had been surprised to discover during his last message from Needle that Stryker had been able to take out Mestizo before Buzzer fried him. Stoner had never thought that Stryker could have been good enough to take out the number-two Guarder in the ranks.

70

Too bad it hadn't been Buzzer. Stoner loathed the man and was ashamed of himself for feeling such intense fear at the knowledge that the number-one Guarder in the ranks was hot on his trail, even if that trail was a false one.

His original plan—to deliver the nuclear pack via an overflight with an Eagle-44J—had been scrapped by the Global Travel Restrictions he had encountered upon his arrival at the Aegis Spaceport; surely Buzzer's doing. He'd had to think quickly after that, and had been able to stow away on the last shuttle flight to the surface before all atmospheric traffic was brought to a halt. Managing to get his hands on a BPG, he had exited the shuttle unbeknownst to the pilot and crew and landed on the upper levels of the Complex shortly thereafter. He felt reasonably secure that Buzzer was off on a wild-goose chase somewhere among the Known Grid-Levels of Space. During that last transmission from Needle, he had also learned that Buzzer went off to continue the hunt for Stoner, probably acting on some false information supplied by Stryker just before he died.

Good old Stryker, loyal to the end.

Stoner had armed the small nuclear pack, originally designed for mining purposes, and placed it in the power generation plants deep within the sub-basements of the U.E.N. Governmental Complex. The radioactive device was concealed inside a shielded casing, the kind used by miners who had to spend good amounts of time in close proximity to the nukes. The shielding had allowed Stoner to smuggle the nuke into the Complex without setting off any alarms tuned to the radioactive components of most nuclear weapons.

It was set to detonate in less than twenty minutes, prompting Stoner to take one last satisfying look around at all the faces that would soon be dead as he made his way toward one of the rear exits of Assembly Center. The explosion of the mini-nuclear device would result in the disintegration of the entire Governmental Complex structure and a good area surrounding it—but Stoner would be long gone and out of range before it detonated. His original plan for using the BPG as his escape vehicle had been replaced by his reservation of one of the thousands of aircars, used to scurry various members of the government to and from the Complex, made all the more easier by Al Samil's access codes. In less than ten minutes, the aircar could have him better than thirty kilometers away from the Governmental Complex. Being seen in the guise of his alias that far away from the Complex when the bomb exploded would eliminate any threat of his being detained for questioning by U.E.N. authorities.

A servant bearing drinks on an elaborate tray suddenly bumped into his side and sent Stoner stumbling to the floor. Stoner gained his balance with his right hand and quickly righted himself, turning to snarl at the careless man. Drink glasses and several bottles crashed to the floor with a mighty sound that echoed off the walls of Assembly Center, and all eyes turned in his direction.

"You idiot!" He rasped and tried to correct the hood that had partially fallen off his head, revealing one side of his face.

The servant, who had bent down to retrieve his tray, now stood to face Stoner, a wicked grin on his face, his eyes icy cold…and a blaster in his hand.

"My apologies," Buzzer said and whipped the butt of his blaster across Stoner's face.

Stoner wheeled away and got caught up in his robes. By the time he regained his stance, Buzzer had slipped to his rear and brought the blaster's butt down on top of his skull with a vicious chop.

Stoner hit the floor, out cold.

"Hold your fire!" Jekel shouted to those Guarders who were already pointing weapons in Buzzer's direction. "Lower your weapons!"

Buzzer held his blaster up toward the ceiling of Assembly Center and tore the wig and glasses from his face. Standing there in one of the formal uniforms of the service staff, Buzzer looked down at the unconscious form of John Stoner and felt the rage begin to boil once again in his veins.

~*~

Stoner was shocked to his senses by several vicious slaps across his face. His arms and legs were bound tight and he could feel the cold metal straps of the bonds that held him. His entire body was vibrating and he soon realized that he was moving, inside a vessel of some sort. There was some kind of weight strapped to his back and his head was pounding from Buzzer's attack.

His vision cleared enough for him to recognize Frank Buzzer standing over him. Buzzer's face was impassive but his eyes still held the ice he had seen before. The Guarder's blasters were both holstered and he had something strapped to his back as well.

Then Stoner saw the wicked looking knife Buzzer held in his right hand and felt his heart pause in his chest.

"Can you hear me now?" Buzzer asked. Stoner nodded.

Buzzer squatted down to face Stoner and remained silent for several seconds. The cold air that was whipping through the cabin from the open hatch of the small transport ruffled Stoner's hair; Buzzer never blinked.

"For the crimes you have committed against the Government, the Guarder Squadron, and the people of the United Earthian Nations, I sentence you to die, John Stoner," Buzzer said. "By the powers given to me by the U.E.N. Judiciary Board, I will carry out that sentence. Right here.

Right now."

"Screw you, Buzzer," Stoner managed.

Buzzer's face turned red at that and his features grew even more menacing. "The nuclear weapon you intended to use on the U.E.N. Governmental Complex is strapped to your back and will detonate in less than four minutes."

Stoner's eyes widened and he began to sweat. "So what about you?" Stoner asked.

Buzzer indicated the parachute strapped to his back. "Don't worry; you won't be taking me with you," he said. "And you won't be getting off so easily either, Stoner."

"You call getting fried in a nuclear explosion getting off easy?" Stoner laughed.

"Yes," Buzzer said evenly.

"So leave already," Stoner urged. "Let me make my peace and die alone."

"You'll die alone, Stoner," Buzzer said. "But you'll also die in pain. This is for Mestizo and for all the other Guarders you are responsible for killing."

Stoner screamed once as Buzzer plunged his knife deep into Stoner's abdomen. The thin red blood felt hot as it surged over Buzzer's fist. He twisted it several times, exposing most of Stoner's internal organs; then he wiped his hands and blade on Stoner's stolen robes.

"Go...to...hell..." Stoner gasped in a barely audible voice, his eyes lingering on Buzzer.

"Yeah; I'll see you there, Stoner," Buzzer said and leapt out of the transport's hatch.

A blast of frigid air beat against him as Buzzer plummeted down toward Aegis. The hum of the small transport's engines soon died away. He had flown Stoner deep into the barren area that surrounded the Governmental Complex for kilometers in all directions. The transport was traveling fast enough to carry it at least a dozen more kilometers past where Buzzer would soon be landing.

More than far enough...

He pulled the cord and the parachute flew open, the sudden deceleration forcing the air from his lungs. He looked to the west toward the transport, which was growing rapidly smaller as it gained distance. It would be just another minute, maybe a little less, he thought, and then this entire nasty ordeal, a dark smudge on the sparkling record of the Guarder Squadron, would be laid to rest. Looking down, he could already see the dust being kicked up in the distance by the ground-car that was rushing to pick him up.

Buzzer continued his mental countdown as he floated slowly to the surface of Aegis and turned his head away from the direction of the transport. The expected blast of intense white light flashed across the sky and just as quickly died away, followed by the muffled sounds of the explosion. A small gust of wind caught the chute several moments later, jerking it slightly to the east. The ground was rushing up to meet him. With bent legs and the skills gained from hours of parachute training in his past, Buzzer landed in a slight roll across the hard packed soil of Aegis.

As the ground-car came to a skidding stop about ten meters from his position, Buzzer was gazing at the small white cloud that was slowly drifting toward the heavens about fourteen kilometers to the west. That cloud was a form of closure for Buzzer.

Now, he could finally say his final goodbye in his own way to Mestizo. Now, he could sleep easy with the knowledge that John Stoner was dead.

~*~

Jekel looked up from his desk and saw the figure of Frank Buzzer standing at attention in the doorway to his office. "Come in, Buzzer," he said and motioned to one of his chairs.

"Thank you, sir," Buzzer said and quickly seated himself. "I was hoping to get a minute of your time, sir."

"You can have more than a minute," Jekel said as he turned away from his desk monitor and gave Buzzer his full attention. "To tell you the truth, I didn't expect you back here so soon."

"There's something important we need to discuss, Sarge," Buzzer said and leaned forward in his chair.

Jekel eyed his best soldier carefully and settled back in his chair. "Does this have anything to do with the fact that both you and Stoner managed to infiltrate this incredibly secure facility a short time ago? That you were both able to perform infiltrations by means that still remain unknown and without anyone having even the slightest clue that either of you were here, inside the Complex?"

Buzzer smiled and said, "It was easier than you think, Sarge."

Jekel sighed, shut off his desk monitor and keyed the control that closed his office doors; he knew that this discussion could take awhile.

"Start talking, Buzzer," he said. "I definitely need to hear this."

MULLENS TALKS VENGEANCE

"I had no idea," Mullens whispered as he saw the grief and pain in the eyes of Frank Buzzer. "The official word on that nuclear explosion was some type of training accident, a field exercise using an ancient drone powered by an older model mini-nuclear reactor that had gone out of control."

Buzzer nodded once and took in a deep breath. Mullens could see that this man had been deeply hurt by the death of his friend and comrade-in-arms, Mestizo. A hurt that he still carried with him, very close to his soul.

He blames himself, Mullens thought. *He holds himself personally responsible for Mestizo's death...*

"I don't know what to say, Mr. Buzzer," Mullens said. "Such news never made it to the nets. I can't for the life of me imagine how such enormous events could be covered up so completely.

I've never heard a single word of this—and it's my job to keep up and record the very types of events we are discussing today."

"I can tell you that news of the rebellion made it to the crime syndicates, Mullens, and plenty of people out there in the Known-Grids knew about it immediately afterwards. But for the most part, what goes on within this group stays within this group and within these halls," Buzzer said. "It's been that way for more than four centuries and it will remain so. Get used to it, Mullens.

Only in circumstances such as these, where one of us is ordered by the U.E.N. President himself, will you ever hear what really happens within our ranks."

"That's utterly ridiculous, you realize that?" Mullens muttered before he realized what he was saying and who he was saying it to. "I mean, of course, your group is very good at keeping secrets—but there are just too many people working in this building, Mr. Buzzer! At some point, information like this is sure to leak out to the public. Just how do you think the legends of you and your kind were created, anyway?'

"The legends were sparked by eye-witness testimonies of the things that happened out in the far fringes, centuries ago, Mullens," Buzzer said and shifted uncomfortably in his chair. "When ordinary citizens saw us at work, saw our training coming through and the things Guarders were capable of doing during the course of our missions...let's just say, they were things that most people have never seen another human being do before. Over time, those old stories have been exaggerated; the mythos surrounding this squadron has grown to epic proportions. All of which works very well for us."

"How so?"

"When I'm out there on assignment, people see me coming and instinctively get out of my way. When I show my Guarder ID and people get a good look at the Falcon symbol, all the old fears and legends come crashing home, and most times I don't have to fire a single round to complete my mission. The people of the Known-Grids fear us and steer clear of us; they don't understand us and can't believe they are actually seeing one of us up close. All of these feelings come together in an instant—and their usual response is to turn their heads away, take several steps to the side and hope we don't notice them. Like I said, all of that works very well for us."

"Is it always that easy?" Mullens wondered out loud. "Are all of your missions usually so peaceful, your targets just throwing their hands up in the air and laying their weapons at your feet without even a struggle?"

"No…not at all."

"So, you're saying that there have been other times, times like today, where you have had to fight for your life? Times where others have had no fear of confronting you, and you had to use your training to survive?"

"Of course," Buzzer said. "There have been many of those times; there are always stupid criminals who think they can get the drop on one of us. The way we handle those types of situations only lends more to our legend. All I'm saying is that, on most missions, we don't have to lift a finger to apprehend our designated targets. But it isn't always that way."

"Has there ever been a time in your experience where your designated targets have managed to take one or more of you out and you had to take on a larger force with lesser numbers?"

"Yes."

"And when that happens, do you call for back-up?" Mullens asked. "I mean, how does a Guarder respond to something like that? When one of your teammates is killed on a mission that called for, say, two Guarders, and now there was only one…do you press on or do you wait for more personnel?"

"You press on."

"Even when the odds are totally against you? When the chances of survival are close to zero?"

"Yes."

Mullens digested that for several seconds and saw that this man was not boasting, not bragging about going into a situation where he was almost certainly going to be killed.

No, this man was telling him about the Guarder way of doing things; *his* way.

"At that point, is it vengeance that drives you on?" Mullens asked. "Is it an anger; or a feeling that some type of payback must be rendered? What could possibly drive you when facing such insurmountable odds; what but a desperate need for revenge?"

"Nothing else," Buzzer said. "Just that, Mullens. No one kills one of us without bringing the wrath of the entire squadron down upon himself. It is part of the Guarder credo; kill one of us and the entire squadron comes gunning for you."

"Has there ever been a time where *you* were in such a situation?"

Buzzer's face grew darker and more brooding at that point—something which Mullens would have believed impossible if he hadn't just witnessed the change. He was about to enter another dangerous place, a place where someone other than Guarders had been responsible for killing one of their own.

Mullens could see by the intensity of Buzzer's eyes that the Guarder would not forgive the historian for asking him to relive these memories; but he couldn't allow the story that was hiding just beyond those eyes to get away.

"Why don't you tell me about it?"

Buzzer lifted his head by barely a centimeter; otherwise his entire body was rigid and unmoving. Mullens could feel the waves of energy flowing off this man and almost felt a crackle of electricity running along the tabletop as he found his gaze glued to the face of the Guarder sitting just meters away.

Suddenly, Buzzer spoke: "We were on a stakeout..."

The New Conflict did not begin with the roar that most people expected "The New War to End All Wars" to begin with. Instead, the U.S.S. suddenly decided, after nearly 70 e-years of total silence, to resume their past bloody history of conquest by first attacking small U.E.N. outposts and various corporate-owned systems along the border separating the Upper and Lower Grid-Levels Of Space. When the U.E.N. Headquarters on Aegis first began receiving reports in 2170 of sporadic attacks by still "unknown" parties, nobody in any position of authority took them very seriously. It was this lack of seriousness on the part of many high- ranking U.E.N. Government officials that ultimately allowed the U.S.S. to establish an upper hand in the early years of the war. It has even been argued that this "upper-hand" enjoyed by the U.S.S. in the war's early days led to an unprecedented U.E.N. resurgence in military growth, weapons production and ship building; all of which combined to turn the U.E.N. war effort into an unbeatable juggernaut that swept the U.S.S. off the interstellar map and into the history books…

(Excerpt:*The U.E.N. Unveiled— The Dark History of Humanity's Greatest Government*by Joseph Mullens)

MISSION FOUR: PEST CONTROL

The silence was unbearable as he crouched there in the darkness and waited for the pending eruption that would bring this boring stakeout to a conclusion.

The last twelve hours had turned up absolutely nothing, a big zero. Four men besides himself were situated in various positions throughout the small marina. Other than occasionally stretching stiff muscles and checking in with each other by sequencer, the five men could do nothing…but wait.

To make matters worse, Orsisenia was definitely not the planet of choice to spend any great length of time on. High-level industrialization and mechanization had plagued the planet for more than three decades. Chunks of existeel, bondite, trash and grime littered every city on the face of the ugly planet. It was no wonder that Orsisenia was considered the interstellar trash dump of the NorthEastern Corporate Grid-Sector. The place was utterly disgusting, not only by sight but also by smell.

And the people in general did nothing to enlighten the planet's lousy reputation. The population of Orsisenia was comprised of the largest assortment of thieves, killers and overall slime to be found anywhere in the Known Grids.

Thus, the planet was not known for its hospitality—and the filthy environs did not make for a good stakeout.

"What a dump," Buzzer muttered to himself as he used the curb to wipe the grime and grit from his boots. His assignment was to capture a shipment of*colboquik*—the newest wonder drug of the NorthEastern Underlords to find a niche in the neighboring systems—as it came into the Delta-Rae Marina. He had hoped for it to happen by day but night had fallen hours ago.

The United Earthian Nations Judiciary Board had been trying to pin something on Kelsington Duncan for quite some time now, but had never been able to come anywhere close.

But tonight…if the Guarders could capture an illegal shipment of *colboquik* on a ship registered under one of his many subsidiaries, and operating out of a marina owned by his parent organization, Duncan Enterprises, they just might be able to make this one stick.

The only thing Buzzer now hoped for was that the ship might actually arrive and unload. The other four men undoubtedly had the same thing in mind. Hammer was positioned on West Dock, Kane on East Dock, Lifter on the upper tier of the marina's main complex, and Bastion was all decked out in scuba gear and under the water near Central Dock.

Being the largest of the three, Central was the most promising dock-site for the incoming shipment. Of course, Buzzer was situated at the entrance to the marina, a point that would be the center of attention once the assault started and the ship's crew tried instinctively to escape. A point that would draw the most enemy fire in his direction. He would be solely responsible for blocking the paths of at least twenty-five fleeing opponents once the action got underway. The thought of it wasn't very promising, but it was the price he had to pay for being the best that the

U.E.N. Guarder Squadron had to offer.

Just being a Guarder in itself was an honor only a handful of men in all of the Known Grids had held. But being considered the best of the best, the top man in the ranks, was something that Frank Buzzer had lived with for most of his career. Somehow, mission after mission, he excelled and succeeded, often against seemingly impossible odds. During most missions, he worked alone. This was the case with most Guarders. But occasionally, some missions required several

Guarders to work as a team. Although he disliked these types of missions, being designated mission leader at least allowed him to pick the players.

Buzzer had a good team with him on this one; Sergeant Jekel had provided him with a list of Guarders who weren't currently out on missions to choose from. Although he knew each of the four men who were with him on this dreadful planet, he had never actually worked together with any of them. Fortunately, Guarder training incorporated techniques that could be adapted to any situation and which took into account any number of team members. He knew he could count on each of them to follow his orders and carry out their mission objectives precisely—and with lethal force if necessary. Each of them was specialized in hand-to-hand combat and weaponry.

The sudden grumble of approaching engines attracted his attention.

A ship, very much like the one he had been expecting, was nearing the Delta-Rae Marina.

Buzzer felt the familiar tingling course through his body as he anticipated the battle scenario that was forming in his brain. He could feel the electrical connections in his nerve endings as they fired; his muscles spasmed under his skin. The fingers of his right hand automatically pulled out his blaster and checked the weapon's charge.

The medium-sized ship was illuminated by the bright lights of the three docks as it pulled closer to the marina. According to information garnered through various sources, the *colboquik* was being transported on small sub-system freighters to an unauthorized landing area in one of the few remaining wooded areas left on Orsisenia, and then brought in to the marina for distribution over the canal system, which crisscrossed most of the planet and allowed sewage and other undesirable materials to drain out of the cities.

Buzzer's eyes focused sharply on the approaching vessel while his left hand unstrapped the half-charger from his back and activated the weapon's small generator with a flick of his thumb.

The powerful weapon hummed to life, raw energy at the ready. Buzzer was at ease with the immense destructive capabilities that were now at his disposal. This single weapon could effectively neutralize the boat if used correctly. But he knew he must wait. He needed some proof for the Judiciary Board to make their case against Duncan. The drugs had to be in his sight before he ordered his team into action.

Through light reflected off the water, he could see the name *Ambrosia* in large black letters across the front of the white ship as it cut its engines and flowed sleekly into the forward position of Central Dock. A few crewmen jumped to the dock and clamped the ship down tight.

Buzzer's eyes scanned the ship, looking for any clue as to what might be hidden in the cargo holds. Behind his icy eyes a myriad of thoughts swam through his mind. He readied himself for what was coming, called on his instincts to bring his body to battle-ready. He prepared his mind for the heart-rending and life-ending screams of his enemy—and quite possibly some of his teammates. He was trained to accept his own death, knew that it would someday come. Maybe in battle, or maybe a long time away. Either way, it could happen at any time. Not many Guarders had been killed in the line of duty over the past four centuries. But memories of some of the more recent deaths came flooding back, filling him with the rage he needed at this very moment.

A very deep, yet very controlled rage.

Buzzer smiled toward the *Sleek-Line* cruiser. He doubted very much that death would claim him this night, out there on the banks of the Elton Canal.

The cruiser's cargo doors opened onto the dock and several crew members began throwing out bundles of various shapes and sizes. Small mobile cranes began loading these bundles on to the tow-motors that had been waiting on the dock.

Phase One: Observation was now in effect. *Phase Two: Search and Seizure* depended on whether or not anything incriminating was seen during this stage of the game.

Buzzer pushed a small button on his sequencer, telling the others to lay low and wait.

The first tow-motor in the line was now fully loaded and a man jumped into the driver's seat.

The small machine revved to life and started up the ramp toward Buzzer's position at the marina's entrance.

Buzzer was all awareness now, every muscle poised and ready. He positioned the half-charger once again behind his back and pulled out his blaster, favoring the smaller weapon for combat in close quarters. The driver looked like an ordinary enough man, not the usual illegal type; but a small bulge under his left arm told Buzzer that he could be wrong in his assessment.

The machine rattled up the grimy pathway leading from the dock and passed through the entry gates of the Delta-Rae Marina. Once it was off the dock, and behind the cover of darkness, Buzzer made his move. It was quiet and quick. A hard jab with the butt of his blaster behind the driver's left ear and the man slumped into unconsciousness. A quick search of the man turned up a small blaster and a work knife, nothing more.

Buzzer used the liberated knife to slice open one of the bundles in the back of the tow-motor. A few small packages tumbled out. He ripped one open and looked inside. Smiling, he grabbed a handful of the small purple pills and dumped them into an empty pocket. It would feel very good to nail down a case against a slime ball like Kelsington Duncan and watch the man cringe under the power of the U.E.N. Judiciary Board.

Buzzer quickly applied cuffs to the still unconscious man's wrists and ankles, dumped him unceremoniously to the ground and climbed into the vacant seat. Turning the machine around, he headed back into the marina and down the ramp toward the *Ambrosia*.

Few crew members paid any attention as he guided the tow-motor on to the dock and to within three meters of the ship before cutting the engine.

But when he climbed up in back and began throwing the small bundles of pills into the canal, many heads turned toward his direction.

"What the hell do you think you're doing?" The ship's captain yelled as he leaned over the side. "I hope you plan on paying for all of that..."

"I don't think so," Buzzer answered flatly. He quickly jumped from the back of the tow- motor, switched the blaster once again for the half-charger, and walked around to the front, allowing the men on both the ship and the dock a better view of him. Jaws dropped in surprise, eyes widened in confusion as they got a look at his Guarder ID, but what he noticed most was the number of hands that were reaching for weapons.

The half-charger came up lightning quick and settled on the captain's chest. "Anyone moves and your captain begins his afterlife!" Buzzer roared and everyone froze in his tracks.

"Who in the hell are you?" The captain growled.

"U.E.N. Guarder, operating under the direct orders of the Judiciary Board to investigate the possibilities of drug-trafficking on Orsisenia." Buzzer stated in a voice loud enough for all of them to hear. "I believe this investigation is over. The drug known as *colboquik* seems to be the main cargo on your vessel, captain. You and your men are hereby placed under arrest. U.E.N. Security Forces will be here momentarily to take you into custody while you await trial for illegal drug-trafficking."

Buzzer paused to let his words sink in. This was the difficult part; the next few seconds would dictate how the rest of this would play out. "Place your hands on top of your heads and kneel down! Do it now!"

The night erupted in an aerial display of charger blasts and explosions. Buzzer picked off two targets before rolling to the right behind the tow-motor. The tow-motor was awash with sparks and fire as several of the enemy focused their weapons on the small vehicle. Buzzer rolled further behind the tractor as he tracked more targets, still firing his half-charger. He ignored the pain of dozens of small cuts and bruises caused by flying debris, and was up and running across the dock in seconds.

Hammer had already taken out three men, and Lifter had eliminated five from his vantage point atop the small marina complex. Kane was effectively pinned down but had managed to knock out one man. Bastion was already out of the water and on the boat, causing confusion and general havoc among the crew.

Buzzer slumped down behind the main gate of the entrance and sent two rounds each into the backs of three men. All three flew forward and lay twitching on the dock. Answering fire hit the position he had occupied just moments before, but only the gate suffered damage. Lifter fired and a man screamed. He had neutralized nine men from his untouchable position so far and the return fire had not yet come close. Screams from inside the ship informed Buzzer that Bastion was doing quite well aboard the *Ambrosia*.

Buzzer could see Kane now, running across East Dock, firing all the way. Two men fell off the ship and into the murky water. The thick slime and grime of the Elton Canal kept the two corpses eerily afloat alongside the sleek ship.

Hammer appeared out of nowhere and decked a man with one swift punch. He opened fire on the open side entrance of the boat and was rewarded with terrible screams. Buzzer caught a man running full speed for the marina entrance out of the corner of his eye. Immediately, he turned to pursue the man. Now that the drugs had been found, the primary goal of this mission was to ensure that not a single man be allowed to escape. If word got to Kelsington Duncan that Guarders were involved with this, and not just some rival drug underlord, the bastard would close this operation down so tight they would never be able to make a connection between the *colboquik* and Duncan's prestigious name.

Buzzer raised his half-charger to fire but dodged at the last instant as he sensed that he was in another man's target sights. Several blasts sailed over his head to smash into the trees that surrounded the perimeter of the Delta-Rae Marina as Buzzer's half-charger skittered away out of reach. With no time to waste, the Guarder pulled out his blaster and answered back with a three- round burst that hit his aggressor square in the chest, lifting the man from the dock and into the water.

The running man made it through the marina entrance but Buzzer was right behind him and gaining ground. Aboard the *Ambrosia*, Bastion had made it to the main cargo hold, leaving a grisly trail behind him. The main door was locked and he raised his blaster.

Lifter had left the cover of the complex and ran through the obstacle course of dead bodies to join Hammer and Kane on the ship. The three men searched frantically for Buzzer.

Buzzer finally caught up to his winded prey and tackled him to the ground. The man came out of his roll with a long gleaming knife in his hand. Buzzer fried him with a single shot between the eyes. The body slumped headless to the ground, the knife still in hand.

Buzzer holstered his weapon and started running back to the Delta-Rae Marina. Bastion fired at the lock on the main cargo hold.

Buzzer reached the marina entrance just as the *Ambrosia* disintegrated in a huge fireball. The enormous blast flattened him to the ground as flaming debris fell all around him. The unseen pack of highly concentrated explosives attached to the main cargo hold's locking mechanism had been very powerful.

Picking himself up off the ground, Buzzer stared at the gaping holes in the three docks that used to make up the Delta-Rae Marina. A quick scan of the grisly scene told him that out of the five Guarders who had landed on Orsisenia just last night, only he remained alive.

On Cazara, a light flashed on a switchboard indicating damage to property on Orsisenia. The switchboard was located on the eighty-fourth level of the Duncan Enterprises Building.

Buzzer felt the hatred rise inside of him. This would not go unpunished. He checked his pocket for the handful of *colboquik* pills. They were there, the proof he needed...but he wanted more. Much, much more than just a prison sentence for Kelsington Duncan.

The decision to go to the Duncan Enterprises HQ on Cazara was already lodged in his brain as Frank Buzzer turned to leave the Delta-Rae Marina. He paused just long enough to make sure that the former driver of the tow-motor, still in cuffs, was not in a coma.

Buzzer wanted at least one prisoner left alive for the U.E.N. Security Forces to interrogate.

Cougar ripped the message off the printer, made his way across the busy Guarder HQ Control Center on Aegis and handed it to Sergeant Harrison Jekel.

"Sir, this just came in from Orsisenia."

Jekel accepted the printout with a look of obvious concern on his face. It read:

...MISSION COMPLETE AND SUCCESSFUL...SCRATCH THIRTY-FOUR ON ORSISENIA—THIRTY NEGATIVES AND FOUR POSITIVES...NOT MUCH LEFT TO BRING BACK...COLBOQUIK RECOVERED ON BOARD SHIP: AMBROSIA...LINKED TO DUNCAN ENTERPRISES... TARGET IS KELSINGTON DUNCAN...WILL REPORT SOON...B...

"Good Lord," Jekel sighed and rubbed at his left temple. No Guarders had been killed in the line of duty since that mess with Stoner and his renegade Guarders several e-years earlier. Now four more of his men were dead, killed on a mission.

And once again, Buzzer had been there and had survived. The man was the best damn soldier he had ever known...

But now Buzzer was on the warpath. That made him a very dangerous man; very dangerous indeed. Jekel felt sorry for the poor fool who was at the end of Buzzer's wrath. Although Kelsington Duncan was known as a dirty character in U.E.N. Intelligence circles, his name and public reputation were well known throughout each of the four Corporate Grid-Sectors. Duncan Enterprises was associated with so many household items in so many grid levels that the man who headed the organization had earned an enormous amount of respect and approval from the billions of consumers who populated the Known Grid-Levels of Space. Of course, great power had come from this vast popularity and Duncan had become quite greedy as a result. Now, the king of Duncan Enterprises & Affiliates was also the underlord of the NorthEastern Corporate Grid-Sector; a drug-trafficker, industrial smuggler, saboteur, and blackmailer. The man was involved in almost every illegal activity currently being practiced throughout the United Earthian Nations.

Duncan had to be stopped, and stopped quickly, before he secured a firm hold on the free- enterprise system of the NorthEastern Grids. The U.E.N. had not possessed any damaging evidence on Duncan—until now. But with the deaths of four Guarders and proof of drug trafficking on his hands, Duncan would soon go down. Kelsington Duncan could finally be tried and imprisoned.

For once and for all, the man could be put away.

"Yeah, no chance..." Jekel muttered to himself and laughed. U.E.N. Guarders held powers of judge and jury while out on assignments. With Duncan directly responsible for the deaths of other Guarders, Jekel knew what the verdict and sentence would be once Buzzer caught up with him.

Guilty as charged, Duncan, sentenced to death. Jekel also knew that the sentence would be carried out immediately. Buzzer would act quickly and efficiently but Kelsington Duncan would no longer be around to appreciate the good work.

No, Kelsington Duncan would be dead.

~*~

"Kelsington, we have to talk," Tappy Willis sounded very worried if Duncan had interpreted his tone correctly.

"What seems to be the problem, Tappy?"

Willis took a nervous look around the busy employee cafeteria of the Duncan Enterprises Building and settled his eyes on his boss. "Bad news; let's talk in the penthouse."

Duncan was interested now, never having seen Willis so uptight in the two decades since they'd been in business together. He left his food on the table and the two men walked to the lift shafts among a constant harangue of greetings from numerous employees. Once in a lift-car, the trip lasted less than thirty seconds, the door opening up on Duncan's penthouse suite on Level One-Sixty.

"Now, what's so damn important that I had to miss lunch, Tappy?" Duncan asked. "This is serious, Kelsington."

"Well then, why don't you cut out the small talk and tell me already," Duncan said sharply and took a seat behind the desk in his study.

"Yesterday we received a damage report from Orsi Transportation, your subsidiary on Orsisenia. It seems that something went wrong at the Delta-Rae Marina. Our people were at the marina today and they say nothing's left. All three of the docks suffered damage beyond repair due to a large explosion. Sixteen small ships were also destroyed, including the *Ambrosia*." Willis paused for a moment. "Does the name of that ship ring a bell?"

Duncan sighed and slumped back in his chair. "We were bringing in a shipment of *colboquik* for distribution on that ship, right?"

Willis nodded in confirmation. "We lost over two-hundred-fifty billion worth on that ship last night, not to mention about thirty men."

"Damn," Duncan hissed. "What the hell happened?"

"Our people on Orsisenia say that the U.E.N. Security Forces have been there all day investigating the explosion. It seems that some of the bodies of our men were found, but their wounds were sustained from a battle with energy weapons, such as blasters and chargers, before the explosion blew everything to kingdom come. By the way, all the drugs were vaporized in the explosion; the authorities found no trace."

"A battle?" Duncan frowned. "I wonder which one of my many competitors thinks he has enough power to hit me? Especially in the NorthEastern Grids?

"It could only be Norden Biological or Zacharia Distribution Systems," Willis offered. "Only those two organizations are large enough to even think about staging a power move."

Duncan pondered this for several moments before standing up and pacing around his study. "Did they find the bodies of any of the attackers?"

"Well, that's the interesting thing," Willis said.

"No other bodies were found. Twenty of our men were accounted for by positive ID of body parts, but nothing else was found. The entire ship was disintegrated in the explosion. They found no trace of the attackers."

"Dammit! Don't tell me that whoever attacked that boat killed thirty of my men and didn't even take one casualty! Those guys are trained by the best!"

"What do you want me to say?" Willis spread out his arms in frustration. "That's what the official reports found, Kelsington."

"Who in the hell could pull off something like this and not leave a trace?"

"I don't have any idea."

"Well, dammit!" Duncan swore and plopped back down in his chair.

Willis continued. "Our people got the usual crap from the Security Forces about why all the corpses were carrying guns, but since they were all licensed, and the specific duties of Orsi Transportation call for definite security precautions on behalf of the personnel, there wasn't any trouble. So, for now, the heat has pretty much died down."

"I don't like this, Tappy."

"Didn't think you would, Kelsington."

"I don't know what's going on here but I sure as hell want to find out. And let's make it soon. I want a full report as soon as you find out just what is happening on Orsisenia."

"As soon as I can, Kelsington."

"And tighten the security around this building; I don't want any surprises here on Cazara. Do I make myself clear? I like it nice and peaceful around here, real peaceful. Anybody causes any trouble, dispose of them. Clean and simple. Am I understood?"

"Loud and clear, Kelsington."

"Alright then, that's done with," Duncan stood and straightened his suit. "Now, let's go finish lunch."

~*~

The night was clear and bright with moonlight as the small cargo ship descended toward the landing terminal. The soft white glow-lamps reflected off Buzzer's face as he stared out the portal.

Cazara was just as beautiful at night as it was in daylight. A planetary resort paradise, it was handcrafted to create the utmost in vacation experience. Cazara, the oasis-wonderland of the Known Grids, and home to many thousands of Multi-Grid Level Corporations and other business entities. The perfect place to locate corporate headquarters, both for its pleasurable atmosphere and its constant flow of people.

The planet paradise was the treasure of the stars…and the home of Duncan Enterprises.

The metallic clang of interlocks sliding into place told Buzzer that the docking procedure had been completed. The unloading ramp fell to the hard surface and an instant assortment of crewmen, cargo and vehicles littered the area.

Buzzer crouched back down into the 'Biological Specimen' freight box he had shipped himself in and secured the lid over his head just as the doors to the cargo bay opened and a crowd of people rushed in. The crate was suddenly set into motion and he silently enjoyed the ride out of the ship.

Once safely placed on a transport vehicle outside, he sat and waited for the commotion to die down. After approximately an hour, Buzzer once again activated the unsealing controls, removed the lid and disappeared into the night.

Cazara Center was easily visible at this distance. A deep feeling of satisfaction washed over him. One of those glittering lights, out there in the panoramic view of the sprawling city, was the headquarters for Duncan Enterprises.

The place where he would locate and destroy his intended victim...

~*~

The guard leaned back against the tree, blaster resting at his side, and gazed out into the darkness of the night sky. Nothing was happening around the Duncan Enterprises Building, nothing ever happened around this place. Cazara had the lowest crime rate in the NorthEastern Corporate Grid-Sector and was generally a pretty dull planet. Except, that is, for the vacationers and business people that always seemed to be having the time of their lives.

But for the people who lived and worked on Cazara...well, there was only so much sun, sand and heat a person could take before getting sick and tired of it all...

The hand came out of nowhere, encircling the guard's throat. He tried frantically to grab for his blaster but it was gone from its holster. When he looked up he was staring into the muzzle of his own weapon. The shocking reality of the situation left him frozen with fear while his aggressor looked him in the eye.

"You're pretty damn stupid, mister," the man said as the gun came away from his head and the hand let go of his neck. "Are you always this unprepared while on duty?"

"No, sir," he snapped back, trying to suck a deep breath into his tortured lungs. His heartbeat was still racing but things seemed to have calmed down quite suddenly. The man's tone was cool and authoritative, kind of soothing in a way.

"Didn't you know that Duncan himself has ordered the security beefed up around here?" "Yes, sir, but..."

"No buts, mister!" The stone cold voice cut him off. "You were lagging off. I should actually dock you some pay because of it, too. Lord knows that if Willis had found you out here almost asleep you'd have been out on your ass in an hour—and for that hour he'd be chewing your ass off. Am I right?"

The guard smiled. "Damn right about that, sir. Willis would have dug me a hole and buried me in it."

"All right then, I'll let you off with a warning this time," the man said and handed him back his blaster. "You should have seen the look on your face when I grabbed you."

"You scared the holy hell out of me, sir," the guard said. "I didn't even hear you coming." "That's because you were almost snoring," the mystery man answered and began walking

toward the massive building. "Take it easy and stay alert. Willis is out here too, you know." "Yes, sir." The guard called to the retreating back of the big man as he tried to slow his still

racing heart. Taking another deep breath, he searched his memory in an effort to recall ever seeing the face before...no, nothing. The guy must be new. A transfer or something. He holstered his blaster, slumped back against the tree to steady himself and took another long look at the stars. He doubted very much that sleep would come to him again this night.

Buzzer walked toward the huge building that was the center of Duncan Enterprises. He couldn't shake the smile from his face. The guard had been so scared that he hadn't even asked for an ID check.

Phase-One of this mission, Infiltration, was complete. Phase-Two, Search and Destroy, was just beginning.

~*~

The main doors of the lobby slid open and the receptionist looked up, a look of wonder on her face. "Excuse me, sir, how did you...?"

"Don't worry about that," Buzzer quickly scanned the room. He hadn't counted on there being ten security guards posted throughout the cavernous lobby this late at night but he wasn't worried. The security personnel were quick to act but Buzzer pulled out his official Guarder ID, the metallic Falcon symbol reflecting the room's light, for all to see.

"Put your weapons down, boys," Buzzer said as he gripped the butt of his blaster. These men were all dressed in uniform. The guards outside had been dressed in street clothes; they had probably been Duncan's own personal security force and not just building security. "I am an

U.E.N. Guarder here on official business. I must see Mr. Duncan as soon as possible. I know that he keeps his private residence within this building and is on the property at this moment. Would you be so kind as to let him know that he has a visitor?"

91

"Who shall I say wants to see him?" the receptionist blurted as she frantically searched for the correct controls on her console.

"The name has no bearing on the nature of my business here," Buzzer growled as the main doors slid open and an older man, probably late forties but looking like he kept in shape, walked in.

"What seems to be the problem, sir?" The man asked casually from a distance of about three meters.

Buzzer automatically recognized the face of Tappleton Willis, Duncan's Chief of Security and overall second-in-command.

"No concern of yours, Mr. Willis. This is between the U.E.N. Judiciary Board and Mr.

Duncan," Buzzer replied as the ten security guards approached closer, effectively encircling his position.

"Whatever could the Board want with Kelsington Duncan? Is there some kind of award ceremony or some such thing that he has not yet been notified of?"

"As I said before, Mr. Willis, this is of no concern to you."

Willis looked into the Guarder's eyes, saw the coldness lingering there and quickly looked away. The receptionist whispered into the small microphone attached to her headset and looked up. The room was deathly quiet when she spoke. "Mr. Duncan would speak with you, Mr. Willis."

Willis swallowed hard and cautiously made his way past the Guarder and to the reception desk. He leaned over the console to grab the headset being offered by the small woman behind the desk and slipped it on. "Yes, Mr. Duncan?"

Willis' words were being whispered and the conversation coming from the other end was inaudible. Buzzer couldn't make out a word of it. Willis looked up and glanced toward him. It seemed that Buzzer's very presence had set the entire building on edge.

Willis turned his back to Buzzer, finished the conversation and laid the small headset on the desktop. As Willis turned back to face Buzzer, he gave a slight hand signal to the security guards who were surrounding the Guarder.

Buzzer took a small step back as all ten men swung up their half-chargers and aimed at him.

Willis stood relaxed and smiled. "Would you please come with me, sir?"

"I'm sorry, no."

Willis blinked in reaction to the blunt refusal. "I think that you are far too outnumbered to play these kinds of games, policeman..." Willis drawled the last word as the ten men surrounding Buzzer snickered.

Buzzer unholstered his blaster and brought it up to bear on Willis's head.

The move had been so quick that most of the security guards were still snickering among themselves before they realized the sudden change in events. Willis stared wide-eyed at the small black hole of the blaster's muzzle in front of his face.

"Any one of those men fires at me and I'll be dead. That doesn't bother me; I accepted the hazards of this job the day I was sworn in. But rest assured, Mr. Willis, I've never missed an intended target in my life, especially at this range. If I die here in this building, you will die right alongside me."

Buzzer felt the electricity in the air. Willis was frozen with fear, his eyes fixed on the weapon in his face. The room was silent; the only sound was the heavy breathing coming from Willis.

"Put down your goddamn guns already!" Willis snarled, eyes unmoving.

Eight of the guards responded to this order immediately by lowering their weapons, but the other two looked skeptical. Willis glared at them and snarled. "Do it now!"

"Negative, Mr. Willis," one of the guards rasped as his finger began to tighten on the trigger of his powerful weapon. "This man is outnumbered and outgunned and he is mine."

The huge blast from the half-charger rocked the wall on the other side of the room.

Buzzer came out of his dive and crouched behind one corner of the reception desk. He had fired twice while maneuvering and saw two men go down hard in a spray of blood and gore, one of them being the man who had fired first.

The other eight security guards scattered throughout the lobby, trying to find any cover they could. Willis pulled out his blaster and scanned the large open area for Buzzer. From another position and two blasts later, two more Duncan Enterprises security personnel went down.

Buzzer was up and running now, only seven opponents left in the field of battle. Although he was well aware that the entire complex would soon be swarming with armed security guards, these seven were his most pressing problem. He had to move quickly or he would surely be pinned down somewhere in this room. Buzzer did not intend to allow that to happen.

Poorly aimed fire followed him in his sprint down a side corridor. He swung around on the run, fired several rounds from his blaster and watched another man fall dead as several others who were beginning to pursue dove, once again, to the carpeted floor.

Buzzer turned a corner and fired again, hitting another target squarely in the chest from a distance of about ten meters. The body immediately hit the carpet and tripped up another who was close behind. Buzzer took advantage of this man's sprawl in the hallway and put one in the top of his head; the body spasmed jerkily as blood washed into the carpet. There were now only four immediate opponents left. He raced down a connecting corridor and found himself surrounded on two sides by lift terminals, with a closed door straight ahead. It was a dead end. Cursing to himself, he searched for any type of alternate route out of there. At any moment, any one of the lifts could open up and disgorge another dozen or so of Duncan's guards.

The lone door flew open in front of him and he leveled the first man to show himself with a blast to the mid-section. The door closed quickly but would soon be opening again. Buzzer went to the corner of the corridor and chanced a quick look around the connecting hall, searched for Willis, couldn't find him, and fired on two approaching guards instead. Both men dropped to the floor, neither of them dead but both badly wounded and screaming in pain.

Two sets of lift doors suddenly slid open and men in uniform began streaming out. Buzzer fired quick bursts into one of the cars and saw blood splatter the walls as he quickly leaped into the other car. The five men still inside were taken completely by surprise as the new occupant began to fight furiously. Two well placed kicks knocked down two of the guards. The other three tried to rush him simultaneously in the small space. Buzzer dropped into a crouch and fired his blaster. The lower leg of one man disappeared in a red spray of blood and bone. The howling shrieks pierced Buzzer's ears as he brought an elbow up under the man's chin, knocking him unconscious. Someone grabbed him from behind and Buzzer threw his weight to one side, throwing the man over his shoulder to land headfirst against the lift-car's control panel. He heard a sickening crunch, and the body slumped to the floor as the car abruptly began to climb.

The sudden buck of the car threw the last man off balance and Buzzer took the clear shot at the man's head. Buzzer found himself breathing hard as he scanned the five men and determined any remaining threat. Only two of the men were conscious and moaning, grasping their badly bruised groins, the targets of Buzzer's first two kicks. One other was unconscious and bleeding heavily, one's head was bent at a very lethal angle and the headless one would never move again.

Buzzer leaned against the wall and tried to control his breathing. The two conscious men would become potential threats once they regained their composure, and thus had to be rendered inoperative, at least temporarily. He bent down and grabbed each of them by the jaw.

"Clench your teeth hard," he told them. "Or you'll bite off your tongues."

The two guards looked at him through pained and confused expressions just before he rammed their heads together. Both men slumped on top of each other, unconscious.

Quickly scanning the control panel, Buzzer punched in for Level Fifty-Six. The car rapidly decelerated and came screeching to a halt. The doors opened. Buzzer was ready for a firefight but there was nothing there to meet him. The sounds of people in the surrounding offices reached his ears slightly. It seemed that even at this late hour, Duncan Enterprises still bustled with activity. He would make it a point to steer clear of the innocent employees.

He stole a quick glance into the corridor and found it empty. Buzzer punched in a command for the lift-car to stay put on Level Fifty-Six and walked out of the car, blaster up and ready.

The sound of other lift-cars approaching made him swing suddenly toward the shafts. Three sets of doors slid open and guards began pouring out. Buzzer burst into action. His back-up mini- blaster filled his left hand and both guns began firing on the ill-prepared security guards. He fired at men, light fixtures, control panels, and everything else that would cause confusion as he dove back into the lift-car he had just vacated and destroyed the car's control panel with a quick blast. The car immediately began to descend, following its pre-programmed fail-safe procedures in case of damage.

This little quest of his had fast turned into something ugly, he thought as he tried to plan out his next move. The car rocked violently as it came to an abrupt stop, stuck between levels.

Buzzer was thrown to the floor of the car but quickly scrambled over to the destroyed control panel to see if he could remedy the situation.

Blasts from weapons powerful enough to be half-chargers shook the car as guards fired from the open shaft above. Buzzer understood now just what they intended to do. If they could succeed in destroying the mounting clamps which held the car to the shaft, the lift-car would plummet more than forty levels and he would be crushed on impact from the force of the downward plunge.

The sudden rush of rapid falling told Buzzer that the guards had succeeded. He blasted a hole through the roof-hatch, leaped to grasp the jagged edge, scrambled out of the lift-car and stood on top. In the very next shaft, another lift was climbing up, probably full of fresh security guards eager to join the hunt. Leaping off of his doomed car, he landed hard on the roof of the other.

The loud thud caused him considerable pain and the sudden attack of angry voices coming from inside the car made it clear that the men inside knew that something strange was going on up top. Buzzer had a momentary vision of the men below blasting their way through the roof-hatch of the car—and blasting him to pieces in the process.

The car he'd just leapt from disintegrated as it hit the bottom of the shaft. Buzzer quickly reached into a pocket and brought out a single marble grenade. Activating the tiny explosive device, he blasted a hole through the roof-hatch, threw it inside and flung himself to the side of the car.

In less than three seconds, the men inside discovered the small object, realized its purpose and began to panic. The small explosion buckled the walls of the car and silenced the men inside forever. Buzzer couldn't wait for the smoke to clear and jumped into the hatch as fire poured down from above. The men who had destroyed the mounting clamps on the original car were now firing down on this one but the car quickly passed their level and kept on climbing. Blood and body parts littered the floor panels and walls of the damaged lift. He looked over the damaged but still operational control panel and punched in for Level One-Sixty, Kelsington Duncan's penthouse suite. The panel declined the command and asked for a security code.

Buzzer had no idea what type of code would be used by Duncan himself so he settled on punching for Level One-Fifty. He would work his way up from there, play it safe and test out the area.

He hadn't realized how much security Duncan possessed. Even if these men were not really qualified for their positions, their sheer numbers and firepower proved them to be serious threats to his chosen mission. He had also miscalculated Duncan's nerve and gall.

The man had ordered the death of an U.E.N. Guarder, an act that would bring the wrath of every single Guarder in the ranks, all two hundred of them, upon him. The Squadron wouldn't rest until Kelsington Duncan had paid for such an act, paid equally, with his own life. Sergeant Jekel would make damn sure of it.

But for now, Buzzer was still alive and Duncan was his target—a man responsible for most of the illegal drug-trade in the NorthEastern Corporate Grid-Sector, a host of illegal practices and countless murders. Although Duncan himself had probably never directly pulled the trigger on any other man, his verbal commands had been responsible for nearly three thousand deaths over the past several e-years. The U.E.N. Judiciary Board had never collected enough solid evidence, concrete proof, to put this man away for his crimes.

To obtain such proof was the official reason that Guarders had been called in on the investigation, but Buzzer wasn't naive enough to think that Duncan's crimes were the only reason the Board would like to see his empire come crumbling down. The economy of the entire NorthEastern Corporate Grid-Sector would benefit greatly if the operations of Duncan Enterprises & Affiliates were to be disrupted. Free trade and new markets would spring up everywhere and many more big businesses would be attracted to Duncan's former turf. Duncan's vast organization was just shy of monopolizing four hundred interplanetary markets. If his power was stripped and his operations discontinued, the opportunities for the local businesses to thrive would be unlimited. The eventual extinction of drug lanes in the NorthEastern Grids would also benefit the entire quadrant. The major supplier of *morphus-3,socoa, nytrodrome, synth*, and *colboquik* would abruptly disappear. Connections and dealers would dry up, especially with the increased presence of the U.E.N. Military that would be sure to follow Duncan's demise. Users would have no choice but to move to the areas where addictive drugs were still available.

Yes, the Board was not only concerned in wiping out one ugly character and his shady business practices, but they also wanted to see the cleansing and subsequent rebirth of a major portion of Grid-Space. The big picture was the real interest here, not just justice.

Buzzer didn't actually care about the politics of it all; he just had one thing on his mind. Four good men, fellow Guarders, had died just days ago and he meant to seek vengeance on the man who was responsible. Kelsington Duncan was somewhere in this building, Buzzer could sense him, feel his fear. Soon he would find the man. And soon after, this mission would end.

The lift-car stopped on Level One-Fifty and Buzzer stepped out. Nobody was there to challenge him. The entire floor was totally quiet. In no time at all, he found the stairs and began his journey upward.

Kelsington Duncan was now all that mattered…

~*~

The security guard entered the stairwell on Level One-Sixty and found it empty. Humming to himself, he took a quick look down. This level was a good ways up, he decided, and turned back toward the door.

Buzzer let go of the pipes running along the ceiling and landed on top of the man. The guard went down hard but struggled to bring his weapon around, too scared to scream for help. A fist connected with the bridge of the guard's nose, flattening it across his face. The man's head snapped back and he tumbled down the stairs. Buzzer leaped down after him, picked him up and prepared to hit him again but the body was lifeless. A huge gash in the back of his head and the odd angle of his neck told Buzzer that much.

The uniform could come in handy, despite the blood spilled down the front of the shirt, and Buzzer quickly made the change. The half-charger felt good in his hands and the two blasters had found homes concealed within the uniform.

After stashing the corpse back up amidst the pipes, he opened the door and stepped into Level One-Sixty. Just five guards had been positioned in the stairwells to wait for him. Each had been handled quite easily. Six other guards were sitting around lazily about ten meters away. This part of the level was made up of Duncan's private office and several executive offices. The other side of this level contained Duncan's plush living quarters.

So he had chosen the wrong stairwell. It had been a fifty-fifty chance anyway. This only meant that it would take him a little longer to complete his mission. Pulling the *DE&A Security* cap down low, he proceeded into the central corridor. Nobody gave him a second glance as he made his way toward the main offices. Buzzer could see by the placards positioned on two doors in the corridor that the two largest offices belonged to Willis and Duncan. The door to Duncan's office was closed tight, his personal receptionist on duty at her desk just outside, while the door to the other office was wide open and inviting. It seemed that Willis didn't rate a receptionist of his own.

The Security Chief and second-in-command of DE&A was busy chewing out the security personnel downstairs on some sort of intercom. The words could be heard clearly from Buzzer's position in the hall. Very quickly and quietly, Buzzer entered the large office and locked the old fashioned hinged door behind him.

Willis spun around with a look of anger on his face. "What the hell do you want?"

"I'll start with you," Buzzer said as he removed his cap.

Willis froze as Buzzer brought up the half-charger. His eyes went wide with terror as he switched off the intercom. "All right, just what is it that you want here, Guarder? You've caused us enough pain and misery as it is."

"I want Kelsington Duncan's head on a silver platter to bring back to the Judiciary Board." "That's a rather morbid way of putting it, wouldn't you say?"

"Not at all, Tappy," Buzzer smirked. "It's the truthful way of putting it. I want him dead. I am an official Guarder of the United Earthian Nations and my word on such matters is law in the Known-Grids."

"Under what charges do you justify death by execution?"

"Under several charges of murder, mostly. Not to mention that your boss is the major supplier of illegal drugs in the NorthEastern CorporateGrid-Sector."

"Where on Mr. Duncan's record can you find a verdict of guilty on murder charges?"

"Four members of my team found out what it's like to be dead the other day on Orsisenia. I'm sure you received a damage report from the Delta-Rae Marina."

Willis turned pale at the mention of Orsisenia. "So, what does that mean?"

"It means that four U.E.N. Guarders were killed that night on one of Duncan's ships in one of Duncan's marinas after a large shipment of *colboquik* was discovered in the cargo hold. I hold Kelsington Duncan personally responsible for that."

"I assure you, Mr. Guarder, that Mr. Duncan had no knowledge..."

"That's bullshit, Willis!" Buzzer roared. "You know as well as I do about the drugs, the killings of hundreds of innocent people who may have one day posed a threat to DE&A, and all the other illegal garbage that Duncan is involved in."

A knock rapped against the door. "Is everything all right in there, Mr. Willis?" Both men froze as the knocking continued. "Mr. Willis, are you alright?"

Buzzer held his weapon steady and took a step closer. "Answer him."

Willis cleared his throat nervously. "Everything's fine, I'm fine, it's all right."

The guard outside the door recognized the emergency-code in his Security Chief's words and immediately began tapping the office-entry code into the door panel outside the office.

Commotion outside the door made it clear that the other guards had also been alerted. "What now, Guarder?" Willis sneered.

Buzzer pulled out his blaster and aimed it at Willis. He wanted to kill him, sure, but not just yet. He needed to know just where in this building Duncan was hiding, since he could no longer feel the man's presence on this level.

"Stay put, Willis," he snarled and fired twice. Willis screamed in agony as both of his legs exploded. The broken man crashed to the floor. Buzzer spun on his heels and brought up the half-charger. The weapon roared once and a major portion of the door disappeared. The man behind it issued one short scream and was silent.

Sporadic fire came through the large hole in the door, hitting nothing but walls and furniture. Buzzer fired the powerful weapon again and the hole in the door almost doubled in size. More screaming rewarded him but the answering fire was growing more concentrated. The guards had grouped together in a last ditch effort at survival.

"I am still in here, you fools!" Willis screamed through gritted teeth at the members of his security staff pouring fire into his office.

Buzzer ditched the large bulky weapon, quickly searched his pockets and brought out five of the tiny marble grenades. The small explosives ought to take care of the little problem in the hall, he thought. With his thumb, he activated all five of the balls and brought back his arm to launch them out of the hole in the office door.

The blast caught him in the right shoulder as his arm sprang forward. Four of the mini-bombs made it through the door—but one landed on the plush carpet inside the office. Buzzer rolled along the floor with considerable pain in his shoulder. His light body-armor had saved him from most of the blast but he still bled from several minor wounds.

As he came out of the roll, landing on his knees, he realized that a live marble grenade was in this very room with him. Barely a second had passed since he had activated the small bombs.

Willis was staring wide-eyed with terror at the small grenade, the mini-blaster he had shot Buzzer with still in his right fist.

Buzzer glared at the man in disgust and raised his blaster. "Goodbye, Mr. Willis..."

The weapon bucked in his hand and Tappleton Willis took the blast in the side of his head, his brain matter splashing red and gray across the far wall.

Buzzer knew the little explosive device would detonate momentarily. Time seemed to pass very slowly when life could be measured in mere seconds. In one frantic move, he picked himself up off the floor and launched his body at the only available escape route—the office windows. As he blew out the windows with his blaster, he realized that he had not taken the time to think about his location before throwing himself out of windows on the building's one- hundred-sixtieth level. As he passed through the remnants of the thick plate glass, the explosion ripped through the room.

Buzzer could feel the heat and flames envelope him as he began to plunge.

Most of the executive offices on Level One-Sixty were destroyed by the blast, the bulk of the explosive energy coming from the ignited contents of the security staff's armory. The existeel wall that split the level in half saved Kelsington Duncan's penthouse suite from any extensive damage.

But just about everything else on the other side was destroyed, including the still twitching body of Tappleton Willis.

~*~

The bright lights and mass of reporters that crowded the large conference room did more to annoy Kelsington Duncan than anything else. The events of the night before had put him in a bad mood to begin with, and now all of the rapid-fire questions were just plain pissing him off.

"I'm sorry, ladies and gentlemen," Duncan announced, hands held high in the air. "I've said all that I have to say at this time. Thank you all for your patience and consideration during this very trying day. My spokesman will answer any other questions which you may have."

Duncan left the small stage amid a throng of voices, all calling out to him, but he listened to none of it. His security people cleared a wide path through the crowd as he left the conference room. For once, he regretted the attention that the press always surrounded him with each and every time something 'big' involving Duncan Enterprises transpired. This little situation of his was one bit of publicity that he could live without.

So far, his people had come up with a decent cover story to explain the devastating explosions that had rocked the upper level of his building. The press seemed to be buying it so he wasn't too particularly worried. The most important thing he could think of right now was the way he should explain all of this to the Judiciary Board of the United Earthian Nations. The Guarder who had come for him yesterday was dead. Duncan had acted without thinking when he ordered the man's death and now he truly regretted it. He was now a marked man. A price would be placed on his head by the mysterious Guarder Squadron unless he could convince the Board that he was innocent.

As far as he could tell, only a handful of people on his staff even knew about the Guarder and all of these people could be easily silenced in the future if warranted. Silence was indeed golden in situations such as these.

But this one Guarder had cost him the lives of more than fifty security personnel, including Willis, and had caused some very extensive damage to the structure of his headquarters. The lobby was a wreck, lift-cars and shafts had been severely damaged, and most of the office area on Level One-Sixty was gone. As far as he knew, this one Guarder had also been behind the recent death and destruction on Orsisenia.

Billions and billions worth of property and personnel had been destroyed by one man within the last few days. Now that he thought about it, he knew that he would have one hell of a lot of explaining to do to the authorities.

The lift doors opened on to his quarters. He blinked his eyes in surprise. His mind must have been grids away; he could not remember walking to or entering the lift. His tired brain was pounding in his skull; the dull ache had been there all night.

The huge wall screen blinked to life at his command and he went into the kitchen. The sound of the news reverberated throughout his living quarters. Of course, the main story focused on the events surrounding himself and his company late yesterday evening. The report of his close brush with death particularly amused him.

He poured himself a good-sized glass of wine, Borandian 2532, the best in his collection, and walked into his lavishly decorated and oversized living room. The glass dropped from his hand and spilled its contents into the eggshell white carpeting. His eyes widened at what he saw, his jaw gaped and all color drained from his face.

The sight of the Guarder standing there, leaning against the giant screen, aiming a sinister looking black blaster at his chest did little to calm his already erratic nerves.

Buzzer had been badly burned, bruised and beaten by the force of the explosion of the night before. The tremendous blast had hurled him through the window of Level One-Sixty and covered his body with a multitude of first and second degree burns. Dozens of small slashes and gashes marked his arms, neck and face. The ten-meter fall to the balcony on Level One-Fifty- Seven had also banged up his left shoulder, hip and knee. The large gash across his forehead had matted his hair and face with dried blood. The tattered remnant of one of Duncan's own security uniforms was also splashed with blood, especially at the right shoulder.

The eerie sight of the specter before him terrified Kelsington Duncan. The Guarder truly looked as if he had risen from the dead and had returned to seek vengeance, had returned to drag Duncan screaming into the dark realms of the netherworld.

Duncan's throat dried up immediately, and his voice was stricken with fear as he spoke. "How...how did you manage to...to survive the blast?"

Buzzer tried to smile but the resulting face made Duncan cringe even more. "I'm a Guarder, Duncan," was his only answer.

Duncan tried to compose himself. His mind reeled with the implications of his present situation.

"I've heard things about you people, the Guarders. Incredible things, legends. But I never actually believed any of that..."

"We're the best, Duncan," Buzzer said and commanded his body to stand straighter. Although Buzzer was badly shaken, the blaster still pointed unwaveringly at Duncan's chest. "But I must give you and your organization some credit. I've never encountered this many obstacles on a mission before. This was a true challenge to my skills and training. I have to thank you for the opportunity to prove myself worthy of my rank."

"Was it you on Orsisenia?" Duncan rasped.

"Yes, it was. But the four men who came with me didn't have so much luck. I left Orsisenia and they did not. At least, not alive anyway."

"Four Guarders? Four Guarders died in that marina? On the *Ambrosia*?" Duncan suddenly understood the reasons behind this man's rage, this one extraordinary man's relentless hunt. "I didn't know anything about that, I swear to you."

"Save the politics for the public, Kelsington," Buzzer waved his hand at the man in contempt. "Sit down, already. I want to explain to you why I'm going to kill you now."

"Kill me!" Duncan was taken aback by the statement but slumped into the chair next to him as commanded. "You can take me back to Aegis to stand trial for whatever charges you have brought against me but you won't kill me, Guarder. I'm much too powerful a man in this Corporate Grid-Sector to be disposed of so hastily."

"You're very cocky, Duncan," Buzzer said and fixed him with a steely glare. "But you still don't get it, do you? I am a Guarder, appointed by the U.E.N. Judiciary Board to defend their best interests in any way that I see fit. While on duty, I hold the supreme powers of the Judiciary Board to act as judge and jury. To pass and carry out sentencing. To dispense justice. The courts would drag this case out for a very long time if I brought you back to Aegis. I do not find that to be in the best interests of the Judiciary Board. My word is law out here; and death by execution is totally justifiable under these circumstances. So, in layman's terms, when I shoot you dead you will have been legally executed in a court of law of the United Earthian Nations. Caseclosed."

"You are insane! Get a grip on yourself! You are talking about cold-blooded murder here," Duncan laughed. "You are a law enforcement officer. How can you kill in cold blood and still have pride in yourself?"

"Very easily, Duncan," Buzzer answered. "You can beg and plead all you want but it won't make a difference. You will not change my mind or my sentence. This has been decided for quite some time."

Duncan's face grew even more worried. He stuttered several times before getting his voice back. "Do you have any idea just how far my influence reaches throughout the Known-Grids? I can make you very wealthy, very wealthy indeed..."

"Save it," Buzzer cut him off. "You're dirtier than anybody I know. You are involved in some of the worst illegal activity to ever hit the NorthEastern Corporate Grid-Sector. Frying you will make a lot of people very happy, including me."

"Listen, whatever grudge you hold against me, we can work it out. There's no problem we can't overcome. Take me back to Aegis, lock me up and put me away, but for chrissakes, don't kill me!"

"You should have been thinking about the consequences before you got into all of this nastiness, Kelsington. The drug world is dog-eat-dog. You above all people should know that. Without hesitation, your men on Orsisenia opened fire on me and my team, even after I pulled out my badge and announced who we were. Upon the first shot, the decision was made that your Orsisenia operation would be destroyed. Guarders don't hold back. We particularly don't like to be shot at either. What brought my men down was not the pathetic efforts of your people on that disgusting little planet, but an explosive device attached to the doors of the main cargo hold aboard that ship. An illegal explosive device whose sole purpose was to kill anyone, including officers of the law, who tried to enter the hold. That counts as conspiracy to commit pre-meditated murder of law enforcement officials, and is grounds for execution by itself. Add, on top of that, my four teammates who were aboard that boat when it blew, and the fact that you ordered my death last night. Screw all of the other charges against you, Duncan. Prison would be too good a place for a man like you, someone who could instigate a riot and possibly escape. I couldn't allow that. I would just have to waste more of my time hunting you down and killing you then. I think I'll save myself the trouble and kill you now."

"I get it; you're trying to scare me, right?" Duncan asked. "Well, it worked. I'm shaking in my shoes, okay. Your little terrorist tactics were successful so just slap on the cuffs and take me in."

Buzzer smirked and shook his head in resignation. "What? What is so funny?"

"You..." Buzzer said and staggered over to where Duncan was sitting. The few steps seemed to take forever to the man who owned Duncan Enterprises. The gaping black maw of the blaster came closer; the Guarder's eyes peered icily into his own.

"Go ahead, read me my rights." Duncan pleaded, the tears now flowing freely down his face as he realized that his attempt to bargain his way out of this one was failing. "I won't resist, I'll go freely..."

Buzzer pressed the muzzle of the blaster to Duncan's forehead and looked down at the man seated before him. Several seconds of complete silence followed and Buzzer could feel the trembling of the smaller man.

"What a waste..." he muttered and pulled the trigger.

The blast thundered through the room and Duncan's headless body tumbled out of the chair to the floor with a dull thud. Buzzer stepped over the steadily growing deep red stain on the carpet, holstered his blaster and left the room.

~*~

Buzzer sat alone on the rock in the middle of the small lake. Cazara's sun was just setting behind the mountains. The beautiful dusk sky was a sight that Buzzer had never seen before and he soaked it in. The stark contrasts in color astounded him. Little things like a sunset could still be so fulfilling...

It would be a long trip back to Aegis and the U.E.N. Governmental Complex which housed the Guarder HQ. That is, if no other missions had since been assigned to him. The return message from Jekel should reach his sequencer within the next day. He had purposefully routed his original message to take the long way around; giving his body some much needed time to recuperate.

In the meantime, he would allow his wounds to start healing and explore the wonders of this planet paradise. Cazara certainly did live up to its reputation.

Buzzer was happy. For the first time in a long time, he felt really happy. It was tough getting over the death of friends, teammates and colleagues. He had come close to the proverbial edge of death himself a time or two. There weren't many things left in this universe that could make a man feel satisfied with life. But, if even for only a brief time, he would seriously consider enjoying himself. The opportunity hadn't presented itself for a while.

Now, sitting here on this rock, he considered how good it felt to be happy. He was just plain glad that there were some things in life that could still be appreciated...like a sunset...

MULLENS APPROACHES TODAY

Silence ruled the conference room for almost a minute before Mullens shifted in his chair and sifted through all that he had just heard.

"Kelsington Duncan...the news agencies all reported that he had committed suicide after what happened in his building the night before. The fact that you were able to survive all that had happened is simply incredible..."

"That's the way it's done, Mullens."

"Is that the way all Guarders do things?" Mullens asked. "Or just you?"

"We're all trained in the same way, by the same man and by the same code," Buzzer said. "We all do it the same way."

"Then why am I sitting here interviewing *you*, Mr. Buzzer?" Mullens asked. "There are two hundred of your squadron at all times, correct?"

Buzzer nodded.

"Any of them could have been singled out for this, including your Sergeant Jekel. Why you?" "Luck of the draw, I guess."

Mullens laughed at that and saw the slightest hint of a smile cross the Guarder's lips. It was an expression he had not seen this man make since the interview started, an expression that almost seemed uncomfortable on that dark face, but he was glad to know that the Guarder could experience a moment or two of levity in his life.

Glancing down at his mini-pad, he saw the time left on his limit quickly counting down in the upper right hand corner of the tiny screen. *What else to ask? There's still so much I need to know. Damn the Judiciary Board for only giving me two hours with this man,* he thought, *his memories could fill two full days at the very least...*

"My time with you is almost over, Mr. Buzzer," Mullens said and sighed. "Perhaps we should move this conversation along to the events leading up to today."

"How much of it do you want to know?"

"Well, how much could there be?"

Buzzer actually did laugh at that and leaned forward in his chair. "If you want me to start at the beginning, this could take a while."

Mullens glanced down once more at the countdown on his mini-pad and knew that he absolutely needed to hear this story in order to accurately record all that had happened just hours ago. "Yes, then, please start at the very beginning and tell me everything that occurred which culminated in your amazing feat of earlier today."

"Listen, Mullens, I'll say this one last time," Buzzer said, all seriousness once again. "I did not do anything special today. I am a Guarder. What happened today—that's what I do. It's my job and I pride myself on being good at it. But in case you didn't realize it, there were several other Guarders involved in that mess besides me. We worked together as a team, and very well I should add, since we don't often get that opportunity. But we were a team nevertheless and it was the efforts of every last one of us that you need to record, not just mine."

"Of course, Mr. Buzzer, of course," Mullens said and motioned for the Guarder to continue. "All right," Buzzer said and searched his memory for the best place to start. "The Grids were being rocked by several incidents, all seemingly unrelated..."

During the twelve e-year span of The New Conflict, the U.E.N. began training a special unit of commandos in the finest arts of hand-to-hand combat, marksmanship, heavy weapons handling, spacecraft/aircraft piloting, espionage, intelligence gathering and survivalism. Soon known by the code name Guardian, *the training program that produced these ultimate soldiers was to be used as a major tool in the ongoing war against the U.S.S. and beyond. The first team of these specially trained commandos to see action in The New Conflict quickly made it more than apparent that their superior training had been worth the effort. That historic first team of twenty men and women would go on to log a total of 17,200 confirmed enemy kills before the war was over. By the time of the signing of the Treaty of 2182, a total of five twenty-member teams had been set loose upon the U.S.S. Of that first hundred, only seventeen had been killed in the line of duty. But by the end of the war, those hundred elite commandos had scored an astounding 114,700 confirmed enemy kills. This impressive figure was extremely significant to U.E.N. Military experts of the time. Significant enough to warrant the creation of a special branch of the U.E.N. Military dedicated to continually improve the most successful training program in military history...*

(Excerpt:*The U.E.N. Unveiled— The Dark History of Humanity's Greatest Government*by Joseph Mullens)

MISSION FIVE: RANKS OF RED

Mouabi Abuka, President of New Africa, sat stiff-backed in his plush office on the fifteenth level of the Administration Building, scanning a seemingly endless supply of reports and proposals. Being the lone presiding force of a planet as large as New Africa would seem like no easy task, but lately President Abuka had found the job utterly boring and monotonous.

New Africa was an incredibly large and beautiful planet, which attracted billions of tourists each cycle—and kept most of its government officials living the wealthy life. The planet generally ran itself. Abuka's immediate subordinates kept complete control of the localized political groups and thus kept the native population happy. Many tourists ancestral to the original African continent on

Old Earth visited the tropical planet several times a cycle. Over ten billion InterGridactic dollars were dumped into the economy each cycle through these people alone.

Another one-hundred-twenty billion was circulated by the remainder of each cycle's tourist population.

Overall, New Africa made a pretty hefty profit from the vacationing masses. One huge advantage was the fact that New Africa was a tropical paradise all cycle long. A glorious eternity of utopia-like climatic conditions, resulting in a continuous flow of off-world tourists, kept the planetary economy running smoothly. The complete opposite of the desert-like environment that was Old Earth's African continent, New Africa was a pleasure seeker's wonderland. Although it did not rival the extreme popularity of Cazara, king of the tropical resort worlds, New Africa held its own within the SouthWestern CorporateGrid-Sector.

Mouabi Abuka was quite content with his advantageous position at the head of the New African government. Coming from the wealthiest family on the planet, his rise to power had not been very difficult. In fact, the presidency had been guaranteed to him by his father's powerful connections more than five cycles before he had assumed the position.

Now, at the age of thirty-one and in the best physical condition of his life, he was an important member of the Universal Corporate Council. Extremely intelligent, well educated and charismatic, Abuka's well-known and favorable reputation had made his name known Grid- Wide.

Whenever people thought of the planet New Africa, the name Mouabi Abuka came to mind.

Abuka had used his power and privileges effectively during his career to accomplish his wide range of goals; and the fact that he had not abused his powers of office made him all the more glorified in the eyes of his people. He was no dictator, no tyrant, only a leader—and one who performed his job well. People the Grids over approved of him and almost every decision he had made during his administration.

As the President of New Africa, it seemed Mouabi Abuka could do no wrong.

The blinking red light on his desk panel attracted his attention. Leaning over, the well-built New African lightly touched the blinking light and a smooth, soft computer-synthesized female voice filled the room.

"There is a Mr. Rhafid Azid on-line for you, Mr. President. He says it is quite urgent that he speak with you."

109

Abuka thought the name sounded familiar but he couldn't match it with a face or an organization. "What firm does he represent?"

"He stated that he is a member of the Universal Freedom Front."

"Display the history of that organization," Abuka ordered and a series of clicks and slight buzzes filled the com-link for a few brief seconds before the computer displayed the data on a small screen embedded in his desk top.

"Universal Freedom Front—splinter faction of the Universal Freedom from Tyranny Movement," Abuka read aloud. "The foremost terrorist organization operating in the NorthWestern Corporate Grid-Sector. Said organization not known to operate in the SouthWestern Corporate Grid-Sector. Zero files on splinter faction."

Abuka smiled, eager for the chance to engage in conversation with an actual terrorist. "Patch him through immediately."

The computer complied and the blinking red light was replaced with a yellow one. Abuka reached over and touched the light, connecting the line.

"Hello, Mr. Azid. How may I be of assistance to you?"

"President Abuka," said a thickly accented Azuridian voice, totally devoid of emotion. "I need say just one word to you, my good man. May you take it with you into eternity."

"And what may this mysterious word be, Mr. Azid?"

Silence lingered over the line for a moment before Azid replied, "Goodbye..."

The small nuclear explosive device planted in one of the lower sublevels, far below Abuka's chair, instantaneously received its specified frequency and promptly detonated.

The Administration Building and an area of fourteen kilometers surrounding it were disintegrated by the blast.

Over twenty thousand people died instantly as the Governmental Headquarters of New Africa was obliterated.

On the other side of the planet, the on-line connection with the Administration Building went dead on Rhafid Azid. The tall, dark, black-haired Azuridian smiled as static filled the line. The smile was one of satisfaction, of accomplishment; Azid had just caused the deaths of thousands of innocent people.

Rhafid Azid was a very happy man...

Neuron Industries was the largest organization on—and part owner of—Linkston-4.

Linkston-4 was a small planet, but it held a wealth of opportunities for the study of genetic marvels. All life forms on Linkston-4 seemed to be products of fantastic genetic mutations. No two specimens of any species on the planet consisted of the same genetic make-up. Each newborn, whatever it might be, a budding twanist or baby braka, was drastically and incredibly different from its parents. Every birthling, budding or hatchling brought something totally new to the planet.

This, of course, made the process of species and family classification almost impossible; but the scientists of Neuron Industries stationed on Linkston-4 were constantly working on some method of grouping or categorizing each species' newest forms.

The vast amount of information which was being gathered each day required an equal amount of recording and paperwork, just to keep up with the rapid rate of change that seemed to affect every species on the planet.

This tedious work often resulted in many late nights sitting in front of a monitor for the employees of Neuron Industries, trying to soak up a seemingly endless visual display of facts and figures.

Dr. Paul Kindler hated this part of his chosen profession but he could easily forecast many more such nights lying ahead of him. Whether he liked it or not had no bearing on his present situation. He had accepted the position to head the entire Linkston-4 operation over eight e-years ago because of the initial data, fascinating material that had come in from Neuron Industries' first seeker-satellite. This data, unbelievable though it had seemed, convinced Kindler to join the project and travel to the distant and mysterious planet.

Now, almost a decade later, Dr. Paul Kindler was the most renowned scientist and geneticist in all the Known-Grids. The biological and genetic wonders of Linkston-4 had piqued the interests of over eighty billion people. As a result, at the tender age of thirty-seven, Paul Kindler found himself writing the reports, narrating the documentaries and acting as the primary spokesperson of the Linkston-4 operation at hundreds of press conferences.

Dr. Paul Kindler sat back, tore his eyes from the monitor screen and laughed at the irony of it all. Coming from a tremendously wealthy and successful family, well-known and respected in the NorthEastern Corporate Grid-Sector, Kindler had chosen to pursue a career as a geneticist primarily to *get away* from all the glitter and glamour of celebrity status.

The scientific community had an age-old reputation for keeping out of the spotlight and letting others accept the credit for their accomplishments. This low-profile image was something that Paul Kindler had desperately wanted and needed in his life. The sleazy, slimy world of the jet-set held no place for him; or no *comfortable* place, he thought to himself.

The high position in the family business offered him by his father was the chance to live the good life, the easy life, the life of the rich. He had emphatically turned it down. Instead, he had been determined to make it on his own and live his life in privacy. This he had achieved…until he had made a name for himself as the spokesperson for Neuron Industries' Linkston-4 operation.

Now, Dr. Paul Kindler was the most famous member of the famous Kindler family. Kindler had to laugh. Life's little twists and turns could be all too funny sometimes. A small noise in the outer laboratory caught his attention.

"Who else could be up at this hour?" He asked himself and laughed again. He stood and stretched his cramped muscles.

"Dr. Kindler, are you there?" A female voice called from the other room.

"Yes, in here," he answered and looked back to the monitor.

"Hello, Dr. Kindler," the unfamiliar voice said from the open doorway.

Kindler spun around to greet his unexpected visitor and was stunned at the sight of the woman in the doorway, blaster held high and aimed right at his chest.

"What is the meaning of this?"

"Quiet, doctor; this will take but a moment," the stranger said. "What do you want here?"

"Dr. Paul Kindler, you will become an example for the rest of the universe of our true strength and power," she said.

"An example? How?" Kindler questioned.

"In death, my good doctor."

The icy chill of the reply rendered Kindler speechless.

"The Universal Freedom Front hereby sentences you to die for our cause in order to prove to the United Earthian Nations that no one is safe from our organization. Not even manipulators and exploiters such as yourself."

Kindler just stood there, his face a mask of shock and confusion, as the terrorist pulled the trigger. The blast drilled through Kindler's chest and continued on to explode against the wall behind.

Kindler died with his eyes wide-open and his mouth forming the question that had been in his mind.

Why?

The convulsing body hit the floor about three meters from where Kindler had been standing. Marita Anzani watched the corpse until it stopped twitching and then left the office.

~*~

CargoLiner-X4J729 had lifted off from Temperest on time with its usual complement of personnel and load of freight but an additional item had been unexpectedly added to its' manifest just prior to lift-off. While the Captain had been filing his final flight-plan with Temperest Control, special orders had come in from the U.E.N. Judiciary Board approving the acceptance of a single passenger. The tall mysterious man dressed in black, armor and weapons included, had boarded uneventfully and quickly disappeared into the small compartment allotted him.

None of the crew had seen this shadow man since his arrival and crewmembers who had passed his room had heard absolutely no sound emanating from the small cubicle.

Rumors had been circulating aboard the huge freighter during the entire trip to Aegis—the man was a spy, a U.E.N. strongman, a protected government witness, or the most outlandish one of all, a U.E.N. Appointed Guarder.

Whatever or whoever the man was, one thing was clear—he was a man of high importance within the U.E.N. Government.

The crewmembers had never seen such a dark and brooding man. The stranger was big, at least six-feet-three-inches tall, and had a physique that reeked of excessive strength. Although only seen for a few moments while boarding, this lone individual had managed to spook the entire crew. The Captain felt it too. It was the man's eyes, those black hollow eyes, that had disturbed his crew the most. One look at those eyes, however brief, revealed the pain and death that this man had suffered through in his lifetime. A presence of death enshrouded this mysterious man like an aura; they could almost see the shadows that lingered within him as he had made his way to his quarters.

And, being that the crew came mostly from the superstitious stock of the Berking System, he was considered a taboo—a symbol of eventual catastrophe for the cargoliner and its crew. For centuries the cargoliners of the Known-Grids had been manned primarily by Berkings, a people who tended to take routine and standardization to the extreme. As a result of their fastidious nature, anything that disturbed the normal ebb and flow of a flight was considered a bad omen. Historically, the unexplained occurrences and bizarre events that had transpired on many voyages where deviations from the norm had taken place seemed to provide a basis for the Berkings' superstitions.

These men would only be happy once the strong silent traveler left their ship. They would be very happy indeed once the small cubicle which had housed him was decontaminated, erasing his presence. When they docked on Aegis and he debarked, then would be a time of rejoicing and celebration.

But, deep down inside them all, they knew that extreme caution would have to be exercised until this gloomy aura of foreboding had passed through the hull of their ship.

~*~

Cabriolet was a peaceful world. It had been discovered and settled over two and a half centuries ago by a small group of independent researchers who had financed the entire operation, including the construction of their own interstellar ship, a multi-trillion dollar undertaking.

The original settlers had all been good friends and, as the colony grew over the years, the good relations had remained constant. No wars had plagued Cabriolet's past. No native murderers had ever walked through its cities. No significant crimes could be found to mar the perfect record of this Utopian society. Everybody had an equal share of everything and all inhabitants had everything that they needed. Life on Cabriolet was good for everyone.

And when it came to holidays and celebrations, the Cabriolets were first and foremost in enjoying themselves. Especially on First Settler's Day. The entire planet took on a party atmosphere on the one day each orbit that marked the anniversary of the original settlers' first arrival. Lavish parades and ballroom gatherings were customary on most planetary holidays but First Settler's Day brought out the best in the Cabriolets.

The most prestigious event on First Settler's Day was the Parade of the SpokesPeople, held in Cabriolet's capital city of Targa. Here, the most famous and celebrated men and women on the planet took part in a ride through the streets of the capital, waving and smiling to the people in their usual joyful ways.

Prime Spokesman for Administration Thomas St. Clair loved the Parade of the SpokesPeople.

Having the most important task on Cabriolet, it was his job to know the people's wants and desires and to relate this to the U.E.N. Judiciary Board when dealing in legal governmental policies and procedures.

St. Clair loved his job. It was mostly taken care of by the people themselves. The only hassles came when dealing with the all too prim-and-proper bureaucratic members of the Judiciary Board. But since he only had to deal with them about ten times each Cabriolet orbit, roughly one-point-seven e-years, he did not mind his job at all.

The parade always made him feel good. The feeling of satisfaction associated with seeing the happy smiling faces of thousands upon thousands of men, women and children was indescribable. It made him love life all the more when he rode through Targa in the open aircar amidst the cheers and laughter of his people.

His reign as the closest thing that Cabriolet had to a ruling power, now almost two decades long, had passed almost uneventfully. His charismatic powers of speech and his wide appeal to the masses had made him famous the grids over. His speeches at universally broadcast press conferences and debates had established Thomas St. Clair as a vocal power in the upper echelons of the SouthWestern Corporate Grid-Sector. His voice held clout when it came to Corporate Sector decision making. People generally listened to the wise older man when he offered advice and knowledge.

In general, not a bad word could be said about Cabriolet's Prime Spokesman for Administration. He was fair, he was practical and, most of all, he was happy.

And happy men always made the best leaders.

St. Clair sat back in the body-form cushioned seat and thanked the Lord for all the happiness in his life. Memories of days gone by filled his head, one great flood of joy. Life had been just like this, one long happy parade, ever since he could remember. And Thomas St. Clair knew, deep down, that he would be happy for as long as he lived. He would take his lifelong happiness with him gladly to his grave. He thought of how lucky he was to have such an attitude toward life and living, when so many poor fools on other worlds get so depressed at times that suicide was their only possible means of escape. What a dreadful concept, suicide. St. Clair could not discern what would drive a person to commit such an act of finality.

Having dismissed his momentary droll train of thought, he went back to smiling and waving at the people, all the thousands of happy smiling faces; men, women, and children. Every single one of them happy to be alive and living on Cabriolet.

Thomas St. Clair never heard the crack of the custom-made, hi-powered, long-range projectile rifle—nor the whine of the bullet that ended his life.

Juan Ortiz watched through his sniper-scope as the specially designed forty-four caliber slug exploded on impact with Thomas St. Clair's forehead. A gory spray of blood, brain and bone showered the others in the car as the now headless body of the Prime Spokesman for Administration slumped to the floor of the aircar in a quivering heap of death.

Ortiz stood on the roof of the Gathering Hall and lowered his head in silent prayer for the deceased. The scene below was one of pure chaos. Never before had an assassination occurred on Cabriolet and it was clear that the citizens milling about the body below had no idea of just how to cope with the situation. Some of them were screaming, some crying, some running and some just standing with blank expressions on their faces. The entire parade had come to an abrupt halt and not a single person had a clue as to what should be done.

Ortiz looked at the hand-crafted projectile weapon and thought that the thing belonged in an antique shop somewhere. But he wasn't about to complain; the gun had performed its job and performed it well—the only job it would ever be called upon to perform.

Dropping the rifle, he bent down to pick up the spent shell casing, which had the words *Universal Freedom Front* etched on its side. He gripped it in his fist and laughed at how easy it had been. He thought twice about heaving the empty casing over the side of the building as per his instructions. This was no ordinary world; if he didn't leave the casing right here on the roof next to the very weapon that had sent its slug toward his target, these backwards people may never make the connection between the Universal Freedom Front and the assassination. As it was, with all the evidence staring them in the face, there was a chance that this tiny bit of a confession would not be found.

Ortiz took one last look at the ball of confusion that was the scene below and laughed at the naiveté of these Utopian imbeciles. They didn't even recognize a good killing when they saw one.

Lifting his eyes from the scene below, he took in an eyeful of Cabriolet's picturesque countryside. What a shame, he thought as he let the spent shell casing slip from his fingers and fall back to the rooftop, that this would probably be the last time he had a chance to visit this insane asylum that these people called home.

With that thought in mind, he made his way to the exit and down to the street below, to lose himself in the crowds of stupefied idiots that seemed to surround him.

~*~

The Jehova System belonged completely to the Catholic Church. The priests of Old Earth had picked up and left the mother planet several centuries ago, even before the New Conflict had spread its disease among the Known-Grids.

Yes, Jesus Christ was worshiped on nearly every colonized planet in all the Known Grid- Levels of Space.

Pope John Jacob Firenzza III had just recently written an epic manuscript covering the vast history of the Catholic Church Organization as far back as it could be traced. The mammoth twelve-volume history was currently being published by the Catholic Church Press and being prepared for its first mass distribution to over two thousand worlds. With an average of just over one hundred Catholic Churches per each colonized planet, with each church receiving at least one copy of the history—some having ordered five copies each—the high priest of the Catholic Church was absolutely positive that his work would be well appreciated.

And well appreciated it should be, after all the hard work he had put into it. Long hours of monotonous referencing, searching and fact-finding on countless worlds had worn him out considerably since he had started the project. Now that it was done, he had retired from all of his traveling and returned to Vatican, the headquarters world of the Catholic Church.

New Vatican City was a sprawling metropolis of office buildings and leisure facilities, which was spread out over an area of two hundred square kilometers. The Catholic Church had become an extremely successful business enterprise over the past two centuries, raking in annual revenues currently averaging over seven trillion InterGridactic dollars.

A healthy portion of this went to Pope John Jacob's yearly allowance. Needless to say, the Pope was one of the wealthiest men alive. But Pope John Jacob didn't flaunt his riches. He wasn't one of those popes who dressed in flowing golden robes and wore an excessive amount of flashy jewelry. No, Pope John Jacob was one of the most well-liked and well-respected popes of modern times. The fact that priests of the Catholic Church were supposed to possess nothing more than what they needed to survive had no meaning to the Catholics of the Known-Grids.

Their pope was their one best link to the Almighty in this universe and it didn't matter to them if he was one of the richest. The followers of the Catholic Church consistently fed enormous amounts of money into the church every single Prayerday, thus making themselves poorer and making the church richer. Some people, rebels to the church, accused the priests of being nothing more than thieves, charlatans, and phonies who exploited the vulnerability of the masses for their own benefit.

It was funny, Pope John Jacob thought to himself, that he was able to sympathize with these people because, in a way, what they were essentially saying was true. But the church meant more than just money. It gave people the Grids over something to believe in, something to hope for and look forward to after the craziness of their lives was over. The belief that there was something better waiting for them on the other side of the black curtain of death was worth more to them than the dollars they doled out once a week, every week. The Catholic Church provided a service, an essential and necessary service, to the populations of the stars. Without that little bit of hope in their lives, who knew what insanities would be released upon the Known-Grids. For desperate people with nothing to live for quite often cared not for the lives that were forfeit by their actions. So, by keeping the peace throughout the Known Grid-Levels of Space, the Catholic Church was an integral component of human society.

This is how Pope John Jacob justified his rank and honor and wealth. In retrospect, he was correct in his belief that people needed someone, something to confide in. Just look at how long the Catholic Church had survived as a profitable organization. But, deep down in his heart, he knew that the church could very well get along with a lot less than what it had. As receipts grew steadily larger each e-year, annual revenues had continued to hit peak all-time highs throughout the last half-century.

Guilt was not the best of emotions to suffer through.

And this guilt is what led the Pope to the confessional booth to pray to God the Almighty, and Jesus Christ his Savior. The enormous cathedral which was the core of New Vatican City was as silent as it could be, just the way he liked it.

A faint sound, perhaps the scrape of a slipper on the fine red carpeted aisle, alerted him to the presence of a visitor. The curtain on the receiving end of the confessional was brushed aside and someone knelt down to pray.

Pope John Jacob Firenzza III wondered at just how the priest had known that he was here and slid aside the partition. "Yes, Father, I will hear your confession," he said as he watched the brown robed figure hunch down in front of him.

"Forgive me, Holy One, for I have sinned and will sin again," the priest said.

118

"In what ways have you sinned, Father?" He asked, genuinely curious now.

"I have killed many men, Holy One," the man replied. "And felt no remorse thereafter."

Pope John Jacob was genuinely shocked at what he had just heard from the man in the other side of the booth. "Under what circumstances, Father, can you justify such horrible actions?"

"When it is for a cause, Pope John Jacob, the cause of our New Era," the voice answered.

"If this is true, Father, then you say that every man who declares a cause may take the life of another human being at a whim?" The Pope queried.

"No!" the priest exclaimed. "This cause is the only cause of our New Era, a cause which justifies itself and all the actions utilized to uphold its righteousness in the eyes of the Lord. The cause justifies all concepts of death and dying for the greater good. Even if this death is dealt by my hands."

"You are quite mad, Father, quite insane, indeed," the Pope said as he weighed his options— all heard confessions were confidential but this man had openly confessed to a multitude of murders and had claimed that he would do so again and again until his so-called 'cause' was fulfilled. "I will help you, Father, I will aid in healing your warped mind. God is within you as he is within all of us. Do not fear the wrath of God and Jesus Christ our Savior, nor that of the Holy Ghost. The Holy Trinity and the strength of your belief in it and all it represents will make you whole again. The fact that you came here to speak to me, to clear your soul of these internal horrors which you have bottled up inside, shows that you are seeking help. And this help I will provide, I assure you."

"I am sorry, Holy One, but you can not help me," the robed man said. "I need no help or religious healing, for my mind is not warped. I am at one with God, Jesus Christ and the Holy Spirit and I do not seek their forgiveness. Only their understanding and condolences..."

"Then why have you come here to me, Father?" The Pope wondered. "If it was not to seek assistance with the faulty mental pathways you have chosen?"

"Because you, Pope John Jacob Firenzza, are the object of my quest," came the reply. "And now that I have found you and spoken with you...now, I will end your life. It is the will of the cause and I am just an instrument to be utilized. Prepare to meet the creator, Pope John Jacob Firenzza; these are the last seconds that you will experience on this plane of existence..."

"This is absurd, Father," the Pope blurted. "How do you plan to take my life?"

"With this, Holy One," Robert Packard produced a small blaster from underneath his robes and pointed it at the Pope. "You are hereby sentenced to death and must be eradicated from this life. The Universal Freedom Front has willed it to be so."

"Now wait just one..."

The blast cut off the words of Pope John Jacob Firenzza III. His body hit the back of the confessional booth with an empty thud and slid down to the red carpet.

Robert Packard put his weapon back underneath the cloak and stared at the body of the once High Priest of the Catholic Church.

"Rest in peace, John Jacob," he said. "I will pray for your soul..."

~*~

The crew of CargoLiner-X4J729 watched gratefully as the dark stranger walked down the ramp of the docking ring and entered the orbiting spaceport.

Aegis was a huge world, especially when viewed from space. On the surface, the seemingly endless conglomeration of large gray metallic buildings lent the planet an air of depression. The United Earthian Nations' entire governmental body was stationed on the planet. Basically, Aegis was a haven of Officialdom.

The mostly Berkingian crew prayed silently as their strong silent passenger disappeared through the entrance to the spaceport, hopefully never to be seen again. Already the atmosphere on the ship had changed. The freight was almost unloaded and the crew was trying to hurry, so they could leave this dark and brooding world as fast as they could.

After a short shuttle-hop down to the surface, Frank Buzzer entered the Aegis New-Arrival Customs Center and quickly scanned his surroundings. The view screens in the main lobby were tuned to a variety of different networks. He found the one he was looking for and stood in front of it. The news was full of stories about the death of Pope John Jacob Firenzza III, or the assassination rather, though the Catholic Church was denying all rumors of violence on Vatican.

Buzzer knew that he had been called back to Aegis because of the recent rash of assassinations and terrorist attacks that had occurred in each of the four Corporate Grid-Sectors. So far, almost thirty of the most reputable individuals in the Known-Grids, not to mention the twenty thousand who had been killed on New Africa along with the late President Mouabi Abuka, had been brutally murdered. Each of the target's bodies had been found, except for the late leader of New Africa—the small nuclear explosive had disintegrated everything in the immediate area of the planet's Administration Building, a circle with a fourteen kilometer diameter.

In the wake of each incident, U.E.N. Outposts throughout the Known-Grids had received communications from dozens of terrorist organizations, each claiming responsibility.

The targets had seemingly been picked at random from a list of the most popular and influential people throughout the Corporate Grid-Sectors. But even though the obvious pattern focused on the most well-known and respected individuals, the ultimate target was unmistakable—Mr. Harold Calhoun Alderman, the President of the United Earthian Nations.

Not one president of the U.E.N. had ever been assassinated, but if the track record of whatever group was doing all the killing had any bearing, its chances of success in such an undertaking seemed pretty damn good.

But a hit on the president would be some time in coming, Buzzer was sure of that. These people, whoever they were, would want to leave some more lasting impressions on the minds of people everywhere before they went for the gusto.

Buzzer could only speculate at just how badly the over thirty billion Catholics spread throughout the Known-Grids were sent reeling after the attack on the Pope. The Pope...such an innocent target. The man who was believed to be closer to God than any other man alive had been snuffed out with a single blaster bolt. No witnesses. No God-like miracle had saved his life; no spiritual revelations had uncovered his killer. People everywhere had felt the reality of the situation when the Pope had been found in his holy confessional, with a five-inch hole in his chest and a one-foot hole in his back, and very little in between.

The attack on the Pope proved one thing—everyone was vulnerable, no one was safe from the new breed of terrorist. But Frank Buzzito, known in the Guarder Ranks simply as Buzzer, was going to stop this new menace, stop it cold in its tracks. If terrorists thought they could just show up anywhere and kill anyone on his watch, they had another thing coming. Something they would not like, Buzzer guaranteed. He would show them exactly what justice meant, and they would learn it the hard way.

The newscast ended and Buzzer whirled around and caught the hand of the man who had been reaching for his shoulder.

"Thunder..." he said in immediate recognition of the man.

Robert Thunder tensed at the strong fist enclosing his right wrist in a vise-like grip, but relaxed when he saw the smile in Buzzer's eyes. Buzzer immediately released his friend.

"Buzzer," he grinned and the two men shook hands. "It's been some time. Where have you been?"

"I needed some time to myself," Buzzer said, dropping his eyes to gaze momentarily at the floor. "You know how it is sometimes."

"Yeah, I know that feeling exactly, Frank," Thunder said and clapped his friend on the shoulder. "Let's get back to HQ; the Sarge has something he thinks you ought to hear."

Buzzer took one last look at the news on the view screens, then followed his friend out of the main lobby. A sleek black cruiser was waiting for them at the curb outside the main entrance.

"Executive treatment?" Buzzer asked. "That's a first."

"Don't worry about the cruiser, Buzzer," Thunder said. "The Sarge just told me to get a ride and pick you up. He didn't specify what kind of ride." The two men laughed at the small joke. "I just elaborated a little on my own."

Buzzer shook his head and smiled. "You always did live the good life, Bobby."

"Yeah," Thunder answered. "But the real good life won't be mine until I whip you at the competitions this year."

Buzzer's eyes widened in surprise. "You? Beat me in the Inter-Service Competitions?" He asked and laughed out loud, exaggerating on purpose. "A day I am still waiting for, my friend. You'll just have to settle for second place...again."

"Don't be so smug, Buzzer," Thunder smirked and pulled away from the curb. "You're not getting any younger."

Buzzer had no answer for that and sat back and soaked in the sights. Same old scenes—large gray buildings and thousands of people. Yeah, he was back on Aegis; he was back to the only place he could ever really call home.

~*~

The luxury aircar raced toward Cazara Center, better known as Glitter City. The scenic overview of Cazara's countryside was something that Clark Von Neuton would normally take the time to appreciate. But, as it was, he was already ten minutes late for the third quarterly meeting of the Universal Corporate Council.

He knew that his colleagues would wait for him to arrive before they proceeded with the meeting, but that would just serve to focus the group's attention on him when he entered Conference Hall.

"Damn," he muttered as they crossed into the airspace over Glitter City.

"We're almost there, sir," the chauffeur called back as he piloted toward the landing deck on the roof of Conference Hall.

"Just set me down, Danny," Von Neuton said. "As soon as you can."

"Yes, sir," the chauffeur said and Von Neuton sat back and sighed. Yeah, he would catch hell from the other fifty-five members of the Council—or fifty-four members, he corrected himself, remembering the recent tragedy on NewAfrica.

If it hadn't been for that unscheduled press conference at the Engells Spaceport he would not have been late. The constant nuisance of being a prime target for press attacks had plagued Von Neuton for over seven e-years now. The InterGridactic Audubon Society, of which he served as president, was the single most popular and most productive humanitarian organization in all the Known-Grids. Almost ninety percent of all the business entities of the four Corporate Grid- Sectors sponsored designated representatives to his organization's bi-monthly meetings and this percentage had been growing steadily for years.

All in all, about eight hundred million members, both organizations and individuals, belonged to the InterGridactic Audubon Society. And Clark Von Neuton was very proud to have led such a prestigious group for the better part of the last decade. He was a very important man in the universal scheme of things. The decisions of the InterGridactic Audubon Society, all of which he personally approved before allowing them to be implemented, affected the lives of almost every human being in all of the Known-Grids. Issues dealing with workers' wages, planetary economics and quality-of-life standards, as well as many other subjects concerning people's lives, were the main focus of the organization's operations.

The InterGridactic Audubon Society also regulated the rights of the animal and plant populations of every single planet in the U.E.N. During the first decade of the organization, the

I.G.A.S. had been instrumental in the approval of legislation that ultimately converted the North American continent of Old Earth into a sprawling wild-life preserve that included at least two members of every species on the planet, both plant and animal.

Von Neuton smiled and then laughed. The I.G.A.S. had recorded many significant accomplishments over the past few centuries. The group's political power and influence was so vast that even the mighty U.E.N. Judiciary Board on Aegis flinched when an audience was requested to discuss new and important issues.

The aircar touched down lightly on the brightly illuminated landing deck. Security clamps immediately fastened the luxury sedan tight to the surface as the vehicle's engines whined down to an idle.

The chauffeur looked back at Von Neuton, "Watch yourself, sir, the cabin will depressurize in a few seconds." The tell-tale hiss of air-seals unlocking followed. "It's safe to debark now, sir."

"Oh, really?" Von Neuton laughed, thinking of the sneers and snarls from his impatient colleagues that awaited him in conference hall. "I guess I should get in there sometime today..."

"Don't worry, Mr. Von Neuton," Danny Martin said. "Those men and women may be colleagues of yours but they are beneath you. You stand head and shoulders above them."

Von Neuton laughed at the man in the driver's seat. "Looking for a big tip, Danny?" "The doors are unlocked, sir," Martin smiled. "Ready when you are."

"All right, I'll see you in a couple of hours." Von Neuton grabbed his jacket and his hat and reached for the door latch.

"I'll be on call, sir. Just say the word when you're ready to leave."

"I hear you, Dan," Von Neuton said and opened the door of the aircar.

The small yet powerful pack of explosive jelly which had been connected to the rear-door locking mechanism detonated at once, followed by a much larger pack attached to the underside of the main engine housing. The sleek gray sedan erupted in a violent shower of flame and debris that took most of the landing deck with it.

The other members of the Universal Corporate Council were lucky that the plexisteel reinforced roof and walls were built to withstand the extra pressure of landing aircars. Otherwise, the explosion would have leveled the entire building.

Instead, only the landing deck and upper-level storage compartments were lost in the blast. All that was left of the aircar were scattered bits and pieces mixed with the concrete and metals of the landing deck. What was left of Clark Von Neuton, his chauffeur and the two landing deck attendants, could fit into an average-sized garbage bag.

Kenneth Kobalsky watched the explosive demise of the President of the InterGridactic Audubon Society from his vantage point down the block. Now these petty executive puppets would know just how vulnerable they were—all of them. It was much too easy, the task of killing. It would have been just as easy to have planted the bomb inside Conference Hall itself and bring the entire Universal Corporate Council to an abrupt and fiery end.

But that would be too easy, much too easy for Kenneth Kobalsky. The members of the Universal Freedom Front were having far too much fun knocking out their targets one at a time, except for their show of force on New Africa.

But the day was coming. Yes, soon the Universal Freedom Front would make its grand statement to the four Corporate Grid-Sectors. A gesture of complete and utter control that would bring the United Earthian Nations government tumbling to its knees. Then and only then would the Universal Freedom Front be satisfied. Once they proved to the people of the universe that not even the most powerful authorities could stop them from achieving their goals, they would have the undivided attention of the InterGridactic masses that they desired. Every man, woman and child alive among the stars, all eighty billion plus of them, would fear for their safety, fear for their lives, fear everything.

And that was the power they sought—the ability to strike fear in the hearts of every person alive was just the kind of power that the Universal Freedom from Tyranny Movement desired. For, until the people of the Known-Grids realized that they were not in control of their own lives, they would not feel the need to break the bonds of authority and seek their own individuality, their own personal freedom.

And when the people finally believed that they needed to be freed, the Universal Freedom Front would step in and take control of the U.E.N. The Universal Freedom from Tyranny Movement wished this to be so and the members of the Front were acting toward that end. They would show the people of the Known-Grids just how happy a communal system of government and total freedom could make them.

Kenneth Kobalsky longed for that time to arrive. But for now, he had completed his task. It was time to leave Cazara and its city of glitter. He started the small utility vehicle and steered through the obstacle course of concrete and debris.

As he passed the steps of Conference Hall he flicked a small medallion out the window. The trinket with *Universal Freedom Front* engraved on both sides bounced a few times before falling to rest on a clear spot of the street.

125

Before the first police cruiser arrived on the scene, Kobalsky was lost in traffic and well on his way to the Engells Spaceport.

~*~

Frank Buzzer walked through the doors of the Headquarters Complex of the United Earthian Nations Guarder Squadron. He passed through the interconnecting halls amid a series of greetings and acknowledgments as he made his way toward the meeting chambers.

Bobby Thunder had stopped in the lobby to get the scoop on what had happened over the last three hours. Buzzer had no more care for the news of the day. He had just suffered through a long and boring journey to get back to Aegis and he was eager to begin working on his new assignment.

As he progressed deeper into the complex, he found himself alone in the silence of the great halls. Buzzer loved this place; he loved everything about it, everything it stood for. The Guarder Squadron had been protecting the interests of the U.E.N. Judiciary Board for several centuries now. The Guarders were the most skillful, most talented and most trustworthy soldiers in all the Known-Grids. They were also the deadliest people alive. Being the only military unit that the United Earthian Nations Government entrusted with confidential operations, these two hundred superior soldiers acted as couriers, warriors, diplomats, and equalizers—in short, they could be called upon to perform any function. Nothing was impossible, no odds too great. Their incredible fighting skills were feared throughout the Known-Grids; nobody alive wanted to attract the wrath of an U.E.N. Guarder—no one who was sane, that is.

Of all the Guarders in the ranks, Buzzer had the honor of being the best. Proven time and time again, he filled the position well. His record was sparkling. Mission after mission brought success after success. He had not failed on any assignment thus far in his twelve e-years in the ranks and he showed no signs of slowing down. He had competed in the past twelve consecutive annual U.E.N. Inter-Service Competitions and had been crowned champion during each of the last eight.

Because of this, Frank Buzzer was very well respected by both those in the upper ranks of the various U.E.N. military branches, and most of the major players in the Corporate Security sector. His status within law enforcement circles made his name greatly despised by the criminal element of InterGridactic society, as well. Buzzer was considered the ultimate soldier, and an invaluable one at that. He had been through many close calls in his career as a Guarder, but he had come through victorious each and every time. Little could be said for those who had opposed him...little could be found. He had been given the toughest assignments, and the complete freedom to use his own best judgment in carrying them out, satisfying his superiors at every turn.

Buzzer respected his position within the ranks of the legendary fighting unit. He did not consider himself a living legend, as he was regarded by most military types. He was just a soldier doing his duty. He sought no recognition, he wanted no fame; he only wanted to be the best at what he did...a goal he had achieved eight e-years ago.

Now, he just lived the dangerous, mysterious life of a Guarder because it was what he loved to do, all he really knew how to do. He was satisfied with his work, and that was a feeling that statistics showed only four percent of the entire InterGridactic work-force shared with him. The Guarder Squadron was a brotherhood, where everybody looked after everybody else. All for one and one for all, as the ages-old saying went.

The doors to the main conference room were standing wide open. Buzzer walked in and stared at the huge mural that occupied the opposite wall. The majestic image of the falcon— strong, swift and silent, a natural predator— stared back at him. That universal symbol of strength also symbolized the U.E.N. Guarder Squadron. A smaller version of the same symbol hung from Buzzer's neck on the end of his identification necklace.

The falcon...Buzzer could relate to the solitary bird of prey. He knew exactly what it was like to journey alone through the insanity that life created.

He had made few real friends in his lifetime. Most of them were dead and buried. His father, a former Guarder, had been the most influential factor in his decision to apply for the U.E.N. Military Academy when he was a teenager. His excellence and outstanding performance while in that prestigious institution had gained him a spot within the U.E.N. Governing Guard. With two successful tours in the Judiciary Board's own personal defensive unit on Aegis under his belt, he had assumed a position within the lower ranks of the Guarder Squadron.

Following in the footsteps of his father and grandfather, he quickly climbed the ladder of ranks until he earned a spot within the top twenty best soldiers in the entire squadron. Less than an e-year later, Francis Vincenzo Buzzito won first place at the annual U.E.N. Inter-Service Competitions—and he hadn't let go of that spot since.

A loud thud behind him aroused his attention. The immense, powerfully built form of Sergeant Harrison Jekel stood in the doorway behind him. "Good to see you, Buzzer."

"Same here, Sarge," Buzzer smiled and walked over to grasp the large man's outstretched hand. "It's been a while, Harrison."

"Yeah, too long. But it always seems that you come back here each time just to be sent out again." Jekel paused and stared into Buzzer's eyes. "You already know what your assignment is, don't you?"

"I have a pretty good idea..."

"Well, let's hear it then."

"Okay," Buzzer said and sat down at one side of the conference table—the top of which displayed a map of the entire Known Grid-Levels of Space. "There's been a recent rash of assassinations in all four Corporate Grid-Sectors. A lot of important people have been fried. There seems to be only a single set pattern—highly important individuals with government or corporate associations—and the targets next in line are virtually unpredictable. Based on the victims that have been fried thus far, we could come up with a long list of potential targets, but it would be impossible to cover them all. And lastly, many terrorist organizations have claimed responsibility for each killing. So, my mission will probably be to determine the identity of the killer or killers and eliminate them."

Jekel smiled and nodded his head. "Pretty good, Buzzer, you've hit it right on the head. Except you don't have to determine the group's identity. We've taken care of that for you."

"Great, less research works for me," Buzzer said. "Fill me in."

"Well, there's one group that has left its ID marks somewhere in the vicinity of each strike," Jekel explained. "They call themselves the Universal Freedom Front. They seem to be a splinter faction of the Universal Freedom from Tyranny Movement. But that group has only been known to operate in the NorthWestern Corporate Grid-Sector, not all four sectors. The Judiciary Board has received a statement from them, among hundreds of statements from other two-bit terrorist groups. Their statement said that they will continue in their attempts to eliminate all forms of authority and power in the universe until they are able to take control of the U.E.N. Government."

Buzzer laughed at the meaning behind the message. "So they're planning to assassinate President Alderman sometime in the near future."

It was a statement, not a question.

"Do we have people covering him?" Buzzer asked.

"Yeah, I have five Guarders on him at all times, including Governing Guard personnel," his commanding officer said.

"Five Guarders?" Buzzer's eyes widened in surprise. "Why five of us for one man? One, at most two, could do the job just as well."

Jekel sat down, the chair creaking loudly as his great bulk lowered into it. "Frank, right now the U.E.N. can not afford to lose Harold Calhoun Alderman. That man is the only thing that holds this government together. If he were to be assassinated, the entire governing body would be thrust into chaos. Between the Judiciary Board and the Universal Corporate Council and all the other divisions, we would have an all-out war among the various branches on our hands. I wouldn't doubt it if the Universal Freedom Front actually did take control after something like that." Jekel paused to let that sink in. "This little penny-ante organization has taken out some of the most important people in the governments of the Known-Grids. I'm sure you've heard of the hits on Von Neuton on Cazara, Dr. Kindler on Linkston-4 and, God rest his soul, Pope John Jacob."

Buzzer nodded and Jekel continued.

"Well, there're many more where those came from. We can't figure out *how* these people are getting as close as they are without being detected. They have planted bombs on the personal vehicles of some of their targets; they have infiltrated some of their victims' personal chambers. For chrissakes, Frank, they set up a goddamn nuclear in the basement of the Administration Building on New Africa! When that device went off, the entire planetary government body got fried along with it. Not just President Abuka, mind you, but nearly every damn member of the administration was in that building when it blew.

"These people are professionals, Buzzer. It's obvious that they've received the latest training in terrorist tactics and that they are extremely well funded. They could have been trained by any one of ten thousand terror organizations in the Known-Grids; but since we know that they are linked with the Universal Freedom from Tyranny Movement, we are pretty confident that they were trained by one man."

Jekel opened the folder he was carrying and handed Buzzer a Hi-D photo of a dark haired, dark skinned man displaying all the telltale characteristics of Old Earthian Arabian descent. "That's Rhafid Azid, professional terrorist."

"I've heard of him," Buzzer replied as he studied the face.

"This group's tactics match those used by Azid over a decade ago when he was in his prime.

He's pretty much become invisible since then, but these assassinations parallel many of the killings that Azid pulled off almost perfectly. In fact, the similarities are so close that we think that Azid may actually be working with the perpetrators on this project. And if Rhafid Azid has resurfaced to continue where he left off...let's just say the Judiciary Board feels it would be in the best interests of the U.E.N. if he were to be terminated. And that's where you come in."

Buzzer tore his eyes from the old photo and smiled at his commanding officer. "When do I start?"

Jekel nodded and stood. "You'll be working with a larger than normal team on this one and you get to choose the members. Any five Guarders in the ranks, Buzzer, take your pick."

Buzzer turned to face the immense falcon on the wall behind the conference table while he mulled over the possibilities. It didn't take him long.

"I want Thunder, Ramsey, Boa, Talon and Able."

"Good group; they're yours," Jekel said. "Thunder's already here but I'll have the others notified and in transit by tomorrow. You'll be shipping off to Lacusa as soon as possible."

"Lacusa?" Buzzer asked.

"We got a lucky tip on Cazara," Jekel offered. "One of our contacts there saw someone throw a medallion on the rubble of Conference Hall just after the explosion. It had *Universal FreedomFront* written all over it. Our contact followed the man to the spaceport. From there we tracked him and intercepted a brief personal transmission. It was scrambled, naturally; so far, all we've been able to decipher is the mention of Lacusa. It's all we have to go on right now."

"All right, good enough," Buzzer said. "Sounds like as good a place to start as any. I'll want to act on this lead before it gets cold."

"Let me get the transportation worked out," Jekel said as Buzzer handed him back the Hi-D of Azid. "I'll have detailed reports ready for each member of your team before you leave. Get some rest for now, Frank. You're going to need it."

Buzzer looked inside his mind at the mental image he had already stored of Rhafid Azid. "Sarge, who do you have covering Alderman?"

"Mack, Brass, Stalker, Gannon and Joker."

"Huh," Buzzer muttered. "Now I understand the need for five."

Jekel looked sternly at his best Guarder. "Clarify your feelings, Buzzer. If you have any criticisms about members of this squadron then make them known. Your opinion is respected around here; I'd like to know what you think."

"Well, I've worked with all of them at one time or another," Buzzer said. "And the only two I can give much credit to are Mack and Gannon. Brass is a hothead who goes crazy under fire, Stalker thinks he's too good to work with anyone else, and Joker…well, take a look at his record. He's had successful missions but the status reports provide some details I'm not too comfortable with. The man doesn't seem to care about anything outside of his mission parameters. He's like a mech sometimes. I just feel that a better team could have been assembled for this assignment."

"I'll take it into consideration, Buzzer," Jekel said. "Thanks for the insights."

"Don't get me wrong, Sarge," Buzzer said. "Any five Guarders working together can do any job, regardless of their individual characteristics. I just don't care for the way those particular three work sometimes." Buzzer's stare lingered on the huge figure of the Guarder Squadron Commander for several seconds before he turned and left the conference room.

Jekel watched the retreating form of the best soldier in his squadron. Once Buzzer disappeared around a corner he looked down at the Hi-D of Azid.

"I feel sorry for you, Rhafid," he sneered. "You are going to die."

~*~

The luxury liner *Apollo* cruised silently through the vacuum of space as it made its way toward Circus, an amusement world offering entertainment for adult guests only. Circus was a planet where the spotlight personalities flocked to vacation in the sun, sand and surf, and live it up at the casinos, nightclubs and amusement parks. The upper-class resort world always attracted a constant crowd of filthy-rich visitors. Resort worlds would always be very popular among the wealthy of the Known-Grids: Cazara, Aphrodite, Safari, New Africa and Fantasia were just a few other enormously profitable planetary resort institutions.

Only one firm, *Luxury Tours, Inc.*, owned the monopoly on every mode of transportation to and from these worlds. From supply routes to major cruise lanes, Luxury Tours ruled them all.

Luxury Tours—and its parent organization...

The Syndicate had enjoyed the good life for centuries, all the way back to its origins on Old Earth. When the vastness of space was first opened for colonization, an infinite wealth of opportunities became available to their vast organization. The number of new markets in the drug-trade and prostitution rackets underwent a skyrocketing increase in the first half-century. And as mankind spread across the Known Grid-Levels of Space, these markets continued to grow. The Syndicate grew right along with them; it had no choice. The various multitudes of opportunities had to be taken advantage of, after all.

Luxury Tours was just one small firm among a hundred thousand that the Syndicate owned and operated across each of the four Corporate Grid-Sectors. Somehow most of these small business ventures were never legally connected with their parent organization. Luxury Tours was also one of the most profitable of those organizations. The high-class transportation business tended to generate a modest income e-year after e-year. Each tour that the Apollo made across the entertainment circuit sold at an average cost of two hundred and fifty thousand InterGridactic dollars per head—small change compared to the cost of a similar Cazarapackage.

The cash flow was constant in this business; there would always be a wealthy population of filthy rich people who wanted to vacation at some hot-spot resort world. These people often tended to keep the Syndicate's booming drug trade afloat as well. This enormous amount of monetary exchange required an infinite amount of record keeping and updating.

At least that's what it seemed like to Michael Tanzini, President of Luxury Tours, Inc., as he sat in his lavish quarters aboard the Apollo in front of his computer monitor. His blood-shot eyes scanned the millions of dollars worth of figures that were flashing across his meter-wide screen. He suddenly yawned and decided that he had seen enough figures for one night. Standing, he stretched and reached down to turn off his computer.

Grabbing the gray suit jacket from his bed, he picked up the glass of deep red Arnoxian wine and swirled it around for a while before he tasted it and put it down. Smiling, he left his quarters and made his way down to the nightclub. The corridors seemed almost deserted.

"Well, what do you expect from a floating party?" he laughed to himself.

The sounds of music, dancing and hundreds of talking people grew louder in the corridor as he neared Party Hall. Just outside the doors, a drunken man fell flat on his face, turned over and began to laugh. The woman he was with, rather heavily intoxicated as well was also laughing while she tried to help her companion to his feet.

"Stupid bastard," Tanzini sneered and made his way over to the downed patron. Bending slightly, he quickly lifted the man to his feet and rested his back to the wall.

"You all right, buddy?" He asked, lightly slapping his hand against the man's slackened face.

"Yeah, yeah, I'm okay, I'm all right..." the drunk muttered, his lady giggling incoherently. "All right then, why don't you go back to your cabin and crash for the night, buddy?" Tanzini said as he admired the curves of the drunk's lady friend. "How's that sound, huh?"

"Yeah, yeah, crash..." the laughing man said and began to stagger down the hall, his lady following closely at his heels. She turned around once and smiled at Tanzini as they made their way.

Tanzini watched them to make sure that they made it to the lifts at the end of the corridor without losing consciousness. Once the lift doors closed, capturing the couple inside, he was satisfied and turned to enter Party Hall.

The music was loud, people were dancing, the drinks were flowing and his girls were working.

"Just the way I like it," he muttered under his breath as he made his way across the dance floor to the back office.

He stopped off at the bar to order a drink and winked at the bartender. "How's business, Louie?"

"Couldn't be better, boss," the short man answered and smiled as he handed Tanzini a hefty portion of Scotch.

"That's what I like to hear, Louie," Tanzini said and took a sip from his drink. "Keep it up."

"Will do."

"Hey, boss!" The shout came from the open office door behind the bar. "Yeah, Vinnie? What's up?" Tanzini turned to answer.

The large mountainous man, stuffed into a suit two sizes too small, walked over to his superior. "We've got a guy in the office says he's from Neo Roma. He says he's got to talk to you about a matter of the utmost importance."

"From Neo Roma, huh?" Tanzini questioned and drank some more of the amber-colored liquor as Vinnie's huge head bobbed up and down in confirmation. "Does he check out?"

"He didn't give his name, no," Vinnie said. "But the *capo* he mentioned registered loud and clear. Whoever he is, he sure is confidential."

"Is he packing any hardware or just standard?" Tanzini asked and finished off his drink. "He's got a blaster, Series-4207," Vinnie answered.

"Those are only available on Neo Roma, aren't they?"

"That's right," Vinnie said. "The 4207's are Schezetti's own personal model. All of his people carry them."

133

Tanzini mulled this over for a few moments and set the empty glass on the bar-top. "Stay close, Vinnie, and keep alert, huh? I don't know what this is but it don't feel right. I don't like it."

"This guy's nothing, boss," Vinnie reassured him. "Jordan's already in there with the guy and I'll be right there with you, too."

"All right, keep your piece handy." Tanzini pressed his arm down and felt the cold resistance of his own piece in the holster under his armpit.

The two men entered the office, Tanzini eyeing the visitor as Vinnie bolted the door.

"Hello, friend," Tanzini said and shook hands with the man. "So how is old CarloSchezetti? Is he still up and around or has age finally caught up with that old dog?"

The man sat silently and scanned the room. The door was locked; he was now trapped inside with three men, all armed and ready to blow him away at the first sign of trouble.

"Mr. Tanzini, I must speak with you alone. If you don't mind, sir."

"Well, that's a problem, you see, because I *do* mind." Tanzini stood over the man. "There's nothing that you can't say in front of my two associates. So, just state your piece and let's get back to the party. Do you hear what I'm saying?" Tanzini smiled and sat opposite his new guest.

Salvatore Mariosa took a deep breath and stood. "I must insist, Mr. Tanzini, that I speak with you alone."

"Oh, Christ!" Tanzini shouted. "Just say what you goddamn came here to say and then get out of my face! Forget about this 'I got to talk to you alone' and spit it out already!"

Mariosa burst into action as Tanzini was screaming. One hand went inside his jacket and pulled out the Series-4207, the other hand went to the back of his belt and unsheathed a small dagger.

Vinnie and Jordan were both taken completely by surprise, impressed as they were by Tanzini's sudden vocal outburst. Nevertheless, they were professionals and they were acting as such. Both had their weapons clear of their jackets and were aiming toward Mariosa in less than three-tenths of a second.

Mariosa was moving now; a flick of the wrist buried his dagger hilt-deep in Jordan's sternum.

In the same motion, he ducked down as Vinnie fired.

The blast exploded against the back wall, rocking the small room. Mariosa leaped at Vinnie and fired twice as he moved. The first blast ripped the giant's head from his neck; the second took most of his insides with it as it exited through his back.

Mariosa caught the convulsing body before it hit the ground and spun it around, just in time for the corpse to take the brunt of the blast from Tanzini's weapon.

On the other side of the office, Jordan's eyes rolled up into the back of his skull as his body experienced the shock of cardiac arrest, the small knife having pierced his heart.

Mariosa hit the floor at the same time as Vinnie's corpse did, then he aimed at Tanzini's feet and fired. The President of *Luxury Tours, Inc.* screamed in horror as his left foot exploded, leaving nothing but the bloody exposed bone of the ankle.

Tanzini hit the floor hard and lost his gun. The blood of three men was staining the blue carpet, turning it purple.

"Jesus Christ, who are you, man?" Tanzini shouted in between screams as he writhed around on the floor in pain.

Mariosa, splattered with blood, stood up slowly and stared at his victims. Two dead and one helpless…and he hadn't even suffered a scratch. Blood was spurting from the stump that was Michael Tanzini's left foot.

"I'm going to kill that back-stabbing Schezetti!" Tanzini screamed. "You tell him that, asshole, he's gonna die just like you!"

"I am not from Neo Roma, Mr. Tanzini, and I do not work for Carlo Schezetti," Mariosa said, staring long and hard into Michael Tanzini's horrified eyes.

"Who in the hell are you?" Tanzini muttered. "What is this?"

Salvatore Mariosa knelt down beside the sobbing wreck of the man who headed one of the Syndicate's most prestigious and profitable organizations. "I am a representative of the Universal Freedom Front, sir. Our group has designated you to serve as an example of our intelligence and cunning. You must die for our cause."

"What? Now, wait a minute," Tanzini pleaded as Mariosa touched the barrel of his weapon against the man's slick forehead. "Look, we can make a deal! There's a lot of money in this business. We'll be partners, huh? Fifty-fifty split. What do you say?"

"I am terribly sorry, Mr. Tanzini, but I have my orders."

"Now you listen," Tanzini growled. "Your petty-ass little movement doesn't know just who in the hell they're dealing with, do they? We are the Syndicate, my friend, a family who doesn't forget this type of thing! My business partners are gonna fry you once they get a hold of you, and whoever it is who controls your organization too, so why don't you just save us a whole lot of trouble and call the doctor down here. Like I said, we'll be partners and no one will be the wiser. How's that sit with you, huh?"

Mariosa laughed at the bleeding man's last begs for mercy. "Goodbye, Mr. Tanzini..."

"No...!" was all the Syndicate man could say before Mariosa fired. Tanzini's head disappeared in a gory spray of blood and bone. The body shook and shivered as it realized its death.

The terrorist holstered his blaster and unbolted the door. The noise of loud music and dancing people had drowned out all sounds of the scuffle. Mariosa, bloody clothes and all, melted into the mostly oblivious crowd and disappeared.

Louie Arone, the young bartender, noticed Mariosa as he left the office alone and grew quickly suspicious. Leaving the bar unattended, he walked over to the office, opened the door and looked in.

Less than five minutes later an unscheduled shuttle departed from the lower deck of the

Apollo and headed out into space.

Salvatore Mariosa grinned to himself as he worked the controls.

~*~

Taylor Young listened intently as his director explained exactly how he wanted the next scene done.

"Okay, Taylor, after you jump down from the pipes and break Jackson's neck, you swivel around and open fire with the charger on those guys down the corridor. You got all that?"

"Yeah, Harry," Young answered and the director lightly punched him on the arm as the actor took hold of the pipe overhead and lifted himself up.

"All right, everybody ready?" The director yelled, and various grunts of affirmation answered Harry Snyder. "Good! Now...one, two, and...action!"

Taylor Young—the Hi-D entertainment industry's number-one leading man and box office draw for the past four e-years—was just about halfway through his sixth *Mike Tractor: Antiterrorist* movie. His overwhelmingly popular alternate identity had taken him from a two-bit, out-of-work actor to a multi-billion dollar superstar celebrity in less than half a decade.

This particular installment had Mike Tractor infiltrating a StarLiner full of terrorists, in an attempt to plant a bomb near the energy core of the ship's reactor. This particular scene was his attempted escape through the terrorist-cluttered corridors of the big ship.

The action started, and Young jumped down from the ceiling pipes, took a hold of veteran stuntman Crane Jackson's head and, with that trademark Mike Tractor flair, proceeded to 'break his neck.' Jackson followed through with the motion and hit the deck expertly, quivering and convulsing in an all-too-accurate depiction of death. The sickening bone-crushing sound effect would be added in later, during the editing process.

Next, Young swirled his body around and lifted his heavy-charger in the direction of the other stuntmen-terrorists. He had been through all of this thousands of times before, in hundreds of scenes and endless retakes. His prop rifle would start spitting out harmless rays of light, the weapons of the 'terrorists' down the hall would do the same, explosions would illuminate the set, booms would rock his eardrums and then Harry Snyder would yell, "Cut!"

Young sent a steady stream of rays down the corridor, the stuntmen 'dying' in dramatic fashion. But something was wrong; he couldn't quite figure out what was different this time…then it hit him—one of the stuntmen was steadily advancing. He wasn't firing; he just kept walking forward.

The actor laughed to himself, thinking that the man was new in the business and was trying to lend the scene a little more life and color.

Swinging his rifle up, Young let out an echoing war whoop and blasted away at the approaching 'terrorist.' The man was startled and temporarily blinded by the sudden focus of light beams but he quickly responded by bringing up his rifle and firing back at Young.

The man's charger erupted several times, the blasts lifting Taylor Young from his feet and flinging him across the set. Young's chest exploded in a red gory mist; the explosion of gore from his back was much larger and bloodier. Young's body hit the far wall of the set with a sickening thud and slid slowly to the floor panels.

Andrei Yurgov kept firing his charger as every person on the set hit the floor and covered their heads from the multitude of sparks and explosions which were blanketing the area. As he reached the exit, Yurgov dropped his weapon, ripped off his costume and ran for his vehicle in the parking lot.

It was several minutes before people started moving around on the set again. A crowd had formed over Taylor Young's mutilated body. The actor's eerie smile was frozen in death.

Harry Snyder suddenly realized that his number-one source of income was dead—not Hi-D dead, but *really* dead.

The newly unemployed director walked off the set, shaking his head and muttering all the way back to his quarters.

Crane Jackson walked over to the exit door and picked up the assassin's discarded weapon. He thought that the stenciling on the side of the charger, which read *Universal Freedom Front*, would interest the authorities to no end.

~*~

Lacusa, a strange planet on the fringe of the SouthWestern Corporate Grid-Sector, was mostly composed of metallic ores. The incredibly large planet, almost twice the size of Aegis, held the grid's largest planetary deposits of thutonium and quranium, and was the number-one exporter of the two radioactive ores.

Positioned just far enough away from its star to be subject to a constant state of autumn-like climatic conditions, the planet had been settled by a small fleet of ships only two centuries before. But this tiny group of settlers quickly grew and began to take advantage of the vast amounts of metals of which the planet was composed.

The planet was named after the man who had led these settlers on their long journey. Steven Lacusa, renowned scientist and engineer of his time, had finished his research of the Metal World, as the planet had been known back then, while enjoying a visiting professorship at the University of Corpura. With his research completed and his curiosity piqued, Lacusa decided to go out into the stars and claim the immense hunk of metal for his own.

He, and a group of eight hundred colleagues, family and associates, had made his dream come true. Now, the *planet* Lacusa was the number-one exporter of metallic ores in all the Known- Grids, and the *family* Lacusa still provided leadership to the planet's population.

Victoria Lacusa, Crown Queen of the Metal World, entered the Royal Banquet Center amid a roar of shouts and applause. The huge gala celebration in honor of

138

her quarter-century reign as queen was just getting underway. Surrounding her were the usual set of five royal guards and the rest of her cabinet, Lacusa's Presiding Court. The beautiful middle-aged woman was smiling broadly, soaking up the waves of emulation coming from her people. Frank Buzzer walked directly behind the Queen, disguised as a member of her guard.

The entire building had been swept earlier by Buzzer's team of Guarders and had come away clean of all known types of explosive devices. Sensors did a pretty thorough job when searching for explosives, especially those with nuclear devices. But since Lacusa was so rich with radioactive materials, the sensors had a hard time distinguishing between different signals. This worried Buzzer slightly, but he was confident that a nuclear explosive planted anywhere within a twenty-kilometer radius would have been detected by their sensors.

The absence of bombs probably meant that the assassination attempt would be done from approximately one kilometer away, sniper fashion. But right now, with the queen of Lacusa walking elegantly through the Royal Banquet Center, Buzzer was ready for anything.

Boa and Ramsey were positioned within the crowd; eyes peeled and trigger fingers at the ready. Able and Talon were outside the building with magniviewers. Thunder was lost somewhere up in the ceiling structure of plexisteel beams and girders, armed with a customized heavy-charger, reworked to ensure that the blast could be focused on specific targets at long ranges instead of spreading with distance. Basically, the weapon had been converted from a maximum target penetration firearm to a sniper's dream.

All five of them were in constant communication with Buzzer through their command sequencers. As of this moment, all things were green. Nothing out of the ordinary or even close to suspicious could be found in or near the banquet hall.

The celebration party proceeded uneventfully for the entire afternoon, and continued unabated into the evening hours. Buzzer was learning that Lacusians did not tire very easily. The people were still dancing energetically, the conversations were going strong and the music was still pounding in his ears despite the ever-growing lateness of the hour.

Queen Victoria consistently and adamantly refused to remove herself from the spotlight all day long. The stubborn woman had not been anything comparable to cooperative since the six men from Aegis had arrived. She insisted that the Judiciary Board was grossly overreacting and was confident that no one in the entire universe would want to see her dead.

No matter how much Buzzer had pleaded with her majesty to bring the spectacular gathering to an end, the Crown Queen of Lacusa had just laughed and waved him off. This, of course, made Buzzer's job much more difficult than it should have been. But obstacles were the one thing that Buzzer still loved about his job. There was nothing better than coming through a challenging mission unscathed and victorious.

Buzzer stood just behind the great throne on which the Queen was seated; he eyed the crowd. Nothing. This entire planet had turned up a bundle of nothings, an absolute zero. His frustration level rose every time he thought that all of this could just be the result of a bad lead.

"Buzz," his command sequencer sounded in the voice of Bobby Thunder. "There's someone down there all dressed in black robes. It could be either male or female, I can't determine from this far up."

Buzzer quickly glanced up at the crowded framework of the ceiling but could not locate Thunder anywhere. "It's been moving slowly but steadily toward Queen Victoria's throne for about the last ten minutes. It's about forty meters from your position, approaching from the northeast. Do you see it?"

Buzzer scanned the crowd and spotted the dark foreboding figure.

"Yeah, Thunder, I got your bogie in my sights," Buzzer said. "It looks vaguely female in its movements underneath all those robes. She could be just a decoy…if she proves to be anything at all. Keep alert and be ready."

"Understood," Thunder said and Buzzer's command sequencer went inactive.

The dark figure continued its forward motion, occasionally stopping to look around. Buzzer noticed that during these short pauses the figure always looked toward the queen and then moved on.

Buzzer's brief glimpse of the face inside the hood revealed female features, confirming his earlier suspicions.

"Thunder," he called softly into his command sequencer and received a grunt in response. "You might as well take aim on this one. She seems pretty intent on the queen. Just wait for me, I might be able to take her down before you let loose from up there."

"No problem, boss," came the response.

Buzzer quickly but inconspicuously grabbed his blaster from his hip holster and primed it for action. Boa had also noticed the woman's ultimate destination and was quickly trying to work his way through the crowd to head her off.

"I've got her in my sights; standing by," Thunder's voice rasped from behind his right ear.

"Good job, Bobby," Buzzer answered. "Keep her there."

The woman was within ten meters now and closing fast. Buzzer could see no sign that she was armed.

Then, the Royal Banquet Center suddenly erupted with a series of explosions of bright white light and roaring sound. A heavy-charger had begun firing way down by the south gates, hitting everything from tables to people. The screams of the dying and terrified filled Buzzer's ears with an angry assault of noise as he tried to pinpoint the location of the lunatic with the charger.

Ramsey sprang up out of the crowd and drilled a hole through the shooter's back. The shooter's chest exploded, the internal organs splashing across the floor as his body dropped.

Less than two full seconds had passed since the man had opened fire. For Buzzer, everything seemed to be moving in slow motion. Out of the corner of his eye, he saw the woman, his original suspect, whip off her robes and raise her own heavy-charger. With an intensity in her eye, she blasted away two members of Queen Victoria's royal guard. The cavernous room was a mass of confusion and hysteria, sheer chaos, as the crowd went into a panic and desperately clawed at the exits.

Before the woman could squeeze off another shot, her body exploded.

Buzzer dove at the queen, knocking her to the floor and covering her body with his own as he aimed and fired at the attacker. Thunder had let loose three concentrated blasts from his customized heavy-charger and Boa had aimed and fired his blaster from less than ten meters away. The combined energy of all those rounds had made contact with the woman's small body simultaneously, causing it to explode, sending a grisly shower of red, gray and pink for meters in all directions. There was nothing left of the small figure…at least nothing big enough to recognize once the smoke cleared.

Buzzer knelt down and helped the queen to her unsteady feet. "Sorry for the rough ride, Queen Victoria, but it was necessary to ensure your safety."

Victoria Lacusa had a look of utter shock in her eyes as she slowly nodded and allowed Buzzer to assist her.

"It is quite all right, young man. Quite, quite all right," she said with a slight tremor in her voice. "Thank you, by the way, for saving my life."

"You're very much welcome, your majesty," Buzzer said and sat her down on her throne. "Thunder," he called into his sequencer. "Is that all of them?"

"All that appears to be in here," Thunder answered. "But I'll keep my eyes peeled."

"Ramsey, are you in one piece?"

"Yeah, but our target doesn't appear to be," came the reply.

Buzzer walked to within inches of where bits of the bloody black robe had landed.

"Damn," he muttered to himself, angry at the fact that he had no prisoners to question. Taking a long slow look around, he holstered his weapons and walked back to the throne. Ramsey and Boa were both there, standing on either side of the queen, their weapons drawn, concentrating on the movements of the terrified crowd.

Victoria Lacusa, now somewhat recovered, smiled at Buzzer as he turned and approached her. "I don't know what to say..."

"Don't worry about it; I can understand why you were skeptical." Buzzer removed the cape and helmet of Lacusa's royal guard that he had been wearing, and dropped them to the carpeted floor. "But whenever we are assigned to a mission, your majesty, you can rest assured that something of vital importance is at stake. Our time is not something which we waste."

"I know that now," the queen replied. "I should not have been so difficult earlier but nothing like this has ever happened before. I do hope you can forgive me."

"Forgiveness is not the issue, Queen Victoria," Buzzer said. "Just be more cooperative with us in the future if we ever find it necessary to visit Lacusa again."

"You will have my total cooperation in that event, young man," the queen answered and lightly clasped his hand. "But let me say that I hope never to have need of your kind again."

Buzzer nodded knowingly at the Queen and stepped away from the throne. Boa and Ramsey fell in step behind him.

"Ramsey, check the outer halls just in case. If it comes down to it, shoot to injure."

"Will do, Buzz, but I just don't feel it anymore. There's nothing else threatening in this

building."

"I know," Buzzer muttered as Ramsey ran off. "Bobby, you can come down from there now. It's over," he called through his sequencer.

"Yeah, I thought so," came the reply.

Yeah, Buzzer knew the feeling all too well. Warriors could always sense danger. It was a weird feeling that all of them had, a deep sense of darkness that brought both the body and mind to battle-ready just as something was about to go down. And just as quickly as these rushes came when danger arrived, they disappeared totally once the danger was gone.

That's what Buzzer felt now, a total nothingness. The deaths of the two attackers had ended the threat to Victoria Lacusa's life but he had no way of knowing who was next on the hit list.

"What now, Buzzer?" Boa's question broke through Buzzer's thoughts.

"We leave Lacusa," Buzzer answered. "They wouldn't dare try here again. Not after their first major failure. Security is going to be stepped up to the maximum around here now. No need for us to hang around."

"Buzzer," Ramsey's voice came over his sequencer. "The halls are clear. There's nothing out here."

"All right, meet us outside," he answered. "It's time to go."

~*~

Rhafid Azid paced back and forth impatiently across the black tiled floor.

The middle-aged Azuridian had lived with terrorism for more than three decades, nearly all of his adult life. And he believed deeply in the cause of the *Movement*.

The cause of freedom, freedom for all, for every person in the entire universe. This was the cause of the Universal Freedom from Tyranny Movement since the organization sparked to life over a quarter of a century ago. Although he believed deeply in the cause, he was intelligent enough to recognize just how distorted it had become over time.

The Movement wanted freedom, sure—freedom for all. But only on one condition—that the leaders of the Movement could step in and take the reins of the U.E.N. Government on Aegis once that freedom was achieved. Yes, freedom for all, but only if the Movement could define that freedom in their own way and be the power which regulated and dictated exactly how the people would enjoy their particular brand of freedom.

But the Movement was the Movement, and it would go on with or without him. This being so, Azid figured, why not go along for the ride, and reap as many of the benefits as he could?

Azid had disappeared from Azuridia at the tender age of thirteen, leaving his family and friends behind with no clue as to what fate had befallen him. Years later, already an accomplished terrorist, he had learned that his death certificate was official and that his life had become a part of history. His funeral had been held, a modest ceremony of family and friends, and a small monument placed in his name. By now, everyone on Azuridia had forgotten about Rhafid Azid.

But the name Azid had not been forgotten, at least not in the realm of InterGridactic espionage and terrorism. In his early days as a terrorist, Azid had made a name for himself with the assassinations of several major Grid-wide business leaders and a few bloody acts of terrorism. After more than two decades of building up his ruthless reputation, and gaining a spot for himself on more than two hundred individual law enforcement agency most-wanted lists, he took a breather and decided to disappear from the scene of InterGridactic terrorism.

Just recently he'd made the decision to show himself again. He had accepted a mission from the Movement's ruling committee to implement a new task force, a splinter faction of the best people in the Movement, and put their master plan into operation.

All had been going quite smoothly—up until yesterday. After over thirty successful operations, Lacusa had been a total disaster. Fawn Mistel and Georgei Tamanko had both been lost in that fiasco.

Azid could not figure out what had gone wrong. His research had shown that Queen Victoria Lacusa's royal guard would be no match for his two operatives— especially when both of them had been well-armed with heavy-chargers.

But, even with the odds in their favor, the sobering fact remained that the two agents had been eliminated and Queen Victoria was still alive and well.

As soon as this news had reached him, Azid had recalled every agent who was out on assignment and had arranged a meeting. Something had gone wrong. Somehow, certain people had found them out and had been waiting for them. He was absolutely certain that the deaths of his agents had not been caused by Lacusa's measly excuse for a royal guard, but rather by a well- trained military force.

The room was crowded with the members of his team. Thirteen of them were now with him, cramped in the little room of this old mansion located in the sprawling city of Gustalton. Yukon was a cold and dreary snow-world of dense populations and industrial centers. No one would take notice of the group of men and women who were convening in the abandoned mansion that was the former Judicial Building of Gustalton. The citizens of the planet were much too busy being miserable to worry about a bunch of people getting together for a discussion.

Not even the authorities on Yukon, what few there were, would question him and his associates for their unauthorized visit to the old mansion. At most, they would get a grumbled, "Get the hell out of here," and that would be all. This was why Azid had chosen Yukon forhisheadquarters. It had only taken two days to get his team assembled on the ugly little planet.

"Rhafid," a dark man seated at a small folding table broke the silence. "What happened? What disaster caused you to call us all here?"

Azid stopped pacing and stared at the man. He allowed his stare to roam and land on each of the others as silence ruled the room for almost a full minute. Only the heavy breathing of the room's occupants provided any sound.

"Please, just tell us already," another man said. "What was so terrible?"

Azid sighed and slumped down into a seat. "My friends…the Lacusa mission was a failure. Two of us were lost and Queen Victoria still lives. I am afraid we have been traced. Somehow, somewhere, somebody found out about the Lacusa mission. There is no actual evidence of it from what I've been able to learn, but I am certain that trained professionals were behind the termination of our agents. I do not believe the reports which say that one of the Queen's guards killed Fawn, and the details of Georgei's death remain mysteriously unclear."

The room remained silent as the small group pondered the deaths of their friends. The man and woman had been a couple, and had operated as a team for quite some time, even before Azid had recruited them for the Universal Freedom Front. Together, they had pulled off over fifty successful missions for the Movement and six others with Azid.

But their seventh had been their last. The Yugoslastian, Tamanko, had been one of Azid's best men in the field and his fiancé had been almost as valuable. Their loss would be hard felt by the team.

"This leak makes our group vulnerable. We can not allow this to happen again! Any one of you could have been traced or spied upon." Azid paused to allow that to sink in. "Maybe it was Tamanko and Mistel themselves, who knows? All I know is that in order for this team to operate successfully together, there can be no more leaking of information! Not one! Is that well understood?"

All members nodded their heads in agreement, none of them willing to speak after Azid's outburst. The dark brooding Azuridian looked them over—his people, every one of them. The two deaths had gotten to them, he could tell; it was in their eyes.

"Now, the deaths of our two colleagues will not go unanswered, will they?" The question was an attempt to facilitate some sort of positive reaction from the group. "Will we let them die for nothing?"

"No!" Riccardo Batista shouted. "We shall make the tyrants of our society pay for this! Our friends will be avenged!"

"He is right!" Azid answered. "We will strike more frequently now, and inflict more gruesome punishment on our targets than a mere charge to the head! After this, we will let society know that fighting back at us is futile! We will fight them until every last one of us is dead or dying! Either they kill all of us or they suffer the consequences! Am I right?"

"Yes!" The group shouted in unison.

"This tainted society will pay, Rhafid," Juan Ortiz spoke solemnly. "They will all pay..."

~*~

Frederick Cayson walked through the open doors and into the shuttle bay of the huge warship. The U.E.N. Battleship *Coyote* was sitting in space-dock off Purvis, the only moon that Aegis had to offer. The military warship had been due for an overhaul for the better part of the last decade and had at last pulled into Purvis Spaceport several months ago for the much needed repairs.

A test-firing of the battered old ship's newly refitted engines was scheduled, as soon as all unnecessary personnel could be evacuated from the vessel.

"Ready to debark, Sir," Cayson said and saluted the man with the clipboard.

"You're late, ensign," his CO snarled. "What have you been doing all this time?"

"Nothing, sir," Cayson said, standing at attention. "Just squaring away a few things before our leave, sir."

"Very well then, soldier," the officer said and pointed to the only shuttle left in the hangar bay. "Now get your ass on that shuttle. I don't have time to waste on laggards like you. Move it!"

Cayson practically leaped onto the small vehicle, the officer right behind him. "Everyone, secure seats and buckle down," the hangar deck chief yelled.

"Yes, sir," Cayson grumbled and swallowed down his thoughts before his mouth got him into trouble. Now only the commander, bridge personnel and the engineering staff were left on board the old gray behemoth, sixty people in all.

The small vehicle lifted from the floor of the shuttle bay and began its descent.

The warship was huge. It was hard to believe that men could build such a thing, and harder yet to believe that it could ever be destroyed. The enormous hulk looked majestic as the shuttle descended. Gleaming gray and strong, the ship's hull was covered with powerguns. A sense of strength, of enormous power seemed to emanate from the old ship. A veteran of over forty conflicts, the U.E.N. *Coyote* had seen better days, and better than ten captains, but it was still one of the most imposing ships in the entire fleet.

It was a shame, Cayson thought to himself; a terrible but necessary shame.

A subtle rocking meant that the shuttle had docked on Purvis. The sound of air escaping meant depressurization. The men and women on the shuttle quickly unstrapped themselves as the exit doors sprang open.

"All right, people! Move! Move! Let's go!" The chief shouted in Cayson's ear.

The shuttle emptied quickly and Cayson followed the group of navy personnel through the tunnel and into the Purvis Spaceport. Everyone split up and went separate ways—some to view the test-firing and others to the recreation room.

Cayson walked to the nearest bathroom and entered. Once locked inside a stall, he hurriedly took off the military uniform, exposing casual wear beneath, and tore the false chin from his face. Blue contact lenses followed the phony facial piece into a garbage chute. After washing his face clean of all residue from the fake chin, he tagged a phony ID to his chest, slipped on a pair of nondescript glasses, and left the bathroom.

The test-firing was minutes away when he boarded the Aegis-Purvis shuttle and headed toward the huge headquarters planet of the U.E.N. government.

As the brand new engines of the old warship commenced the test-firing sequence, the mini- nuclear explosive device attached to the reactors detonated.

The U.E.N. *Coyote* instantly disintegrated. An enormous explosion followed which flattened the Purvis Spaceport and killed over eight thousand people.

A slight shock-wave rocked the Aegis-Purvis shuttle, but aside from that the small ship had not been affected by the blast.

Frederick Cayson smiled inwardly as he perfectly played the part of just another shuttle passenger, shocked and confused by the scene of destruction outside the viewport, for the rest of the ride to Aegis.

~*~

"Sarge!" Cougar called as he entered the mission control center and scanned the area for his CO. After several seconds he spotted the huge form of Harrison Jekel leaning over a technician's shoulder, staring at a bank of scanner screens.

Cougar quickly made his way over to the sergeant and handed him the data-sheet.

"This just came in from Buzzer, sir," Cougar said and Jekel tore his eyes from the screens and grabbed the sheet of Hi-D. The message read:

...HQ—LACUSA MISSION IS COMPLETE...ROYALTY IS INTACT...SCRATCH TWO NEGATIVES...ALL POSITIVES RUNNING SMOOTHLY...SOME LACUSIAN CASUALTIES... NEGATIVES IDENTIFIED AS MEMBERS OF THE TARGET GROUP...ALL POSITIVES NOW ENROUTE TO X...NEXT COMMUNICATION SOON...B...

"Good job, Buzzer," Jekel muttered under his breath as he handed the Hi-D message back to Cougar. "Things are looking up, Cougar. Buzzer's on a roll."

~*~

Buzzer sat silent on his bunk aboard the immense Slavix CargoLiner. Talon, Boa and Ramsey were lined up across from him in the cramped little room, quietly talking among themselves and leaving Buzzer alone with his thoughts.

Before leaving Lacusa, Buzzer had requested that any results derived from the autopsies of the dead terrorists be transmitted on a specific frequency to his command sequencer. Once those results had come in, Buzzer decided to go after a hunch. There was something in the coroner's report about an unusual excess of rock salt erosion on the boots and clothes of the one assassin who, for the most part, had remained intact. That, coupled with an unusually high content of minerals in the blood and brain tissue samples that had been collected from both assassins, essentially caused by drinking large amounts of untainted spring water, led Buzzer to his decision on their next destination.

Yukon wasn't the only snow-world in the SouthWestern Corporate Grid-Sector, but Buzzer remembered once hearing about the unusually high amounts of natural minerals found in Yukon's spring water. He also remembered that Yukon's industrial centers and metropolitan areas were constantly covered with a fine coating of rock salt—a much cheaper substitute for some of the more expensive snow-removal techniques—to keep the streets clear and snow-free.

The autopsy findings could only be explained if the two corpses—or one corpse and one collection of smears—had spent some time on Yukon. A temporary headquarters of the Universal Freedom Front might still be operational on Yukon. That is what Buzzer was hoping to find on the world of snow and ice, where the highest temperature Fahrenheit ever recorded was twelve degrees.

Right now, Buzzer would settle for just an empty building with a few clues. Anything that would lead him to Rhafid Azid and the rest of his sick demented followers.

The door to the small compartment slid aside as Thunder and Able walked in. Able joined the group of three across the room and Thunder took a seat next to his mission commander.

"What's up, Frank?" Thunder asked. "You look distracted."

"No, I'm just trying to sort out our mission plan," Buzzer said. "I can't wait to get my hands on Azid. It will be my personal pleasure to fry that bastard. I can taste it."

Thunder smiled and clapped a hand down on his friend's shoulder. "Now, that sounds like Frank Buzzer."

Buzzer smirked at Thunder's half-hearted attempt to cheer him up. "Is everything all right with the ship's crew?"

Thunder leaned back against the cold unyielding wall of the bulkhead before responding. "The captain of this tin can is just as cranky and uncooperative as Slavix captains are reputed to be," he sneered. "He kept complaining about how the U.E.N. keeps trying to boss the small guy around, and how the two days of lost travel time that this trip to Yukon will cost him will make him look bad to his superiors. You know, the usual, but we told him to contact Aegis and file a credit voucher with the Claims Office for the amount of his total cost. No doubt he'll probably charge a couple of thousand more than he needs to, but travel time costs are always hard to pinpoint. He'll get away with it."

"Any estimates on our arrival time?" Buzzer asked.

"Yeah, about twenty-two hours from now, Aegis Standard," Thunder answered. "So what's really the matter, Frank? How come you look so glum?"

"I don't know, Bobby," Buzzer answered. "This one just doesn't feel right. You and I are both sitting here on several billion tons of scrap metal coasting through space, instead of being back on Aegis helping to guard President Alderman. I'm itching for something to happen, something that will lead us to Azid. I hope Yukon doesn't turn up empty."

"Come on, when's the last time one of your hunches landed a zero?" Thunder said.

"That's bullshit, Bobby, and you know it," Buzzer answered. "Always question things, think them through for yourself. Following someone blindly is a quick way to get killed. You guys all think that I'm some kind of expert when it comes to strategy, but I'm just following a hunch like any other Guarder would under these same circumstances. Just a hunch, with nothing else to go on. I hate to think of what's going to happen when the time comes for me to be horribly wrong about something. When my first disastrous failure comes as a mission commander, what's that going to mean for me? I'll be thought of as tainted, as a screw-up whose time has come, and all because my mission record has managed to remain clean since I joined the squadron."

Buzzer paused for a moment and Thunder let the awkward moment pass in silence.

"Damn, Bobby, that rookie Otter has screwed up twice already and nobody ever said a word.

Failures are just a part of the job, right? Almost like he's expected to screw up every once in a while, just like everyone else. But not me, no, Frank Buzzer could never mess up a mission. Because if I did, Bobby, I'd be nothing. All in one shot, that spooky Buzzer mystique would be gone. The faith and respect of my teammates, and of my CO, would be gone. I've been trying to block that type of pressure for so long now that I'm almost convinced I know how to do it. But I don't. It's there, always, and one day it's going to get one of you or somebody else killed."

Thunder remained silent and cast his eyes downward. The sudden onslaught of emotion by the usually quiet Buzzer had briefly stunned him.

"I'd never lose respect for you, Frank," he managed. "You are the best in the Guarder Squadron, and you'll go down in the books as such. No one questions your authority or your integrity, no one ever has. And I doubt that you'll ever fail, Frank. You're just too good at what you do."

"You see, that's exactly what I'm talking about, Bobby," Buzzer said. "I'm not some kind of god out here, do you realize that? How come you guys all trust your lives to me without a single word? No questions, like I know what I'm doing out here any better than you guys do. I am directly responsible for making sure that the members of this team stay alive. And that's a lot of pressure, Bobby. Watching friends and teammates die is not a lot of fun. Believe me, Mestizo's death taught me that much."

"Damn, Frank," Thunder whispered. "That was a long time ago."

"Yeah, I know, but it still hits hard, Bobby. Very, very hard..."

Buzzer took a deep breath and sighed. "I'm sorry, man. I didn't mean to lay all that on you." Thunder looked into the eyes of his friend, the greatest U.E.N. Guarder who had ever lived, and saw the confusion and uncertainty boiling there, deep inside.

"It just proves that you really are human, Frank," Thunder said. "Don't you think we all go through this stage? Death doesn't exactly stir up many pleasant thoughts. But it surprises me that this stage of confusion is just hitting you now, after more than twelve e-years. It hits most of us about the third or fourth. If you think about it, Frank, you really are something extraordinary when you operate out here in the Grids. You just have to accept it; you are the best out of all of us and have been for quite some time now. No matter what you do out here, win or lose, no one in all the Known-Grids is going to think that you screwed up. Believe me, the U.E.N. knows that Frank Buzzer is the number-one Guarder in the ranks. If something goes wrong, it may or may not be your fault. But when that happens, you will make it right, like you always do. It's your nature. No one would ever think that you personally caused a mission failure. I don't mean to put you up on a pedestal, but hell, you've been up on one for so long already. You've got nothing to fear about how we think of you or will think of you in the future, Frank. We'll never think that you're washed up or past your prime. Who in his right mind would ever think to criticize your actions or your mission records? Don't worry, Buzzer, you're only thirty-two, and that's far, very far, from washed up. Do you hear me?"

Buzzer smiled then and started to laugh. He tried to control it, keep it under wraps, but it soon escalated out of control.

Thunder couldn't help but smile as he watched his friend, cheerful for once.

"What? What's so funny?" Thunder asked and started laughing, too, much to the surprise of the other four men in the room. Moments later the laughing fit was over and Buzzer rubbed at his eyes to clear them.

"Damn, Thunder," Buzzer said. "That's the longest speech I've ever gotten out of you. Man, did I ever need a laugh like that. That was great stuff; put me on a pedestal...you're hilarious." Buzzer started laughing again and Thunder just shook his head.

"Any time, boss," Thunder said, chuckling himself. "Any time."

Buzzer kept laughing, though mostly to himself now. He had never heard anyone talk about him to his face in such a way before. And especially, he had never coaxed such an admission of respect and admiration from Bobby Thunder, the Guarder who just happened to be number-two in the ranks. Of course,

Thunder had been the number-three Guarder before the death of Tony Mestizo during a mission some time ago. Mestizo had been Buzzer's best friend, and his loss had always hung dark and heavy over Buzzer's soul. Buzzer had been mission commander on that particular assignment and he had always felt directly responsible for the loss of Mestizo.

Death...that word kept popping up in Buzzer's mind lately. The thought of his death, or the deaths of any of the five men with him on this mission, just turned his stomach. Only over the past few e-years had the members of the U.E.N. Guarder Squadron been forced, once again, to fire their weapons in defense of their lives on so many occasions.

For centuries the Guarder Squadron had operated silently and efficiently throughout the four Corporate Grid-Sectors, mythic figures, the stuff of legends. But five e-years ago, a group of renegade Guarders had nurtured their greed for wealth and power into a rebellion against the Guarder Squadron. Secretly forming an elite mercenary unit, they had attempted to recruit as many other Guarders into their group as they could. They also set their sights on eliminating any Guarders who refused to turn traitor.

Mestizo had been killed during the mission to put an end to the rebellion. Buzzer's wrath and hunger for vengeance had quickly eliminated this threat, cleanly and efficiently. His final act of that particular mission had given Buzzer the greatest sense of satisfaction in his life.

But the treacherous deaths of just that handful of Guarders, a group of soldiers who up until then had been considered invulnerable, had recently prompted countless attacks on Guarders all across the Known-Grids. So, once again, it was up to the members of the Guarder Squadron to prove their soldiering skills to the entire population of the universe. To prove to the Grids that they were still a force to be reckoned with, a team of the most well-trained, most gifted and most lethal soldiers in existence.

Buzzer had been forced to use his blaster and various other weapons more times since that mini-rebellion than he had ever had to before in his career. And every time, he had come away from his encounters victorious.

Unfortunately, the same could not be said about some of the other Guarders who had been on the receiving end of death since then.

After the rebellion, it had suddenly seemed as if open season had been declared on Guarders and, for the first time in history, the members of the Guarder Squadron were on the hit-lists of every major illegal operation in the Known-Grids. Everywhere they went, on every mission, or so it seemed, people were gunning for Guarders.

The Guarder Ranks had responded with a vengeance to this open-season policy and had proven to the Grids that anyone responsible for the death of a Guarder would not live long enough to enjoy life, not with Guarders on their tail. The legend of the undying wrath of the Guarder Squadron had been established several centuries ago and the Guarders of today were doing all they could to uphold it.

Slowly but surely the people of the Known-Grids were beginning to regard the Guarder Squadron with the respect and subtle tinge of fear that they had always been accustomed to in the past. And no other Guarder had gained more respect from his actions than Francis Vincenzo Buzzito, Guarder ID—Buzzer. He had been the prime target for the criminal element ever since the rebellion fiasco had shaken the Guarder Squadron down to its very core. But, after numerous altercations and countless mission assignments, he had come away from almost every incident unscathed.

Physically, that is. Mentally, Frank Buzzer had experienced an overwhelming amount of stress in his career. The fabric of his mind, which was once rough and coarse, had been torn in many places and, as a result, had become somewhat weaker.

But Buzzer was aware that this process was taking place and had been doing his best to correct it. For some reason, crazy as it seemed to himself, Buzzer knew that Bobby Thunder's speech had restored his confidence and had lifted him up again, had set his mind to mending itself once and for all. Now everything would be all right; Buzzer felt sure of it. His former state of mental uncertainty, of teetering on the edge between confidence and denial, had been eradicated. His friend's praise had been the missing link in the chain of his twisted thought patterns. And now that the system had been repaired it could begin to run smoothly again.

Buzzer felt better already. Bobby Thunder had helped his mission commander out in more ways than he could ever realize.

As Thunder sat laughing, Buzzer just smiled at his second-in-command and gripped his shoulder. "Thanks, Bobby, I mean that."

"Like I said, boss, any time," Thunder replied, just a little bit confused.

"All right, guys," Buzzer stood and spoke sternly, his former humorous demeanor gone as quickly as it had come.

"This is what I think is going down on Yukon..."

~*~

Fred Murphy, Midge Porseitz and Marita Anzani sat in the small terminal room, staring intently at their respective monitor screens crowded with data. Sal Mariosa and Steven Todd were downstairs in the recreation room, lounging around since they weren't due to leave on their new mission until the morning.

The rest of the old mansion was empty and silent. The heat had been comfortably set at seventy-five degrees Fahrenheit. This made it very pleasant while inside the house…and very hard to step outside into Yukon's formidable climate. The constant cold could inch its way past any and all layers of clothing, to freeze the unwary who dared to stay outside long enough. But as an out-of-the-way, quasi-headquarters, Yukon passed the test. Nobody wanted to set foot on the icy planet to begin with, let alone begin a lengthy search of its mostly barren continents.

Planted in the center of Gustalton, the planet's foremost industrial center, the old mansion provided quick and easy access to the Bering Spaceport and most of the major financial institutions. Another advantage was the ease with which members of the Front could slip into and out of crowds unnoticed. Yukon afforded the Front an almost complete blanket of obscurity and invisibility, a luxury desperately sought by every terrorist organization that had ever existed.

A luxury which the members of the Universal Freedom Front cherished.

Midge Porseitz stared at his monitor with amazement. A satellite picture of the immense Slavix CargoLiner filled the screen. Porseitz had never seen anything like it.

"When did that thing dock, Midge?" Anzani asked as she quickly glanced at the object of his sudden attention.

"Early this morning," the small, sniveling rat-like man answered. "It's been there for a while."

Anzani went back to her screens, a look of disgust on her face. She would never understand why Azid had admitted that little runt into the Front. As far as she could tell, the man was an imbecile, a child whose almost total attention could be captured by the mere appearance of an InterGridactic CargoLiner. She had heard that the man was very good, actually excellent, with a blaster, and even better with a charger. But it took more than aim to be successful in this business. Intelligence also played a huge role. A quick trigger-finger could never compensate for the brains with which to use a gun effectively.

Beside his apparent Neanderthal mentality, the small man smelled like a rotting corpse, had breath to match, and wore more filth than he did clothes most of the time. A despicable example of a human being, to be blunt, she thought to herself

154

with amusement. Nevertheless, if she had to work beside people like Porseitz in order to support the Movement's cause, then so be it. Her petty grievances had no say in the overall goals of the Front. She would do what had to be done to make their unit successful and nothing less. Even if it meant working side by side with a piece of slime...

A sudden noise attracted her attention. She seemed to be the only one in the room who had noticed. The sound seemed to have come from outside but she couldn't be sure. Leaving the terminal room, she walked downstairs to the recreation room and found Todd and Mariosa sound asleep.

"Did you two hear anything just now?" She asked, shaking the two men awake. Both of them grunted negatively and fell back into their hibernation. Anzani sighed in disgust at the two lazy slobs, pulled out her blaster, primed it and continued on with her search.

Another slight sound started the blood pounding in her head. It had come from the kitchen, a room which should be empty with everyone else in the house accounted for. Another sound, a creak of a door, and the slight scrape of a foot on carpet caused her finger to tense on the weapon's trigger. Whoever these visitors were, there was more than one of them and they hadn't been invited.

The option to go back into the rec-room and wake the two sleepers for backup passed fleetingly through her mind, but quickly departed once she realized just how much noise the dreary fools would make in the otherwise quiet house—just maybe alerting the uninvited guests to their presence.

Sounds, small and almost inaudible, were coming closer and closer. Marita Anzani's terrified form stood silently in front of the door to the kitchen, in anticipation of the intruder's entrance.

The footsteps seemed to stop just beyond the door, only meters away. Anzani tried to stifle the sounds of her heavy breathing but could do nothing to control it. The door seemed to move, microscopically at most, but it had definitely moved. She was certain of it. She was also certain that her blaster's charge would drill through the flimsy door and anything else that was standing on the other side. Her finger pulled the trigger.

The blast was deafening. Anzani caught the brunt of the charge in the back, the force of the blast flinging her into the kitchen door.

Boa opened the door and stepped over her crumpled corpse, which had slid to the carpet leaking internal organs, fluid and blood. When Buzzer's blast had shattered the window and plowed through her shoulder blades, Anzani's gun-arm had been thrust up toward the ceiling, sending her blast through the floorboards to explode into Midge Porseitz's computer terminal. The monitor exploded,

155

sending thousands of shards of glass splinters deep into his face, throat and chest. The wave of glass particles literally tore him to shreds, penetrating the inner recesses of his brain and opening a huge gash in his throat. Midge Porseitz died quickly, his last vision being that of a Slavix CargoLiner.

Buzzer climbed in through the shattered window as Boa flipped him a quick thumbs-up.

Thunder and Able also entered the living room. Ramsey and Talon were on the roof, trying to enter the mansion from there. Activity upstairs made it clear that they weren't alone in the huge old structure.

"Take the east, we'll take the west," Buzzer called to Thunder and Able and the two men quickly departed the room.

Buzzer ducked by instinct just as a charger blast exploded against the remnants of the kitchen door. Boa answered back with two quick shots as Buzzer crawled toward the doorway across the room. More blasts came crashing into the room, setting drapes on fire and making toothpicks out of furniture.

Boa upended a small metal table and took cover behind it as he poured more fire into the open doorway. Buzzer crouched just beside the doorway from which the weapon's fire was coming and signaled to Boa to provide cover fire. Boa released an onslaught of blasts into the hall as Buzzer stood and glanced down the short corridor.

Two men were crouched at the end of the hall, firing heavy-chargers aimlessly. Taking a breath and steadying himself, Buzzer crouched down again and checked the charges on his weapons. Both blasters still had over three-quarters power left.

Blasts kept firing down the hall until Buzzer signaled Boa to stop. Immediately after Boa's weapon stopped dispersing fire, Buzzer threw himself into a low roll and pinpointed both targets. He squeezed the trigger of one blaster three times in rapid succession and the corridor was suddenly quiet.

From the other side of the doorway Buzzer saw Boa signal that it was all clear. Mariosa had been hit twice; his head was gone and his chest was oozing. Todd had been drilled through the gut and was just barely alive.

A single shot rang out from upstairs and a thump sounded on the ceiling above him. Then all was silent in the large house.

"Boa, check out the rest of the west side of this place," Buzzer said as he holstered one blaster but kept the other primed and ready. "I'm going to try and get something of value from this zombie."

Boa nodded his understanding and took off.

Buzzer knew that it was over; that feeling always came in strong once the action died down.

Kneeling beside the gasping terrorist, he grabbed the back of his neck. "Where's Azid?"

The dying man tried to spit in Buzzer's face but ended up spitting on himself. Buzzer reached into the open cavity of the man's abdomen with his free hand, grabbed a handful of the ravaged intestines and pulled them out into plain view.

The man's eyes widened and he screamed in horror, nearly choking on his own blood.

"Again, where's Azid?"

"To hell with you," the semi-corpse managed to rasp. "To hell with all of you."

Buzzer brought his blaster up and pressed it to the man's head. "I can keep you alive and suffering for a good while yet and you know it. That's what's so great about gut-shots, I can torture you forever. At least that's what it'll seem like to you. Or I can kill you quick and easy. You're going to die either way so it's your call. All I ask is that you just tell me what I want to know."

The man gulped down some of his own bile and coughed. "So torture me, then."

Without hesitation, Buzzer thrust his blaster down barrel first into the man's exposed guts.

The inhuman shriek of agony gave him the chills but he needed this information and he needed it quick. Despite what he'd just told the man, life would soon be ebbing away from this one.

Recognizing the urgency of the situation, Buzzer continued with his interrogation. Once again placing the muzzle of his blaster to the man's head, he said, "So what'll it be?"

"Aegis," the terrorist rasped. "Azid's on Aegis. He's going for broke."

"What does that mean?" Buzzer asked.

"It means that he's...going for the primary target."

"President Alderman," Buzzer confirmed.

"Yeah, the president of the U.E.N. He's our...primary target...half of the team is with Azid on Aegis for this hit."

"When's it going down?" Buzzer urged.

"I'm not sure..." the terrorist gasped.

"Don't bullshit me!" Buzzer threatened.

"I mean it, man," his victim said. "I'm not absolutely certain...but I know it won't be for a few more days."

"Why's that?"

"Because I was supposed to complete my mission first," the man said, breathing heavily.

"And what was that?"

"To kill you," he said and gasped again in pain. "You're that Buzzer guy, right? The Guarder?"

Buzzer's eyes turned cold as he absorbed what the man had just told him. This little sneak attack had quite probably saved his own life tonight. Now he would have to warn the Sarge and get back to Aegis as fast as he could. Azid was crazy. He would sacrifice his own life in order to pull this thing off. Killing Harry Alderman, President of the U.E.N., would secure his place in the history books forever. And lunatics like that were the most dangerous of all.

Thunder and Able entered the room, Ramsey and Talon close behind. Boa came in several seconds later. All of them found the same thing—nothing. Buzzer stood and looked down into the fearful eyes of Steven Todd.

"I'll see you in hell, Guarder," the man said just before Buzzer fired his blaster point-blank into the man's face.

Looking up at his fellow Guarders, Buzzer sighed and holstered his weapon. "Let's go."

"Where to?" Thunder asked.

"Aegis...we've got trouble back home."

~*~

Cougar raced through the doors of the conference room and immediately located his commanding officer. The massive form of Sergeant Harrison Jekel stood at the head of the conference table where he was lecturing a group of young U.E.N. Governing Guard cadets.

Jekel frowned at the interruption and motioned to his communications officer. "What is it, Cougar?"

"Sergeant Jekel, sir," Cougar said. "Buzzer just sent word from Yukon."

Jekel watched the eyes of most of the cadets in the room go wide at the mention of the legendary Guarder's name.

"Where did you say?" Jekel asked.

"From Yukon, sir," Cougar said and thrust the Hi-D data-sheet toward Jekel. The leader of the Guarder Squadron grabbed the message andread:

...HQ...FOUND ENEMY STRONGHOLD ON YUKON... SCRATCH FIVE NEGATIVES...ALL POSITIVES ARE RUNNING SMOOTHLY...ENEMY LEADER—AZID—ON AEGIS...OTHER FRONT MEMBERS ACCOMPANYING... TARGET EQUALS HEAD OF STATE...ASSASSINATION ATTEMPT WITHIN DAYS...WILL FIND QUICK MEANS OF TRANSPORTATION...BEEF UP SECURITY...AZID WILL STOP AT NOTHING...BE THERESOON...B...

Jekel handed the data-sheet back to Cougar and took in a deep breath.

"Class is dismissed," he sighed and stormed out of the room, Cougar close at his heels. "Get on the line to the Presidential Offices in the Northern Wing and tell Mack to get his team on alert. Azid can strike at any time now. Also tell the commander of the Governing Guard to get his ass in gear and get his troops on a watch detail. I want President Alderman heavily protected at all times and kept alive at all costs. You got all that?"

"Yes, sir, I'll get right on it," Cougar called as he raced down the corridor and out of sight.

Jekel approached a bank of lift-cars and pulled out both of his blasters to check each weapon's charge. Both read full. He primed them for action and returned them to his holsters.

"Dammit, Buzzer, why is it that every time I get a message from you it seems to be bad news!" He muttered to himself and entered a lift-car. After punching a complicated security code into the destination panel, Jekel stood back as the lift-doors closed and the car started on its way up to President Harry Calhoun Alderman's private quarters.

The president wasn't going to like hearing that a terrorist assassination squad was already on Aegis one bit, Jekel thought to himself and sighed heavily. Especially after these terrorists had already gotten close enough to Aegis and the U.E.N. Governmental Complex to blow both the battleship *Coyote* and the Purvis Spaceport to hell and back.

"What in the hell is happening to the security on this planet?" He muttered as the car steadily rose through the complex.

~*~

Frederick Cayson and Kenneth Kobalsky walked through the corridors outside President Alderman's private quarters. They were on their way to the Oval Offices, the maze of rooms where all the members of the boards and committees met with the president to discuss confidential issues central to the operations of the government.

Dressed in the uniforms of two recently killed Governing Guard, and with very authentic looking imitation ID badges pinned to their chests, they had been roaming the halls of the U.E.N. Governmental Complex for more than two days already. Azid had taken up residence in the congressional chambers after assuming the identity of a fictitious ambassador from Kuriacoa.

The alias had worked for him before and a lengthy record already existed concerning the good ambassador in the Judiciary Board's vast file room. Lisa Durkin was also playing her role as the fictional ambassador's wife quite effectively. Andrei Yurgov, Juan Ortiz, Robert Packard and Riccardo Batista had taken a room in the Aegis New Arrival Lodging Area and were awaiting further orders from Azid.

The three-hundred-eighty-ninth meeting of the U.E.N. Executive Session was scheduled to begin tonight and would probably last well into the next month.

Cayson and Kobalsky had been searching the complex for their next target vigorously since they had assumed the roles of U.E.N. Officers. After asking a frazzled looking member of the administrative staff where they could possibly find the object of their search, the young woman had unwittingly directed the two terrorists to the Oval Offices and directly to their target.

Sergeant Harrison Jekel stood outside the entrance to the Oval Offices, talking to the United Earthian Nations Vice President Nathan Cantor. The two terrorists approached the entrance and stood to the side, acting as if they were on duty.

Kobalsky's finger tensed toward his blaster but Cayson flashed him a glare of warning to relax and ride it out until the time was right. Everything the two men had heard about the commander of the U.E.N. Guarder Squadron had been true. The giant man stood just over six-feet, seven- inches tall and looked as if he weighed a lean and solid three-hundred-plus pounds. The man looked like a walking bull. His bald head reflected the overhead lights brightly; his eyes had a glare of icy stone-coldness.

Intimidating was not the word to describe this man. Much more than that could be said. The two blasters strapped to his body looked worn, as if they had seen plenty of action in their time.

"I don't like this, Freddy," Kobalsky blurted. "Let's just take him now before we lose the chance."

"Yeah, and get fried by the two Guarders over there in the corner, right, Kenny?" Cayson snarled. "Just calm yourself down and ride with me on this one."

Kobalsky glanced over his shoulder and spotted Mack and Gannon standing in the shadows.

The blood drained from his face as the memories of legends flooded through his brain. The deadly accuracy and efficiency of the Guarder Squadron had been told down through the ages. What in the hell was he doing here, messing around with Guarders of all things anyway, he swore to himself, feeling closer to death at this very moment than he ever had before. This outer corridor reeked of death; the gargantuan figure standing just meters away looked like death incarnate.

Cayson could see Kobalsky trembling and sweating, and prayed to God that the nervous bastard wouldn't freak out and get them both fried.

Jekel finished his conversation and the Vice President disappeared behind the doors to the Oval Offices. Their target walked over to his men in the shadows and began whispering to them. Cayson could not make out the words.

Turning to his companion, he said, "Kenny, I'll cover the two Guarders. All you have to do is level your charger at that monster's chest and blow him away. Do you think you can pull that off?"

"Yeah, Fred," he replied shakily. "I just freaked for a minute. Don't worry, I'm back again."

"Good," Cayson said and stepped away from Kobalsky. "When I open up on those two in the corner, you fry Jekel. Put two or three blasts into him and he'll never move again."

"You got it," Kobalsky said.

"Good," Cayson walked briskly down the corridor toward the two Guarders as Jekel walked past him and nodded in recognition of a fellow military man.

Cayson raised his charger and brought it up to face the two Guarders.

Mack's eyes went wide with shock at the sudden appearance of a Governing Guardsman intent on killing him. Gannon whipped out his blaster as he fell to the floor, bringing Mack down with him.

Cayson fired twice, both blasts ripping into the wall where the two Guarders had been standing less than a second earlier. Jekel whirled toward Cayson, his blaster in his hand and already firing. Gannon and Mack fired simultaneously. All three blasts connected with Cayson's upper torso, reducing him to a bloody mess and covering the entire room with gore.

"Sarge!" The shout came out of nowhere and Jekel, acting by instinct, dropped to the floor just as Kobalsky opened fire. The heavy-charger boomed again and again as the terrorist tried to handle the heavy weapon and correct his angle of fire down toward the carpeting where Jekel was rolling away, trying to reach the cover of a pillar.

The twin roars of blasters rang out across the corridor. Brass and Stalker had both hit Kobalsky, one in the shoulder and one in the chest. Kobalsky's body slumped to the carpet, already dead but still twitching.

Blood seemed to be everywhere. Jekel quickly lifted himself from the floor and scanned the hall from behind a pillar.

"It's all clear, Sarge," Joker called as he entered the corridor. "There's nothing behind me. I came as soon as I heard the action."

"What just happened here, Sarge?" Gannon asked.

"There's a force of terrorists on Aegis, already in this building as we just found out, who are gunning for the president. Security has been beefed up but it looks as if these two slipped through. I'll talk to Captain Brooks of the Governing Guard about this as soon as I can. In the meantime, you guys be careful. We don't know how many of them there are or when they're going to hit, so be on alert. Buzzer and his team are en route now. He says that Azid's on Aegis and will stop at nothing to assassinate his target. Keep as tight to Alderman as you can. In fact, Gannon, I want you with the president at all times, in his quarters while he sleeps and in the Oval Offices as he works."

"Understood, sir."

"The rest of you, be careful and stay awake," Jekel said and left the corridor.

The five men watched their leader as he disappeared behind a corner and realized just how close to the end they had all come.

"I don't like firing on a man in U.E.N. stripes," Mack said.

"Yeah, but I'm damn glad we were able to react as quickly as we did," Gannon countered. "That one moment's hesitation on our part was what they were counting on."

"It's no good when men wearing the uniforms of our own military open fire on us," Stalker muttered. "We have to put an end to this."

"That, gentlemen," Joker said, "is exactly why we're here."

~*~

Azid took a deep breath and clenched his teeth as he watched the newscast. The story involved the deaths of two unidentified terrorists, who had tried to ambush the guards stationed just outside the U.E.N. Oval Offices. Azid did not need to guess who the two mystery men were.

It was clear that Kobalsky and Cayson had utterly failed in their mission and that Sergeant Harrison Jekel was still alive. No news of the death of the Guarder, Frank Buzzer, coupled with the fact that Yukon had not responded to calls in days, led Azid to believe that Buzzer had gotten to Yukon before his people had gotten to Buzzer.

First the deaths of Tamanko and Mistel; and now this. He would have to assume that the five he had left on the snow-world were dead also. His death toll now stood at nine.

He only had six members of the Front left to work with, including himself. That increased the odds a little but Azid was confident that he could pull this assignment off. He would do all in his power to complete this mission; to him it was a matter of pride. This had been the first assignment that he had deemed worthy enough of his skills in the last decade and he would be damned if it ended in failure. His life was worth it if it meant success. Azid was ready to die and had been since he swore his oath to the Movement. The Universal Freedom Front had worked like a charm as a cover operation for him and his people. But at first it had fifteen members…now it had six.

Well, six would just have to be enough, he thought to himself as he opened up an outside com-link. Having already attached the de-tracer to the com-link in his quarters, he was confident that the recordings of his calls would result in nothing but static. He punched in the number for the Aegis New Arrival Lodging Area and Andrei Yurgov answered.

"Hello, Andrei," Azid spoke softly. "There's been a change in plans. We're moving up the schedule…"

163

~*~

Six Guarders stepped out of the third docking interlock of the Aegis Spaceport and into the main lobby. The entire trip from Yukon to Aegis had lasted less than two days, Aegis Standard. The multi-cruiser that Buzzer had acquired from Yukon's impounding depot was the fastest vehicle he had ever piloted. Buzzer now knew why the U.E.N. Security Forces had such trouble catching pirates and smugglers. More ships like the one that brought them here should be pressed into active service in the U.E.N. Military.

The ride on the shuttle-hop to the Aegis New Arrival Customs Center took no time at all and an air-car was waiting for them at the exit when they arrived. The six Guarders were quickly delivered to the U.E.N. Governmental Complex. Minutes later they met Sergeant Jekel in the conference room of the Guarder Squadron HQ.

"So, what do we know?" Buzzer asked as he took a seat across from his commanding officer. "You did a good job out there on this mission, Buzzer," Jekel said. "All of you did. But, as

you know, this thing's not over yet. Yesterday, two of those terrorists were actually stupid enough to attack Mack, Gannon and myself outside the doors of the Oval Offices. We fried both of them but Azid's still around. We have been totally unable to locate him at this time but he and other members of his team are probably on Aegis and more than likely in this very building.

Unfortunately, this building is just about as big as most of the cities on this planet. Azid could hit at any time. And the meeting of the executive session is just about to begin. If Azid can get into Assembly Center he may just be able to pull this thing off. With you guys and myself and the others watching Alderman, we'll have twelve Guarders positioned in or around Assembly Center. That should be more than enough firepower and skill to overpower one man, especially a man who has been out of circulation for the better part of the last decade. But we don't know how many people he has here with him. Something is scaring me about this one. There's something different, something strange…and since I can't describe it, I don't like it."

"I guess I don't have to ask if you've swept the entire complex for bombs," Buzzer said and Jekel nodded his confirmation.

Jekel stood and moved toward the door. "I'll admit it; I have a bad feeling about this one. It may sound strange coming from me, but I'm spooked. Azid just came back on the scene like an explosion and has been all but unstoppable since.

164

All I can tell you is to be careful and watch each others' backs. The two terrorists that attacked us were dressed in the uniforms of Governing Guardsmen. I'm telling you, I don't like this one, not one bit. This Azid guy is crazy..."

~*~

Rhafid Azid sat in a high-backed comfortable chair in the middle of the fourth row of desks. Assembly Center seated over five thousand people. All of these seats were presently occupied by politicians from across the Known Grid-Levels of Space. Members of the press stood everywhere, making the arena look much more crowded than usual. Azid could see Robert Packard, disguised as a reporter from the *Prophecy News Network*. Along with his camera, Packard carried a half-charger and blaster concealed beneath his traditional flowing robes.

Playing the role of the fictitious Kuriacoan ambassador was all too easy. Azid sat back and didn't say much. When he had registered as an off-world diplomat inside the U.E.N. Governmental Complex, a place had been automatically set aside for him in Assembly Center. The cold steel of his blaster felt very reassuring underneath his own traditional robes. In minutes, the gun would fill his hand and begin to work his will. Packard would open up on the two Guarders who flanked the president on either side, and the others would try to take out the Guarders and Governing Guardsmen who were patrolling outside the doors. If everything went right, some of them might just get out of the complex alive.

If things didn't go right...well, he didn't want to speculate on that at the moment.

For now, he would wait patiently until he got the signal from Packard telling him that all was green. President Alderman was speaking powerfully, the microphone booming his voice throughout Assembly Center.

Azid scanned the large arena, his eyes coming to rest on a face he recognized. The face of Frank Buzzer—the most famous Guarder in all the Known-Grids. A man whom Azid would take great pleasure in killing just as soon as he assassinated the President of the United Earthian Nations.

Buzzer was just standing there, off to the left of his president. Sergeant Jekel was in the same position on the other side of the stage. How Azid despised these two men. They had made life very hard for him and the Front recently. Especially hard on those members who were now dead.

Yes, revenge would be his in the end, of that he was certain.

165

~*~

Buzzer stood at the back of the stage.

The suspense was killing him. Whatever was going to happen would happen soon, he could feel it. It was one of those chills that traveled up and down his spine and just wouldn't go away. He felt it in the air, he could even smell it, taste it. That was how strong it was.

He slowly scanned the thousands of faces crowding the arena. Sure, some of them looked like suspicious characters. Hell, *hundreds* of them looked suspicious but that was what being a politician was all about. Out of all the guilty faces he could not pinpoint one that stood out from the rest. Not a single face. Despite that, he remained absolutely certain that the action was almost upon them. His concentration level was at its highest, his fingers itching for the trigger of his blaster.

Alderman was still talking loudly, but his words were lost to Buzzer's ears. As he scanned the crowd he made momentary eye contact with one of the ambassadors from some backwater, insignificant little world. Their eyes locked for the briefest of moments and then Buzzer continued his observations.

In the back of his mind, something was nagging at him about that ambassador. Buzzer quickly scanned back and tried to locate that mysterious face. The man was easy to locate, since he was still staring straight at Buzzer.

There was something different, but it was there; Buzzer could just about make it out. The skin tone, the jet-black hair, the uplifted bridge of the nose, the deep-set eyes…Buzzer had studied dozens of Hi-D photos of that face for hours during the past few days. Although they had their differences, like the missing beard and mustache, different hair style and the absence of the heavy acne problem that was apparent in the older images of Azid he had seen, they were one in the same.

Buzzer could not believe his eyes. Azid had been sitting there within the crowd and within easy firing range of President Alderman all the while. Buzzer's eyes burned through the man's skull as each man locked gazes with the other. Azid stood abruptly, knocking over the flimsy desk in front of him and produced a blaster from underneath his robes.

As the Azuridian terrorist fired at the president of the United Earthian Nations, Buzzer sprang into action and tackled Harry Alderman hard, knocking him to the floor. The two men kept rolling across the stage until Buzzer was sure that the president was hidden under sufficient cover.

166

All hell had broken loose inside Assembly Center. Another terrorist had opened fire from way back at the end of the arena. Two members of the Governing Guard were rushing toward the president, guns drawn. Buzzer was about to leave the highest ranking official in the entire U.E.N. in their capable hands when one of the uniformed men went down on one knee and took aim at his chest with a half-charger.

"Get down, Mr. President!" Buzzer screamed as he leapt into the air. The terrorist fired but the blast traveled underneath Buzzer's flying body.

In mid-air, Buzzer collided with the terrorist, both men crashing hard to the surface of the stage. Buzzer came out of his roll and pounced hard on his assailant's chest. Putting his blaster in the man's face he muttered, "Time to die," through gritted teeth and fired. In seconds he was running from the convulsing corpse, looking for his next target.

The other terrorist was already on the floor, less than two meters from where Alderman lay. Gannon was leaning over him, a bloody knife in his hand. Buzzer flipped him a thumbs-up and raced off into the crowd searching for Azid.

Just then, Juan Ortiz and Lisa Durkin burst through the janitorial chamber doors and opened fire on anything and everything that moved.

Jekel recognized distraction tactics when he saw them. He signaled for Boa and Mack to circle around and hit them both from behind while he kept them occupied.

Stalker and Joker appeared from nowhere and opened up on the two killers from the left. The terrorists were ripped apart from the multiple blasts, bits and pieces of them flying for meters.

People, politicians and reporters alike were screaming hysterically and shoving toward the exits.

Harrison Jekel stood from cover and snarled at his men, "Keep an eye on the stage! Alderman's still up there!"

"On the way, Sarge," Stalker called; he and Joker were already on the move.

Only one terrorist, disguised as a reporter, was left firing at the crowd. He seemed to have Able and Talon pinned down effectively but Brass was pouring it on from a difficult angle and getting closer with each blast. As Jekel approached the scene, he was also trying to locate Azid and Buzzer.

Suddenly, Bobby Thunder dropped from the latticework that lined the ceiling and landed directly on Robert Packard. The terrorist's charger went clattering away across the floor as he grappled with the Guarder.

Thunder kneed the man savagely in the crotch and watched his aggressor go down. He quickly wrapped his muscular arms around the terrorist's neck and gave it a vicious twist. Packard's neck snapped like a dry twig and Thunder let the body thud to the floor.

The crowd was still making a tremendous amount of noise, hundreds of panicked people milling about in a hectic state of frenzy. Jekel still could not locate Buzzer or the head terrorist, Azid. But, at least, for now the action seemed to have died down...

~*~

Azid crawled along behind the long drapes at the back of the stage. All of the gunfire had stopped, which meant that he was now alone; the other members of the Front were either dead or dying. But that did not matter. His team might be gone but he could still carry out the mission.

He stole a quick glance underneath the heavy ceremonial drapery and saw Alderman lying prone, presenting as little a target as possible, near the podium. A lone Guarder, unfortunately not Buzzer, was kneeling over him. Assembly Center was echoing with the shouts and cries of the wounded and terrified officials, still scrambling to get out.

Not wanting to attract any undue attention with a blaster just yet, Azid left the cover of the drapes and crept quietly up behind Gannon. He delivered a quick blow with the butt of his blaster to the vulnerable spot just behind the Guarder's right ear.

Gannon immediately went limp and Alderman whipped his head around, stunned at the sight of the Kuriacoan ambassador holding a blaster in his face.

"Mr. President," Azid rasped. "I have waited a very long time for this moment, sir."

"Why would you want to kill me?" The president blurted, shaking with fear. Azid looked into the man's eyes and saw in them the terror of the unknown, of certain impending doom. The most powerful man in the Known Grid-Levels of Space trembled before him.

Rhafid Azid soaked it up. He thrived off of the fear of his prey. "Because your death, Mr. President, will prove to the masses of the universe the Movement's overwhelming power and strength," he said. "Because, with your death, we will move in and take over the government. We will become invincible."

"Those are the words of a madman," Alderman scowled.

"Quiet, you tyrant!" Azid screamed and pressed the muzzle of his blaster to the forehead of the president. "You will die, right here and right now!"

"Not on my watch," an icy voice whispered into Azid's ear.

Before Azid could react, a strong arm came out of nowhere and grabbed his gun hand, thrusting it up and clear of the president.

A single burst of blaster fire echoed throughout Assembly Center. The terrible scream that followed caught the attention of over two thousand people still in the arena. Assembly Center suddenly went quiet.

Azid gripped the bloody stump where his hand and blaster used to be. He quickly went into shock and began to hyperventilate.

"You are a dead man, Rhafid," Buzzer smiled as he grabbed the terrorist by the hair on the top of his head. "I'm going to kill you now..."

Alderman watched wide-eyed as Buzzer put the barrel of his blaster into Azid's open mouth and stared coldly into the Azuridian terrorist's eyes. No other words were exchanged as Buzzer pulled the trigger.

The blast took off the back of Azid's skull and splattered the president with a spray of blood and brain. Azid's body spasmed for a few seconds where it had dropped after Buzzer let it go.

Buzzer's strong hands were suddenly lifting Alderman from the floor of the stage and setting him on his feet. "Are you all right, Mr. President?"

Alderman took several moments to shake his head in amazement at the morning's traumatic events. "Yes, thank you," was all he could manage to say.

"You're very welcome, sir," Buzzer said and holstered hisweapon.

He bent to inspect Gannon and saw that the wound was not serious. Other than the bump, only the Guarder's pride would be wounded. Gannon was lucky to be alive, he thought. If not for the circumstances of the situation, he had no doubt Azid wouldn't have hesitated to kill him. Out of the corner of his eye, Buzzer could see Jekel approaching the stage.

"Good work, Frank," the Squadron Commander said. "Damn, it was a lot closer than it should have been. I would've been screwed if this plot had succeeded. I owe you big for this one, Buzzer."

Buzzer stood and stared back at the dead form of Rhafid Azid.

President Alderman was still trembling with shock at his near-death experience. Alderman was alive; despite one of the most concerted attempts to assassinate a U.E.N. president to have ever been implemented, he was alive. Alderman was perhaps the most influential man in all of InterGridactic politics, from the farthest reaches of the Ceryoiyava System to the outskirts of the Siberi-Vastness. He had been instrumental in unifying the InterGridactic governments after several recent near-collapses and only his continued survival helped to maintain the current state of peace throughout the Known-Grids. An important man had been saved today and perhaps much, much more.

"Make good on that all-expense-paid two-week vacation to Cazara that you've been promising me, Sarge," Buzzer said. "And I think we can call it even..."

MULLENS WRAPS UP

"Absolutely remarkable, Mr. Buzzer, remarkable to say the least," Mullens said and reached across the table with his hand extended. Buzzer rose and gripped the historian's right hand in a strong and assertive grip. "Congratulations to you and your team of Guarders on a job well done today."

"Like I said earlier, Mullens, I was just doing my job."

"Still, it was a very thrilling thing nevertheless," Mullens said and sat back down in the chair.

Mullens's small frame was almost swallowed by the vastness of the oversized chair, a thing obviously designed with much larger men than he in mind. He had seen the whole thing play out on the newscasts live as it happened, President Alderman coming extremely close to death in Assembly Hall before the Guarders sprang into action.

InterGridactic terrorism had never been made so clear to the people of the Known-Grids until the events of earlier today, never before had they seen the gut-wrenching reality of the true political arena in as up-close a venue.

And here he was, sitting across from the very man who was most responsible for Alderman's continued breathing; the man who single-handedly fought with the assassin and killed him in full view of billions upon billions of people. Although nearly all of the men holding cameras within Assembly Hall had stopped filming and begun running once the explosions began, the remote cameras that were fixed to walls and pointed at the podium caught the entire ordeal from dozens of different angles. The news nets had done a spectacular job of quickly piecing all of that footage together into a single flowing image that showed Frank Buzzer blowing the head off Rafid Azid within a meter of President Alderman of the United Earthian Nations.

Simply amazing...

"I believe your time is up, Mullens," Buzzer said, but made no move to get up from his seat.

Mullens looked down at his mini-pad and sighed; his time was indeed about to expire. He looked up and met the eyes of the Guarder one more time. Silently, he nodded at this man, a gesture of respect and gratitude.

Buzzer accepted the gesture and nodded in return.

The slightest whisper of the elaborate doors to the conference room swinging open on nearly silent hinges interrupted the silence and a voice boomed across the room, "Historian!"

Mullens whirled around in his chair and sent his mini-pad skittering across the table. "Yes, what is it, sir?"

Harrison Jekel strode into the room and fixed the small man with a frown. "Your time is up and I need this man immediately, urgent business is pending."

"Yes, of course," Mullens said as he tried to shrink as far back into the seat as possible. Jekel was easily the largest man he had ever seen; the hands of the Guarder Squadron Commander were quite possibly better than double the size of his own. "I am quite finished."

"Good then, please be on your way at the quickest possible speed."

"All right, I just need to get..."

Jekel turned toward Buzzer, ignoring the historian, and said, "Wait for me in my office, Frank. There are some details on your vacation we need to discuss."

"Sure thing, Sarge," Buzzer said, stood and flashed a glance at Mullens. "I hope I was able to help you today, Mullens."

Mullens smiled again as he gathered up his mini-pad and said, "More than you will ever know, Mr. Buzzer. Once again, my congratulations."

"Noted," Buzzer said and strode out of the room.

Jekel loomed less than a meter from Mullens as the small man walked as quickly as he could across the thick carpeting of the conference room. He paused momentarily to take in once more the awesome figure of the falcon which occupied one entire wall of the enormous room. He thought that quite probably he would never enter this room or this section of the Governmental Complex again for the duration of his days in the Historical Division of the United Earthian Nations.

The huge doors swung open at the slightest touch of Jekel's massive right arm and Mullens walked through into the corridor. Jekel stood within the doorway for a moment and the harshness on the man's face nearly vanished.

"You should feel very honored, Mr. Mullens," Jekel said. "That man you just interviewed is quite possibly the very best man you or I will ever meet."

Mullens lifted his head to look into the eyes of Sergeant Harrison Jekel and knew the truth when he heard it.

"I know, Sergeant," he whispered. "I know."

THE END

Table of Contents

About the Author of THE GUARDER FACTOR

   Shawn P. Madison, creator of the Guarder/U.E.N. Universe, currently lives in the beautiful Garden State of New Jersey with his wife and a veritable cornucopia of kids. Although he has written in many different genres, he tends to write mostly science fiction and horror. He has published more than eighty short stories in thirty different magazines and anthologies, both electronic and print, so far this century. Other than his Guarder novels, his collection of short Horror Fiction, THE ROAD TO DARKNESS, was released by Double Dragon Publishing (www.double-dragon-ebooks.com) in April of 2003 and his novella, THE EMPIRE OF THE IRON CROSS, was released by Cyberwit Publishing (www.cyberwit.net) in March of 2019. You can reach Shawn via e-mail at: asm89@aol.com

www.ingramcontent.com/pod-product-compliance
Lightning Source LLC
Chambersburg PA
CBHW081205170626

46813CB00010B/3325